CHRISTMAS COFFEE

A Christmas Story

H. M. WARD

Laree Bailey Press

LAREE BAILEY PRESS

First Edition: NOVEMBER 2016

Originally printed titled as HOT GUY

ISBN: 978-1-63035-248-6 (Paperbacks)

ISBN: 978-1-63035-247-9 (ebook)

Created with Vellum

I
CELYN

My heart slams into my chest like I'm having a fucking heart attack. I pull up Quin's number and press CALL. He's been my best friend since we were in boarding school together, back when we were young kids with big names. Quinton was shortened to Quin, much to his parent's horror. And Quin learned how to pronounce my Celtic nightmare of a name, and made sure no one else said had a chance to call me "Sally-Ann" or other stupid shit kids said to me early on.

In a single breath, I unload all my shit in the longest sentence ever heard. I don't fucking come up for air until I'm done. Panic has its icy fingers around my throat and I can't shake the bastard.

Quin's on speakerphone as I floor the sleek

black McLaren across the Verrazano Bridge and toward eastern Long Island. I'm bobbing and weaving through traffic, gripping the wheel so tight that it might come off in my hands.

I rant for a while and then slam my palm into the steering wheel. "What the fuck am I going to do? I did every last fucking thing that man ever asked of me! I'm screwed, Quin!"

"I'll help you think of something."

"Quin, you don't—"

"KEHL-ahN," he says my name in two sharp parts, cutting my off with the throaty sound of that hard C. "Celyn, seriously. Stop. Don't lose your shit over this. You've handled worse."

Quin gives me the pep talk I need as I drive away from Uncle Aldrich's swank office in Manhattan. "Go have a few drinks, nail some hot chick, and we'll work it out on paper tomorrow."

I grimace and stare at the dashboard, making the same expression I'd offer if Quin were here with me. "Tomorrow's Thanksgiving, asswipe. You're supposed to be at your mother's house."

He laughs lightly, "She can wait."

"She'll kill you." His mother is like Martha Stewart, pre-trial, on crack. Their estate home on the north shore of Long Island is pristine and the holiday will be exceptional, until Quin shows up in jeans and a T-shirt instead of a tie. Formality isn't dead, not in that house.

"Fine, then come with me. Eat turkey, talk turkey, and then poke your eye out with the wishbone, because my fucking Hallmark family is *that* boring. We'll need some drama. If I have to sit through another holiday meal and listen to shit about hedge funds, I'll fucking snap." His voice rises an octave as he speaks so fast that all the words run together.

Quin's family has more money than God, but he doesn't act like it. Not until he's forced into the annual soul-sucking conversations about his future. When we were in college together, Quin nearly cracked from all the pressure put on him by his parents. Yeah, he has a set that's still married after thirty-five years, which is a feat in and of itself. At times, like holidays—like now, with all this shit raining down—it's difficult to not be envious. He has meddling parents. I have an evil uncle. That's it. No kin to call my own, no family watching my back come hell or high water. No cousins or brothers. Quin is my only family.

I assure him, "I'll go with you. Calm the fuck down. Hedge funds are better than this shit."

Quin laughs but there's no joy in it. "I'd trade lives with you in a fucking heartbeat, Celyn."

"Likewise buddy," and I mean it, "but first, I need to get through this shit."

"Tomorrow, Celyn." He urges. "Tonight, let your subconscious do all the thinking. Actually, let your dick do all the thinking. Pound some pussy and get smashed, in that order. It'll give you something to be thankful for tomorrow." Quin laughs and disconnects.

I sigh and rub my hand over my face. It's not a bad plan, but I feel too wound up for it. I'm still pissed. By now I've driven so far out on the Island that I'm passing the county line into Suffolk. Shit. It's another hour to the summer house and an hour back to the city. When I took off, I was irate and started to drive without thinking about where I was going. All I could focus on was finding Ocean Parkway and letting the salty sea air fill my lungs as I gunned it down the road.

I groan and glance around. I left the Parkway behind a while ago, and am flying down an open stretch of Sunrise—a modest concrete wonder with six lanes that connects suburbia to the city. Buildings jut up from the landscape, nothing more than three stories. If you took Manhattan and tipped it over on its side, you'd have Long Island.

I drive like I have a destination in mind. I don't want to go to the normal places tonight. I can't face those people. They all know who I am, what I am. If they find out what happened, I won't be able to bear it.

I drive a bit further and stop just outside of Bayshore, past the mall, in a sketchy part of town. I roll into the back parking lot of a bar and cut the engine. I strip off my jacket and tug on an old gray sweater I left laying on the passenger seat. It's old and soft. Combined with a pair of shit-kickers, I know I can handle myself.

When I walk into the establishment, I'm thinking bar fight. That's why I stopped here. I need to beat the shit out of someone, and lose the anger building inside of me. This gutter looks like the perfect place to do it. But then, I spot this blonde in the corner with her nose in a book. Long tendrils of golden hair fall over her shoulders. Her face is perfect, fucking beautiful, not that I look at it too long because her tits are there in this red ribbed sweater, plump and perfect. I can imagine my hands on them as I kiss her senseless, spread her legs, and fuck her until she cries out in ecstasy.

I walk over to her and stop in front of her table. She's reading a Chilton's manual, which shocks the hell out of me. I pull out a well-worn wooden chair and sit without asking. "Light reading?"

She doesn't glance up at me, just gives me the finger. "Fuck off, buddy. I'm not in the mood." Her petite face remains downturned, her nose in that fat-ass book.

"Neither was I, until I saw you." That makes her look up. She stops for a second, startled. I think she recognizes me, but then her eyes tell another story—blank. She has no clue who I am, which is fucking perfect.

"Nice line. Use it often?" She smirks at me, lifts a brow, and then goes back to her book, turns a page. She opens the index and goes to a previous section and then pinches the bridge of her nose like she has a massive headache. I say nothing, and just watch her for a second. The manual is for Hondas that are over a decade old. I saw one in the parking lot on the way in.

I reach across, and take the book from her even though I know she'll rip my arms off. "Hey!" She reaches to take it back, and I grab her hands and squeeze hard before releasing them. I push the book back at her.

"Listen, I've had a shitty day and from the way you're flipping through the pages of that manual, you're stuck here until you can get your car to start. Honda Civic, am I right?"

She frowns and her lip juts out. It's so fucking

perfect. I want to lean in and taste her, suck that pouty lip into my mouth and nip her.

Her gaze narrows. "How'd you know that?"

I run my hands through my hair and then lean on my elbows, getting closer to her. Her scent fills my head—fuck, she's intoxicating. "Listen, I'll fix your car and then you can spend the night doing funner things, or you can stay here alone. Up to you."

She hesitates. "What do you know about cars?"

I don't answer her. Instead, I get up and tip my head toward the door. "Keys?"

She stiffens, and then sighs as she reaches into a purse that looks like a horse-feed bag. She fishes them out and hands them to me. "Fine, but if you steal my car, I'll kick your ass."

I smirk at her. I like the spunky thing she has going on. This chick isn't a pushover, which means she should be a lot of fun in bed. I offer a lazy smile and lean in close, invading her space and inhaling the perfect scent. "Tell me, honey, how exactly would I swipe a car that doesn't run?"

Her eyes lock with mine. Defiant. "You'd be surprised at what a desperate guy is willing to do."

I choke and laugh at her. "Desperate? That's what you see when you look at this?"

She shrugs and gives me a once over, folding

her arms loosely over her chest. She stands on one leg, which tips her curvy hips to the side, and glares at me, like she's bored. "Does it matter?"

I step closer, her body an inch from mine. I can feel the warmth of her body. She's close enough to touch, but I'm having too much fun taunting her. I feel the words wrap around my lips as I say them. "Desperation and kindness don't mingle."

She snaps, and lunges for the keys. "I don't need charity."

I pull back, letting her body brush against my arm. I hold the keys out of reach and look down into her beautiful face. There's something about her that's so different. I honestly think she may knee me in the nuts, take back her keys, and figure out the Chilton's manual. "Good, because I'm not offering a handout. I never said I was paying, honey."

Her gaze narrows. "Stop calling me that."

"What? Honey? You're not all sweet and smooth, going down?"

She snorts. "Well, you'll never find out, will you?" She raises her brows at me and smirks.

Holy fuck. I love this woman. I can't believe she said that. I lean in close enough to see the tiny freckle that rests on the soft skin just above the bow in her top lip. She stiffens and lowers her lashes, her gaze fixated on my mouth thinking that I'm going to kiss her.

Instead, I stop and whisper as I grin. "Stop thinking about it."

"I'm not," she breathes, but I know she is from the way her gaze drops. She doesn't move. She stays there a breath away. When she shifts her weight, her tits brush against my chest. It's enough to make me want to take her here and now. "Besides, certain acts are reserved for men who are worth it, and you're questionable at best."

"Then, I'll have to change your mind."

She smiles and watches me from under those long lashes. "Once I form an opinion, it doesn't change." Her minty breath washes across my lips as she speaks. It's fucking hypnotic.

"Then, I'll be sure to leave you with a lasting impression—something unforgettable." I turn on my heel before she can say another word, or change her mind, and head toward the door. She follows me out into the parking lot.

I pop her hood, the real one, but see the problem as soon as I sit down behind the wheel. It's basic, but not something that I can fix in a parking lot. I try to crank the engine. It doesn't even sputter and I point to the dash. "See that needle?"

"Yeah, what about it?"

"It means your battery is dead."

"But I just changed it." She deflates slightly. "It's new. It can't be dead."

"Odds are it's your alternator, but someone needs to check it out. A jump won't bring this battery back to life. Hell, it's so far gone that the dome light isn't even coming on"

She inhales slowly, doesn't blink, and then swears under her breath. Hand to her head she says, "Shit. I can't fix that myself." Her book has black smudges and oily fingerprints all over it. I have no doubt that she's been working on the car.

"Not tonight, but given enough time in the light of day, I'm sure you could figure it out." I mean every word of it. There's something about her, I can see it in her eyes. She likes to tinker, to take things apart and put them back together. She's not a grease monkey—it's more than that. It has something to do with curiosity and understanding. She wants to know how things work.

She softens a little. "Thanks. I think I'm going back to plan A for tonight."

"Which was...?"

Her green gaze cuts to the side, landing on me. "Getting plastered and joining AAA so they can tow my car home."

"As amazing as that sounds, I can have your

car fixed in a couple of hours. It'd be ready for you, right here. And I can't help but notice there's a nice warm room right over there." I tip my head at the little Hilton glowing in the cold night. She's shivering, no coat, and doesn't flat out reject me this time. "Which would you prefer? Drinking buddy or getting off with a guy who can make a girl come three times, back to back? It's pretty amazing, at least that's what I've been told." I hold her gaze, shocked she hasn't shot me down yet.

She rolls her eyes and tries not to smile. Tucking a piece of hair behind her ear, she glances up at me. "You don't need to hype yourself. I'm not blind."

"It's not hype. It's a fact, and I felt like you needed the choice. But it is fucking cold out here, so how about picking one. Either way, I'll make sure you forget everything that's bothering you for a little bit. What do you say?"

She sighs loudly and looks back at the bar. She's going to pick drinking buddy. Her body language says it all. Slumped shoulders, apprehension, lack of trust. She's strung tight like she might punch me in the face for the hell of it.

Then she looks down at my hand and takes it, threading my fingers through hers. "Grab a bottle to go, and let's get the hell out of here."

2

CELYN

I have no idea who this woman is and I don't ask her name. She doesn't ask for mine. I grab a bottle of Absolute and check in under an alias, pushing the guy at the desk a hundred when he wants to see my license. He takes it, and suddenly that part isn't important anymore. It's amazing what people will do for a few bucks at this time of year.

A nervous energy radiates from the blonde goddess standing next to me. Her body is tense, all lean muscle, and she's strong. I got that. She's not a doormat and sure as hell doesn't take shit from anyone. I wonder how crazy she is for a second, eyeing that massive purse, knowing damn well she might be insane. There could be an ax in there. The hot ones are always nuts.

Hot Girl follows me to the room and when we walk inside, I flip on the lights. I toss my keycard on the cheap counter and look at the sad little room. The bedspread has that once white look and the room is well lived in. I'm about to turn around and tell her that she doesn't have to do shit with me, that we can drink in here—I'm fine with it—when she shuts the lights off and steps toward me with a look in her eye that's all sex.

She wants me, is thinking about clawing her nails down my back and riding my dick. I wonder if she wants me or just needs an escape. It doesn't matter, not tonight. Her arms are around my neck and her perfect little body presses against mine. Her tits mash against my chest making my dick hard. She smells like vanilla and baby powder. Coupled with that peppermint breath, I could eat her up. Her hair feels like silk in my fingers and when her lips meet my neck, she trails her hands up under my sweater running her palms over my abs slowly, teasing me.

She breathes into my ear, "Open the bottle and let's get to it."

"Anything you want." I crack open the vodka and ask if she wants ice, but she shakes her head.

"Neat is fine." She downs the first cup and then a second one before tugging that sweater over her head. She steps toward me with her golden hair tossed over her shoulders and a black bra that makes her tits look better than the sweater. It's not fucking possible to look at her face when she's this hot. The best part, she has no fucking clue. This chick probably thinks she's cute or pretty. She has no idea that guys like me fantasize about a body like this. She's curvy with a narrow waist and her hips spill down into thighs that I can't wait to get between. She's a fucking seductress with a fairy's face and a saunter that would make a succubus jealous. The girl's got moves.

She pulls my sweater over my head and walks around me slowly, dragging the pads of her fingers across my stomach, side, and then across my lower back. She stops behind me and presses her tits to my back, rocking those sweet hips toward me. I feel her hot kiss on my skin and it takes everything I have to stay still and see how this plays out. Most women wait for me to make the first move. I can count on one hand how many times a woman has controlled me in bed. Most don't even try.

She places a palm on both sides of my waist and asks, "Why aren't you drinking?"

"I thought you'd have a better time if I wasn't totally plastered."

"Plastered would be bad, but a little tipsy

might be fun. Take a drink." She releases me and then walks over to the bed, sits down on the edge and crosses her jean-clad legs at the knee. She leans back on her arms which pushes her chest out, making her body look even more appealing.

She doesn't have to ask me twice. I pour a double and down it fast, before walking over to her. I'm about to push her back onto the bed when she stops me, grabs my waistband, and unbuttons my jeans. The zipper slides down slowly as she watches with fascination. I feel her hand wrap around my shaft and swallow a moan. She smiles as she feels its girth, squeezing me firmly, making me harder, longer with her touch. She slides down my jeans and strips my boxers, leaving me naked and standing in front of her, my erection before her eyes.

She glances up at me from under her lashes. "Is anything off the table?"

Oh fucking hell. She's perfect. I shake my head. "You?"

"No." She takes a swig from the bottle.

I do the same before putting it on the nightstand and lying back against the pillows. I lace my arms behind my head. I glance at her and see her eyes on my face, questions fade when she kneels on the bed and unhooks her bra. She tosses it to the side, and I can see the swell of her tits and those nipples, tight and perfect for me.

I grin at her and command, "Strip. Lose it. All of it."

She doesn't speak, doesn't play coy, or act shy. She obeys and it makes me hard again. The way she slips out of her jeans and panties, she tosses them aside without a drop of shame and waits. I could learn to enjoy this. She goes from being in charge to being compliant. I want to feel her naked body pressed to mine.

Before I can act, there's a knock at the door. I look at Hot Girl for a second and she says, "Go ahead and answer it. I'm not going anywhere." She leans back against the pillows.

I'm torn, I don't want to leave her—not even for a second—but the asshole is knocking more urgently now. I swear and grab my jeans, pulling them on fast, and then pull on my shirt. I walk over to the door and yank it open. When I see who's there, I step into the hallway, closing the door behind me.

Quin is grinning. "Lovely place to spend the night."

I glare at him and hiss, "What the hell are you doing here?"

"Saving your ass. Come on. I stumbled on something, but it'll be gone by morning."

I glance at the door. "I can't walk out on her. She'll never forgive me."

Quin scoffs, "You'll never see her again. Your ass is on the line. Fix it and then nail some other girl. She's a piece of ass, they're all the same."

He sounds completely reasonable, but in the back of my mind, I know this one is different. If I leave now, I shoot any chance I have of being with her to hell.

Quin tugs at me. "Come on. We're running out of time. We have to get there before the shredding company."

"Where are we going?"

"Bardenbey." The company that should have been mine. The company I nearly bankrupted. "It could save your ass."

I walk away from the woman on the other side of the door without an explanation.

3

NOVA

I tug my long hair over my shoulder, away from my sweaty skin, and smile. He's insanely hot. In fact, I could have fallen for him and I know it. To save myself the heartache, I took him to bed. At least that's what I tell myself as I wait for him to come back. There's no way to recover from a one-night tryst with a random guy. I've tried it. There's nothing after that which could possibly live up to the unrealistic expectations that have grown in my mind. If a guy is good in bed, he's usually a total asshole, which is why I had a long string of non-serious relationships until I met Ben. As for the one-nighter type of men, their bedroom skills come from years of dicking around, nailing anything that moves. This guy has mad skills, but there's something else there—a haunted look in his eyes.

Something is gnawing away at him. I sense it, I'm not sure what it is exactly, but the slope of his shoulders and the twinge of regret in his voice makes me wonder. Maybe he's coming off a bad break up too. Or maybe he just doesn't want to be alone. Night is the worst time to be isolated. Every worry I ever had seems to creep up until there's no escape. Being alone makes it worse.

I don't want to think of Ben or what happened. There's a hole in my chest where my heart belongs. Easing the ache for a bit, a distraction of slick bodies and sensations will help. It helped in the past, but the effects don't last long enough. I thought I was done with this part of my life. It's strange to be back in this vulnerable spot. Maybe I use sex as a defensive mechanism, a way to push guys away. The truth is, I didn't plan on stopping at the bar tonight. The day went to hell and the car died just as I ran off from Ben. Luckily, I was able to push it into the nearest parking lot, which was the bar across the street. No one stopped to help, not that anyone ever does. It's not like that here. At this point, my car is mostly duct tape and barely runs, but it's all I have.

I know what I'm doing is reactionary. That if I hadn't gotten dumped, I wouldn't have said yes to this guy. Add up the rejection, cheating, and disbelief and I want to forget for a while. I can't believe Ben was seeing someone else while he was living with me. I can't get past that. What's wrong with me? How did I miss that?

Then I quit. I walked away from a great job. I had no choice. I can't go back there.

I'll have to visit the employment agency on Friday and beg for a shit job that pays too little. People ask me why I'm not in college, or they look at me and assume I'm a student. It makes job-hunting difficult. I'm a social pariah for not continuing my education. There's so much pressure to do what other people think is right. At times, I'm not sure who I am at all. Add in the swiftly approaching holidays and this entire mess is a nightmare. I don't want to think about Thanksgiving tomorrow. I don't want to pretend that it won't suck, that I'm fine. I'm not, but I can put blinders on and keep marching.

One day everything will be all right. One day things will be good again. Until then, keep going and don't stop. If I slow down, I'll fall apart. I can't let that happen.

I'm twirling my finger against the sheet forcing my mind back to thinking about the stranger. His body tells me everything I need to know. He's a pampered ass, one of those rich kids that has time to work out and get rock hard abs and a matching ass. His arms are thick, powerful, but he's careful with me. I like it. I can't wait to see what he's going to do.

I roll onto my side after a second. I glance at the door that hasn't moved. The hallway is silent. His sweater is still on the chair. The pit of my stomach dips. There's no way he walked out, but the sinking feeling in my gut is telling me a different story. I wait another minute or two and pull on a robe and pad over to the door. I press my ear to the door and listen.

Nothing.

I pull the door open wide, throwing it back, hoping he's there, but the hallway is empty.

4
NOVA

Mystery Man is gone, he took off without a word. Mortification sours my stomach and I nearly fold in half. This has never happened before. Ever. What the hell?

I dress quickly with every intention of darting. When I fly by the counter, head lowered and eyes glassy, the man at the counter calls out to me. "Miss! There's a message for you."

I stop and turn on my heel. I stop in front of the long gray desk and he hands me a note.

'Keys will be under the mat in your car first thing tomorrow.'

There's nothing else. No reason for walking out on me. No apology. No mention of an emergency.

I crumple the paper up, balling it in my fist. I can't go home. I have no car. I don't want to see Ben. This has been the worst day of my life. I turn and storm back up to the room. There's a bottle of Absolute with my name on it.

❦

THE NEXT MORNING, MY HEAD IS POUNDING. I don't want to get up. I don't want to face the day. This is going to suck. I dry swallow a few aspirin, shower, and leave the hotel, but not before I pass happy children dressed in pretty fall clothes as frantic parents try to corral them into the car.

It's snowing. Fat white flakes fall from the sky and melt when they touch my skin. It won't stick, but it's enough to make traffic a mess. I groan and wrap my arms around my middle, tuck my chin, and walk faster toward my car.

Part of me expects it to still be busted. The whole thing was a massive play to get into my pants until someone else came along. Being left behind with no explanation stung. Coming off an abrupt breakup, and now this? Well, it's more than I can handle. The best way to deal with it is to pretend it never happened and if I see that asshole again, I'll kick his junk into his skull.

When I make my way across the double

parking lot, I spy my car dusted with a fresh blanket of snow. Crap, it's sticking. Getting a tow truck is going to be even harder.

I walk up to the '89 Honda and wrench open the half frozen door. The keys are still under the mat where I left them for Hot Guy's 'friend' to fix it. I slide into the car and press my head to the steering wheel when I spy my crocheted hat on the floor. I reach for it and tug it on my head. It's freaking cold. I inhale deeply and decide that I should at least try to make the engine turn over. AAA is going to ask me when I tried to start it, so here we go.

I slide the metal key into the socket and twist. The car sputters like it usually does and then turns over. Startled, I glance down at the gauges. The battery needle is where it's supposed to be, rather than hanging limply to the side.

"He did it," I mutter to myself, shocked. But why? He walked out on me. Why the hell would he pay to have someone fix my car in the middle of the night? It must have cost him a fortune to get it done so fast. I don't understand.

The snarky voice in the back of my mind snaps at me. *He pities you and your sad little car.*

I frown. It didn't look like pity last night. In fact, I thought he actually liked me. My skin prickles as I think about him, his touch, and easy laugh. Screw it. I'm not torturing myself trying to figure out why he walked. It's his loss.

Snarky me chides from the back of my mind, *Yeah, keep telling yourself that*.

The roads are a sheet of black glass. My wipers frantically wash away thick flakes as I crawl ahead with the rest of the stragglers who decided to head to their Thanksgiving dinners this morning. Lots of people are going over the river and through the woods to their grandmother's house. I'm headed toward my older sister's house in Deer Park. It's a little town that lies smack in the center of Long Island, about thirty miles east of Manhattan. Think of suburban homes, cape cods and split-ranches, and tons of traffic. The homes have little yards with barren trees that jut up from the frozen ground like skeletal fingers. Add in the cold morning air and the scent of exhaust as I travel east, and I don't have the stomach to eat the muffin I nabbed from the breakfast buffet. Instead, I clutch a cup of mediocre coffee like it's a lifeline.

My chest feels like it's going to cave in. I don't want to think about anything. I try to stare at the road and forbid my mind to wander, but it does. Ben's voice echoes in my ears—*it's been over for a long time. We should both move on.*

He was the one who wanted to date me. He

was the one who wanted to move in. At some point, I stopped doing what I wanted because it made him happy. I had never dated anyone for long before him. I guarded my heart ferociously back then, but somehow Ben got through. And now, it feels like I've been ripped to shreds. Add on the hot guy who wanted me one second and vanished the next and I feel completely mental. If I go crazy, at least I'll blend in a bit more with the family. They're all nucking futs.

The bends in the highway are pitched sharply to one side and the car slips as I take a curve too fast. Swearing to myself, I slow further. I could walk faster. I grip the wheel tighter and lean forward in my seat, trying to see. An old Bonneville crawls up next to me. I'm on top of the steering wheel when I glance over and notice the driver. She's eighty years old with a crocheted cap on her head, hugging the steering wheel with her face so close to the glass that she could kiss it. Something white paws at the back window of her vehicle and I can see that her ancient car is filled with felines. The old woman straightens her knitted cap and adjusts her huge-ass glasses before looking over at me.

It's like she's my ancient twin. Or the worst omen ever. It's like looking into a mirror with a built in time machine. Fast-forward sixty years and that's me. Holy crap.

I rip my hat off my head and toss it in the back seat and give a panicky yelp to myself, "No cats! Never!"

The old lady frowns at me, flips me the bird, and speeds away. I'm left gaping in her wake of white exhaust. I try to speed up but the car loses traction again. I make a mental note never to buy a Bonneville.

My mood drops a few bars into suckage as I near the exit for my sister's place. The last thing I want to see is her Norman Rockwell poster child life, but I don't want to go home and eat frozen leftovers. Being alone will make everything that's happened real. I'll have to face it and that's the last thing I want to do. Besides, the only thing in my fridge is a jar of pickle juice. I ate all the pickles when I ran out of Vienna Sausages. I can't believe I ate those, but it was tiny wieners or dinner with Mom and her million questions.

When I finally get to her pastel gray cape cod, I park in front. A stream of smoke billows from her little chimney. Snow hugs the roof of the picture perfect home. Boughs of holly hang from her eaves, coupled with draped evergreens, and topped with twinkling white lights. It forms a pretty garland that runs the length of her house.

A matching deco-mesh wreath adorns her front door. Sprigs of holly and evergreen poke out from between the bright red and green plastic.

I tried to make a deco-mesh wreath with her this summer. She bought all the materials to make a summertime wreath. The picture looked cute, but when I was done, my wreath looked like a bloated marshmallow with crap stuck to it. I'm not Suzie Homemaker and never will be. Just ask the pickles in my fridge. I need to go grocery shopping.

I take my time moving up the shoveled walk and reach the front porch. The wooden front door is cracked open an inch, behind a glass storm door that's foggy with condensation. I wrap my knuckles on the glass and then poke my head inside. "Tinselly?"

My sister's dark hair swings into the doorway, followed by a face that's a few years older than mine. "Nova!" She's wearing a long brown skirt with a festive sweater, all of which is covered by a ruffled apron with a hand-drawn turkey on the front. She rushes at me, spatula in hand, and gives me a bear hug. "You came!"

When she plows into me, I let out an *oof* sound as I'm bear hugged. I pat her on the back and then pry myself away and smile. "I couldn't pass up your stuffing."

She believes me for a moment and then her face falls. "You were wearing that sweater yesterday." Frown lines pinch between her brows as the corner of her mouth raises.

I avoid her gaze. "Yeah, I sort of had a bad day and didn't have time to change." I feel my face flame. "Can I freshen up?"

Her mouth opens and the spatula rises. I already know what she's going to ask.

I raise my hand, one finger up, and shake my head. "It wasn't what you think. I slept in my clothes. I'm that girl. And for the love of God, please don't mention Ben to mom at dinner. She doesn't know and I can't deal with it, not today. Promise me?" I texted Tinselly last night when I was a little past drunk. Texting while intoxicated is never a good idea. I grimace as I think about the messages I sent. Some were weepy—those were sent to Tinselly.

I told Ben to fuck off a few times. Texted that I hate his guts and hoped he had fun with his new girl toy last night. I may have written some other things too—crass, angry words that I would have never said.

Tinselly's dark eyes rest on mine, sad or disappointed, I can't tell which. She nods and then her lips twist into a smirk as if she knows I had a rebound guy last night. "Well, at least answer this—was he good?"

I frown and swat at her. I don't like lying to Tinselly, but if I tell her what really happened, I'll cry. So, I smirk and whisper in her ear, "He was completely unbelievable."

5

CELYN

THE NIGHT BEFORE

I run my hand over my face and glance back at the hotel. "How the hell did you even find me?"

Quin glances over at me. We're sitting inside his Hummer. He decked the thing out so it's solid black and chrome. He smirks. "If you don't want people to find you, turn off your phone."

I pull my cell out of my pocket and glance at it. "I have that feature turned off." I scroll through the control panel and find the toggle switch for FIND MY FRIENDS. It's on.

"Yeah, I turned it on."

"Damn it, Quin. Stop screwing with my phone."

"You'll be glad I did, because this can't wait. I was at Bardenbey and overheard something I shouldn't have." Quin drives toward the city—Manhattan—in the inky night. It's way past business hours and has been for a while.

"What the hell were you doing there now?"

He glances over at me, like I have no brain. "This absolutely stunning set of tits wanted me. As if I could deny her." He scoffs. "We were in a compromising position, and being an honorable guy, I did the honorable thing and let her rush off before she got crowned office whore. I plan on nailing her another night. She likes to work late, if you catch my drift."

"Yeah, caught it. What does this have to do with me? Because if you're just shitting around with me..." My voice trails off. I just walked out on a woman that was beyond exceptional. There's no way in hell she'll let me explain or take this as anything but rejection. That's why I didn't tell her I was going. Yeah, it was a shitty thing to do, but I couldn't explain. That would require spilling everything, who I am, what I'm worth, and that I'm going to fucking lose it all if I don't figure this out.

"Never. And I said come quick. You could have taken that literally, nailed her, and left."

"I don't walk out on women I just slept with. I'm not that guy."

Quin grins. "I am. You should try it some time."

"I have and it's not me, so move on."

Quin makes a gesture with his hand and then gets serious. "Tell me everything. Start at the beginning and leave nothing out."

I rub my hand over my face, exasperated. "Quin, we already did this."

"No, you gave me the drive-by version. Every man alive thanks you for your brevity of words, but I need details so you need to flip on your chick switch and start at the beginning. Tell me about exactly what happened when your uncle called you into his office. Leave nothing out."

6

CELYN

YESTERDAY MORNING

I'm standing in my uncle's office. It's decorated in opulent woods, all exotic, and every last detail is dripping with wealth. The man spares no expense on anything. When he calls me in here like a goddamned kid, I don't appreciate it. Uncle Aldrich sits in a high back leather chair with his fingers steepled together, silent. His once black hair has grayed over the last decade—probably from raising me—but the man isn't weaker. No, if anything he's grown stronger, more determined to crush me and ruin my fucking life.

My father dying wasn't part of the plan. I never had a mother, well not one that I remember. She died shortly after having me. It was the beginning of a life with the Midas touch, but instead of turning everything to gold, I turn it to shit. Investments have gone south and I lost nearly a billion dollars a few years back. I've never lived that moment down. It shouldn't have happened, but it did.

Shit always happens to me. I single-handedly turned the hottest girl at school into a lesbian. They say it doesn't work that way, but after that, I'm not so sure. One night with me and she started playing for the other team. I was a master in bed, knew every spot that would send her reeling into ecstasy and then some. She clawed my back, screamed my name. When I bullshit with the guys about it—about her—I say I'm glad she found herself, has a chance at happiness and all that shit, but deep down inside I can't help but wonder if it's me.

I mean, how many things can I ruin? When I was eleven, I was standing next to my golden retriever, Sandy, watching a storm roll in. Big beautiful clouds billowed across the sky turning it into a gorgeous mess. A second later all my hair stood on end and lightning struck. Not in a good way. Sandy got zapped, died in front of my pre-adolescent eyes. Uncle Aldrich said these things happen and gave me a new dog, named her Karma. Even after all this time, Karma gives me a wide birth.

But that's the past. Every schmuck has a sob story and mine's no different. I just inherited some of the shitty Ryan luck, that's all. I'm nearly thirty-five, and due for a course of good fortune. Everything changed for Uncle Aldrich when he hit thirty-five. Same for dad, and now it's my turn.

Uncle Aldrich's face is slack as he puts the tips of his fingers together. His facial expression reveals nothing. Classic Aldrich Ryan. The man can look completely serene and then rip your throat out. It's hard to say which way this meeting will go. Actually, I figure it's about taking my seat at the family company next month. Thirty-five years old, MBA, and every box checked to earn my spot on the board of Bardenbey, a multi-million dollar corporation that makes everything from socks to satellites. Dad started the company with nothing before I was born, with the help of his brother who sits before me now.

Uncle Aldrich holds out a hand, gesturing for me to sit. "How are you, Celyn?" He asks the question with complete candor, but I know it's not sincere. We don't see eye to eye on many matters. His job was to keep me alive while I was a child and that's what he did. I survived the isolation, the lack of affection, and the scorn that trickled off of him every time he looked at me.

Uncle Aldrich has always hated me, but I have no idea why.

When I was a kid, I remember crying at Dad's funeral, desperately trying to get Uncle Aldrich to put an arm around me, to touch my shoulder and tell me it'd be all right. I would have taken any affirmation he offered, but there was none. Years passed and every failure, every heartache, was dealt with in solitude, deprived of touch. I wandered the great house alone, wasn't permitted to have friends over or play at their homes—Uncle Aldrich said those children were beneath me. When he caught me playing with the maid's daughter, three quarters of the servants were fired the same night. I was eight when that happened. No one came near me after that, except Sandy.

Now that I'm a grown man, we don't talk much. The mistake put a rift between us, one that should have bled out and died a long time ago.

I slip into the burnt orange club chair and lean back against the tufted leather, placing each hand on an armrest. My French cuffs poke out from under the sleeves of my sports jacket. I place my ankle on my knee and smile at the bastard. "Wonderful, and yourself?"

Uncle Aldrich doesn't return my grin. His clean-shaven face reveals a few more wrinkles than the last time we spoke. The man is stern, harsh, and has been a cold sonofabitch for a long time, but when his wrath faced my direction, well, I'm never standing in that spot again. Which leads to a problem. He's president of the board. We'll have to see each other every day shortly, and make nice. Maybe the old bastard is offering an olive branch.

"Couldn't be better, Celyn." He taps his fingertips together once, glaring at me. "I heard about your recent venture. Didn't go well, did it?"

Spine stiffening, I resist the urge to take the bait, but when he smirks at me, I lose it. I grip the arms of the chair tight and smirk back. "At least I tried."

"Trying doesn't make a man into a success. You're weak, Celyn."

I grit my teeth and try not to fall into this loop again, but it's so damn hard.

Uncle's gaze narrows as he presses the pads of his fingers together. His voice is steel, colder than ice. "This family has no room for failure, and yet here you are." He offers a predatory smile, showing the tips of his teeth as he stills his hands and then places them on the top of the desk.

"You are not infallible," I growl.

"I never said I was, and yet I'm the one sitting here and as I look over your list of accomplishments, it's difficult to say you're anything but a disappointment. If you were my son—"

"I'm not your son." I can't believe I fucking said that. Not again. This is a fight we've had over and over again since I was thirteen and finally had the balls to fight back. I feel my chest rise as I inhale sharply. Rubbing my palm over my face, I inch forward in my seat and place a hand on the edge of his desk. I swore to myself that I'd do the best with whatever I was given. This man is my only family.

"Listen, we've said everything there is to say on this matter, and burned enough bridges. I'm sure you didn't call me in here to rehash the same old shit." The unspoken question hangs in the air, as I wait for him to tell me why he did call me here.

Uncle Aldrich smiles and glances at his watch. The timepiece set him back over half a million, but every rich old man has a closet full of watches, Aldrich is no different. For every major success, he buys another. I have one watch that was given to me when I graduated with my MBA. He handed me a box with a Jaeger LeCoultre. The little piece was worth fifty grand. After I opened the paper and pulled it out, I looked at the inscription on the back.

Written on the silver disc were the words:

I'm very proud of you. –Uncle Aldrich

I was so choked up that I couldn't speak. But before I could put it on my wrist, he reached for the gift and took it back.

He said, "You need to do something worthwhile to earn this accolade. In the interim..." he handed me a different gift.

Confused, I silently opened the paper and stared down at the plastic casing. A black plastic Timex watch was perched within, price tag still attached: $9.99.

When he saw the expression on my face he said, "That is the gift that matches the magnitude of your achievement. You're nothing until you prove otherwise."

I was the salutatorian, second in my class at Harvard. I busted my ass and missed valedictorian by a fraction of a point. But that was then. Years have passed and I never saw the watch again. There were no birthday presents or cake. Simply being born wasn't an achievement worth celebrating.

Aldrich sits back in his chair and places his hands on his desk, his expression unreadable. "I've a bit of bad news for you."

I brace myself, steel my expression, and remain silent. I nod and raise a brow, waiting for him to spill whatever he wants to say.

The corners of his lips rise slightly, making his mouth look like a bloated snake. "After careful consideration, your seat on the board has been revoked." Aldrich spits out the words like nails, not buffering a damn thing.

"You can't do that." I'm the sole heir to my father's fortune. Dad split up the payments and when I could take control of the company. My first million paid in at eighteen years old, then another chunk when I got my MBA. I had to follow in Dad's footsteps, become his legacy, to get the family fortune. I did that. I checked every box, crossed every t, and dotted every i.

"I can, actually. Your father left Reginald Palmer, esquire, with a list of provisions. If certain conditions were not met," he twirls his wrist as if this entire conversation is beneath him, "then your seat would be forfeited and with it your stake in the company."

I'm on my feet, seething, hissing through my teeth. "Why didn't I see this paper before now?"

"Sit down, Celyn," he snaps at me like I'm a dog.

"No, I'm going to see Palmer and straighten this shit out."

"The man is already here. I knew you'd want to see him." He presses a button under his desk and the door to the side of the room opens.

Reginald Palmer is ancient, with snowy hair and timid blue eyes. He's always looked like he was one hundred years old, but today he looks older.

Uncle gestures to me much in the same way he did when I was eight. "Come in, Reginald. Explain matters to the boy."

I stand there, frozen. This can't be happening. This is crazy. I manage to calm myself and sit back down. I incline my head toward Reginald. The guy has always been kind to me, from the day he read my father's will through forming my first corporation. He's patient and kind, which is a rarity for someone in his line of work. Most of his peers are monsters made to devour people, and win at all cost.

Reginald clearly doesn't want to be here. He sits in the seat next to me, tension lining his pasty body. His pin-striped suit fits him well, but then it should. The guy is loaded. He handles all the Bardenbey legal needs.

He clears his throat, but it still sounds raspy. "While I was preparing your father's estate to fully transfer into your hands, and drawing up the paperwork for Bardenbey, a time-sealed letter from your father came due. I remembered drawing up the papers prior to his passing, but years passed and I never thought it'd be an issue."

"What would be an issue?" I ask, not understanding his implications.

Uncle Aldrich cuts in. "Your financial failures —specifically that little stunt where you nearly made the pharmaceutical arm of Bardenbey hemorrhage a billion dollars with your snake oil, RequimX. Remember that? Well, I certainly do. Your father put a failsafe in place to protect the company. In the event that you were not interested, or were unable to fulfill your duties as a member of the board of Bardenbey, he adjusted the will to bequeath the remainder of his estate, including all assets and Bardenbey, to your uncle. The thought was that you'll be very comfortable with the sum already bestowed upon you and—"

I'm on my feet again, fingers clenched to fists, palms sweating. My heart slams into my lungs, stealing all the air. I can't breathe. I can't fucking believe this. Everything I did to get to this moment is being torn away. Silently, I manage to pad to the massive window at the far end of the room and try to steel my nerves. It's hard to stand here and let someone fuck with me like this. The pharmaceutical blunder should have never happened. We did everything we were supposed to do, but we got caught off guard. It cost people their jobs when the cancer cure turned lethal. People died because of me and I've had to live with that. Uncle said it was my youthful zeal that blinded me, the eyes of an idealistic youth deceived me. That mistake haunts me to this day. The money wasn't the worst of it, it was that I robbed people of their last few moments with their families. It's something I could relate to so much, that I wanted so badly. If I could give them a way to live a little longer, then it'd be worth it. In the end, it was my lowest hour and I've paid for it ever since. RequimX was the biggest mistake I've ever made. Now it'll cost me any chance I had at making amends. Well, amends beyond monetary restitution. I already did that, without Uncle's knowledge. It's why I'm broke, save the few status symbols that prove to the world that I'm a Ryan—my car and my clothes.

Staring out the glass pane to the city below, I ask, "Is it true, Reginald? I lose everything?"

Reginald's voice, once booming, is now a timid whisper. "I'm afraid so, Celyn. It could be deemed that you're incapable of serving the company in the way your father desired. Your spending, though not lavish, is beyond modest. And in business, most of your companies have failed to be successful. Unfortunately, if your uncle challenged the court to hear the case, I believe he would win." The old man brushes a piece of lint from his suit, avoiding my eyes. "He could challenge your competency."

"And there's nothing to be done? No way I can prove to you that I am capable? That I can fulfill my father's wishes?" I turn on my heel and beseech the old man.

Uncle scoffs, "You've less than forty-five days. How on earth could you prove a thing by then?" He stands, shoves his hands in his pockets and mutters something about this being utter nonsense.

Reginald doesn't agree though. I see it in his old gaze. He nods to me slowly, "I could arrange a task, terms of which are pre-agreed upon by both parties. Should you achieve the desired results, then your inheritance proceeds as planned. However, if you don't meet the terms of the agreement—there will be no question about the succession of the company to your uncle."

Uncle Aldrich blurts out. "How, Reginald? There are only forty-five days. What could he possibly do in so little time? There's no way."

Reginald pulls a legal pad from his attaché case and starts scribbling. I'm rubbing the scruff on my jaw and trying not to glare at Uncle while we wait. A moment later, Reginald hands me the legal pad. "That would more than prove the issues at hand: frugality, competence, and a solid work ethic."

I blanch when I see what he's written down.

Uncle snatches the pad from me and looks it over. The man starts laughing. "Are you serious? You're giving him five grand for a holiday start up?"

Reginald isn't deterred by Uncle. "Certainly. Most retailers earn over seventy percent of their income in this one month. Thanksgiving is tomorrow. It gives him a few days to get set up."

"What about employees?" I ask, while completely ignoring the pittance offered for the start up. There's a bigger obstacle in the way. "How will I hire people in that amount of time? Management searches take months."

"We'll provide your employees. You decide everything—rate of pay, position, etc. We'll tap into Bardenbey's personnel department to fulfill employee placement, but you have to take care of payroll."

"With five thousand bucks?" I look out the window and consider it. The city is gray today, the sky covered in thick clouds, plump with unfallen snow. There's a sharp chill in the air that makes the pedestrians scurry faster, keeping their chins tucked tightly as they clench their coats at the neck.

Most of the businesses we've started through Bardenbey had a minimum of fifty grand to start up. Petty cash usually has twenty grand. I'd have no money for rent or inventory. I couldn't get most items delivered in a few days anyway, because it's too late in the season. This seems impossible.

Palmer replies after looking up from his notes, "Yes, five grand. And you're forbidden to add to it with your own funds. It's a challenge and that is the point—we need to see what you can do with that amount of money in forty-five days."

I turn and ask, "Who will decide if I succeed or not?" How do we ensure there isn't a bias against me? I glare at Uncle who is standing beside his desk, jaw locked. His expression is void of emotion. The only thing that gives away his anger is the tiny vein throbbing at his temple.

"A secret board will decide," Reginald replies and glances at Uncle, then sighs, "Yes, you have a right to be on the board, as do I. I'm the one who will examine the books and see that profit and paper match. To prove competency you need to net a minimum of two thousand dollars."

I still have no idea what I'm selling, but I think I can manage to earn two grand in a month. Either way, it's this or walk away from everything I worked for. If I hadn't botched that pharmaceutical deal, I wouldn't be standing here now. I took full accountability for that when it happened. I pinch the bridge of my nose and consider it for a moment. I have to do this. I worked my ass off to get here and it's what Dad wanted.

I press my lips together and feel the resolve building within me. I nod once at Reginald. "You have yourself a deal."

Uncle is shaking his head, and snarls, "That's not good enough and you know it, Reginald. This is for the boy to prove himself and with a bar that low, he's likely to trip on it. He has to net the full investment amount by December 31st." His cold eyes bore into me, knowing that the task is highly improbable.

My spine straightens, but I hold back my venom. It won't help now. Startups don't turn profits for years. Asking me to earn that much in that short a period is insane. "That's impractical. You know yourself that most businesses take years to get out of the red."

"Yes, they do, but I have never, in all my life seen someone hemorrhage money the way you do." With every step toward me, Uncle spits out barbs laced with truth. "Your businesses fail because you have no vision, and no leadership skills. You throw money at problems and make small issues into monsters. I'm not letting you near Bardenbey. I'm not going to sit idly by and watch the company your father and I built get ripped apart by some arrogant young prick. Turn a profit of five grand by New Year's Eve. That's my stipulation and it's more than fair with your shitty track record, Celyn. Take it or walk away."

My jaw locks as Uncle stands nose to nose with me. His cold eyes lock onto mine, challenging me to defy him. I won't back down. I refuse to slink away without a fight. I hiss through my teeth, "This is all I have left of my father, and I won't hand it over without trying."

Uncle's lips pull into a lazy smile. "Try all you like, but you won't succeed."

I glance at Reginald and ask, "I have to earn ten grand total, after expenses? Five pays off the original $5,000 to start the business and then I have to profit another five grand on top of that?"

Reginald nods. "Yes, that's the agreement, but it's going to be very difficult, Celyn. You have no stock, no inventory, and aren't likely to get any this close to the holiday season." Reginald looks at me with those old eyes which seem to apologize for Uncle and then fill with pity.

I don't do pity. I'm in a pissing contest with Uncle and if this is the only thing that will appease him, so be it. I jut out my hand toward Reginald Palmer. "Deal."

☙ 7 ❧

CELYN

THE PRESENT

I finish the story and feel the agitation of the encounter flitter under my skin as if it just happened.

Quin nods and raises a brow, his hands still clutching the steering wheel of his Hummer. "Wow."

"No shit. So, what'd you hear at Bardenbey? What was so important that you'd track me down and make me vomit the entire exchange with my uncle?"

Quin shakes his head slowly, his lips parting slightly, and glances over at me. "I can't explain it. You'll have to see it with your own eyes. It sounds —" he shakes his head and takes a deep breath. His hands are strangling the wheel at 10 and 2 as he flies toward the city.

When we get to Bardenbey we go up to the top floor and down the hallway toward Uncle's office. Quin is in front of me, walking quickly, his blonde head glancing up and down like he wants to get in and out without being seen.

I grab his shoulder and stop him. "This is my uncle's office. You were fucking some girl in here?"

"No," he throws my hand off and rounds the corner into the assistant's office. "We were in here. I had her bent over the desk. The adjoining door made her freak out a little bit when we heard someone enter your uncle's office, so I sent her off to the ladies' room to freshen up while I zipped up here. That glass door isn't soundproof." He points toward the frosted glass that separates Uncle's office from his assistant. "I heard him."

I fold my arms over my chest and tip my head to the side. "You heard what?"

Quin's smirk fades and he steps closer to me, and then puts his ear to the glass door. He holds up a finger to me, indicating that I should keep quiet. Quin opens the door and we both walk into the dark room. No one is here. The room is silent, save the soft hum of the computer.

Quin stops by Uncle's oversized mahogany desk and turns toward me. "Your uncle is a dick."

"I know that." Impatience flares across my

face. I try to rein it in, but my nerves are completely shot.

Quin holds up the palms of his hands and says softly. "They were talking numbers. One guy told your uncle that he's been through the books over and over again, but there's no sign of it."

"Of what?"

"That's what I wanted to know, so I hung back after Perky left. Your uncle kept telling him to go over it again, that the man must have made a mistake. But the guy said that he'd done it several times already and the reports don't lie. Your uncle finally let the guy leave and then made a call."

"To who?"

"I don't know, but your uncle told the guy the books were botched, and then verbally castrated the man as if it were his fault and suggested an external audit."

I frown. That's not like him. "Why the hell would he want an external audit? That could turn into a clusterfuck faster than anything else."

Quin shakes his head. "I don't know, but it sounded wrong. He jotted something on a notepad and tore it off. I thought if we could get into his office and find the paper, maybe it could help you out. Something's not right."

I nod, following his train of thought and head toward the wastebasket. Empty. I swear. "The cleaning crew already came through." I pinch the bridge of my nose and lower my head into my hand, thinking.

"Shit man. I wasn't fast enough. I should have come in here when he left instead of getting you."

"No, I needed to see it. The door, and the way sound carries." I glance at my friend. "He didn't hear you two, did he?"

Quin shrugs. "I don't know. He stormed in and was so loud, I don't think he heard a thing. It freaked Perky out. She said your uncle knows everything that goes on in this building. She was worried that she'd get fired."

"If he heard, then there should be a pink slip from personnel in the morning. I'll keep an eye out for it. Actually, I may not have to." It's a long shot, but I know where my uncle keeps that pad in his desk—the pink slips. Most companies don't use them anymore, but Uncle always insisted on keeping a paper trail because computer files can be altered, manipulated. No one can contest a physical signature.

I walk around to his desk and pull open the drawer. The book of pink slips is next to a legal pad with a note scrawled across the page: *429*.

Quin is by my side a moment later, glancing down into the drawer. "What the hell does that mean?"

I shake my head. "No clue." I pull out my phone and snap a picture. Then I run the pads of my fingers over the pink slips. There's no fresh indent on the pad. "He didn't fire her. Not yet anyway."

I glance at Quin, "What the hell does four hundred twenty-nine have to do with anything? Why would he flip out over such a small amount?"

Quin thinks for a moment and answers, "I don't know, but I can visit my perky friend next door to his office more often. It'd be a real sacrifice because there are usually no seconds of this," he rubs the palms of his hands down his abs, "But I could make an exception."

"I thought you didn't nail her?"

He scoffs. "I was nailing her. We were interrupted. I think this chick is an exhibitionist. Could be fun."

I think about the woman I left in the hotel room, about the promise I'd made to get her car fixed. I need to call in a favor. I won't let any of this change me. If I make a promise, I keep it. End of story. "Come on. Let's get out of here."

8

NOVA

THANKSGIVING DAY

Freshly showered and adorned with Tinselly's least bedazzled outfit, I wander toward the kitchen to help. My hair is slicked back into a damp ponytail.

Tinselly is doing five different things at once. She thrives on stressful situations. She's cooking gravy and baking biscuits, while putting the potatoes, stuffing, and turkey on serving dishes. She hands them to Lucas, her husband, and he carries them to the table one at a time.

Tinselly glances my way when I stop in the doorway. "Need help?" I ask.

"Nope. Go sit down. It's going on the table right now."

I was hoping to avoid this part, but if I want food, I need to sit and play nice. Tinselly's table setting looks like it fell out of a magazine and onto the table. Tall tapered candles glow dimly under a cornucopia centerpiece that's filled with flowers, nuts, and fruit. Gold chargers sit under white plates that line the long table and glisten like snowflakes against the plum tablecloth. Matching napkins are folded into pretty shapes, one on each plate.

Tinselly is an overachiever. I love this stuff, but when I try to make it, well—it tends to look like the cornucopia threw up a glue gun.

Tinselly walks in and places a hot dish on a black iron trivet that's toward the end of the table. It's a tight fit, so no one has taken a seat yet. Tinselly waves a hand at us. "Sit! The food's ready."

My eye twitches as I scoot in, crammed between a set of twin toddlers, Lucas, my mother, and my grandmother.

Gran is mostly deaf and somewhat blind, but the woman has the appetite of a grizzly bear. Her little body is squeezed in next to mine, her aerodynamic shoulders sweeping forward from old age, ready to dig in. She's wearing a silvery wig today with bright blue eye shadow.

She snaps at Lucas, "Did you cut the turkey yet?"

Lucas came to this country as a foreign

exchange student, married my sister, and periodically looks like he wants to return to the wilds of Scandinavia. I've never been, so it's filled with polar bears and penguins in my mind. And lots of ice. I imagine everyone wears thick sweaters from Land's End and all the men have beards.

Lucas smiles at me and then answers Gran. "Tinselly wants to cut the bird. She always does a fine job."

Tinselly beams at him, still madly in love. How you can have children and keep the spark in a marriage is beyond me. Between birth and babies, bondage doesn't seem to fit. At least not in my mind, but then I can't even manage to keep my fridge full.

Tinselly opens her mouth to reply, but Gran cuts her off. "A man needs to cut the turkey. It's bad luck otherwise."

I lean back in my seat and gape at Gran even though she can't see me. "Really? Since when are you all 'the man must do it?' You've always said that Tinselly didn't need a man for anything."

Her blind gaze cuts to the side as if she can see—sometimes I swear she can—and she grins. "There's one thing that's much more satisfying with a man—"

Tinselly mutters something I can't make out.

My eyes widen at the remark and I gently

swat her arm, scolding her. "Gran! There are little ears here."

Gran shrugs. "What? You asked. I answered."

Mom is staring at me like she wants to say something but isn't sure if she should. Mom looks older today, her skin paler like she hasn't been outside much. Tinselly is a photocopy of Mom. Add a few years, some polyester, and a massive chip on her shoulder and you have my mother.

After Tinselly carves the turkey and everyone is served, Mom forces a smile and stuffs a fork full of peas into her mouth. When she's finished chewing my skin prickles in anticipation of the question. "So, have you and Ben set a date?"

Tinselly stiffens as she's cutting up the twins' turkey into toddler-sized bites. Her eyes cut over to me and she hovers there for a second, laughs nervously, and blurts out, "They already told you, Ma. They're not ready yet."

I mouth thank you to my sister and start poking at my mashed potatoes that are forty percent butter and one hundred percent amazing. I shovel some into my mouth and feel my bad mood lighten, well, until Mom starts talking again.

My mother doesn't like that reason. She continues prying, "Nova, you can't make him wait forever. Not every marriage turns out like mine.

You need to pull your life together. You've got a nice apartment and a good job. Fill your fridge with food and keep your good man."

Gran cackles, holds up her wine glass and blurts out, "It's time to make the babies."

I laugh from discomfort and shock, but more from the fact that she said it like the Dunkin' Donuts guy. "Gran!"

"You have everything." Gran says.

"No, I don't." I gape at her. Is she insane? I'm broke and if things work out well, I'll turn into the old lady in the cat car.

"Yes, you do. You've had everything to catch a man for a while."

I blanch when she gestures her hand to the side and accidentally swats my girls. Lucas's face turns red as he pretends he didn't see and turns his attention to the toddler nearest him.

"No harm in pointing it out." Gran swats a withered hand at me, making the silver bracelets on her wrist clatter. Gran could be easily mistaken for a gypsy fortune teller with her tiny arms packed with glittering metal and a crocheted shall over her shoulders at all times. The only difference is that Gran's pants are polyester rather than a billowy skirt.

Mom picks up where Gran left off. "Guys like Ben don't wait around forever. If you keep putting him off—" she gapes at me as I suddenly begin shoveling food into my mouth in a very unladylike way. "Novatin Nikolaev!"

Just as Tinselly finally sits down to eat a now cold meal, I scrape the last bit of stuffing off my plate and shove it into the Thanksgiving buffet in my mouth. I feel bad, I really do, but I can't do this right now. The speeches about how I had everything and blew it will reduce me to a bag of tears. No way. I'm out of here.

I stand and hear Gran pish posh me, but Mom just rolls her eyes as if she knew I was incapable of adult conversation. That's totally okay, because it's true. I talk with my mouth full as I wave the tips of my fingers at the twins. "This was so good, Tinselly. Your cooking is amazing. The house is perfect. Add a baby Jesus to the front lawn and you'll be all ready for Santa."

The twins cheer in unison, chubby little hands in the air like they really don't care, which makes their food go flying. Cranberries splat on Lucas's cheek. He acts like nothing happened, and wipes it off with his hand, and licks his fingers before going back to his plate.

Tinselly stares flatly at me, fork in one hand, knife in the other—paused above her slice of turkey. I see it in her eyes. Pity laced with annoyance, but then compassion floods in and wins out.

She knows I'm miserable. I'm treated to a warm empathetic look. "Thank you. If you wait a second, I'll make you a baggie and grab you a piece of pie."

Everyone knows the only thing in my fridge is condensation and an empty jar of pickles.

I'm already walking by the twins, kissing the tops of their heads, and making a beeline for the door. "No need. I'll stop by tomorrow. You wanted to hit the sales, right?"

Tinselly pauses half way to the kitchen and turns. "Yes, but—"

I wave to the kids as I back away and only slow to grab my purse. Tinselly follows me as Mom mutters from the dining table to my brother-in-law about responsibilities and that I need to buckle down. I'm about to lose it. I shove outside without my pocketbook on my shoulder.

Tinselly comes out a moment later. She smiles calmly. "You don't have to do what they did. No one in their right mind gets married that young anymore."

I'm mad, pacing across her sidewalk and onto the crunchy dead grass that's covered in a thin dusting of freshly fallen snow. I want to rant and throw my hands in the air and scream. Instead, I let out a huff and turn back to Tinselly. "You did. Mom did. Gran did. So I'm nearly twenty and have no desire to marry anyone. That doesn't mean I'm some sort of social pariah."

"I know," Tinselly says soothingly. "I happened to find the right guy. Mom didn't. Gran did. The point in all this is that it's your life. If Ben wasn't the one, he wasn't the one."

Tears are prickling at the back of my eyes. She doesn't know why we broke up. I never told her in the text messages. I didn't say anything about the other woman, or that he has a warm bed. I'm alone again. I thought Ben was going to be the one. I thought that he loved me and only me. But he didn't. He cheated.

I feel hollow inside. When people look at me, very few see a teenager, a nineteen-year-old. I've been called an 'old soul' for as long as I can remember. I've seen things that most kids never have to endure. I was a frightened child when it happened and it changed me. But, I'm the wiser for it. It also separates me from the other women in my family, and the rift feels like a chasm at times.

I put my hand on Tinselly's shoulder and smile at her. "You cooked a great dinner and I'm ruining it."

"No, you're not." Her sincerity kills me. She'd do anything for me and I love her for it.

I turn her back toward the house and start her

walking in the direction of the steamy glass door. "Go eat something, play with the kids, and let someone else clean up. Everything looks beautiful and tastes delicious."

She leans into me, refusing to move. "But what about you? What are you going to do?"

I stop pushing and when she faces me, I smile broadly to hide the ache in the middle of my body that threatens to tear me in two. "I'm going to figure out what I want to do with my life. I'm starting over. New job. New life."

9
CELYN

I hate holidays. They sting and seem to draw attention to everything I lost. There are no warm memories to cherish. Holidays with Dad are fuzzy recollections at best, and there's nothing of Mom. I don't remember the sound of her voice or the feel of her arms around me. I know she was there in the beginning, but not having the memory of her scent and her touch feels like a piece of me is missing.

I'm at Quin's Long Island home, sitting in the kitchen, stealing small parfaits off a silver tray while the staff hurries around the large white room, chopping, seasoning, and cooking a Thanksgiving meal fit for a king.

Quin sits on a stainless steel countertop across from me, dangling his feet off the sides. He pops a pastry into his mouth—a puff of the lightest buttery potatoes you've ever tasted coupled with a tiny bit of something that tastes like gravy and bacon bits, all inside a flaky golden crust. It takes a lot of self-control to not eat the entire tray.

Quin licks his fingers and then smooths his dark green sweater. "So, five grand and forty days. What the hell is that supposed to prove anyway? I could make five grand in my sleep."

"Doing what?" I feel my face pinch together as I wait for an answer, and he has none. I lift a hand and point out. "That's the problem. It takes money to make money. If you have no fucking capital, it's a lot harder. That's the point. This whole thing is a test. If I don't pass, then I'll lose everything I've tried to accomplish."

Quin nods, his brows pulling together. "No more payouts?"

I shake my head and pop another pastry in my mouth. "No. The will assumed succession at age thirty-five. Dad didn't think I'd fail. The letter he wrote seemed to be an afterthought, a way out in case I didn't want the company."

Quin plucks another delicacy off a passing crudité tray and pops it into his mouth. When he finishes chewing he asks, "So you need a customer base that already wants whatever you sell. You don't have time or money for ads. You need people lined up from day one."

"With minimal overhead, and a skeleton crew to staff the place. And I think it needs to be a consumable product. Something that people come back for over and over again. Something cheap that I can get my hands on today. I can't get stuck waiting on a truck for deliveries that never show."

Something clatters on the other side of the kitchen and the chef swears. A maid rushes by and cleans up the fallen tray as more kitchen workers walk around her like she's not there. There's a hum to this place, the way people work together to make fine food at all hours of the day is alluring. It's not frantic, but it moves quickly. I've always admired Rupert, Quin's chef, and the way he runs the kitchen.

Rupert is an older man, thick through the middle, dressed in a perfectly pressed white chef's coat with gray pants. He walks to us with a kettle in his hand, "Would you like some tea or coffee?"

Quin nods. "Coffee."

I can actually feel my brain thinking. It takes the concept, crunches numbers swiftly and I blink it away. Those numbers aren't wholesale. The markup is there, but I hesitate.

Rupert is watching me, waiting for my answer. Instead, I ask, "Where do you get your coffee?"

He seems startled. Rupert smiles kindly and explains, "From a handful of suppliers. Then we make the blend in the kitchen, one for breakfast, lunch, dinner, and dessert. Plus seasonal blends and special creations for parties."

I can see it, I know what I need to do. Coffee. It's a highly consumed product. It's like milk—they use it as an example in business classes. Everyone needs it. Everyone sells it. It's the repetitive nature of the consumer purchasing the milk from one place that makes it a profitable item to sell. The same thing could be said about coffee. People are crazy about their caffeinated cup of java. The markup is easily three hundred percent. Add things like soft drinks that have a four thousand percent markup and I can see it working.

I've been quiet too long. Rupert is still standing in front of me. "Can I watch you make the blend?"

Rupert beams with pride and nods. "Certainly. There's nothing to it." I follow him across the kitchen with Quin on my heels. The guy has known me forever and knows I've thought of something.

"Coffee? Are you serious? You don't have the

money to open a shop and hire a bunch of baristas." Quin talks to my back, and shakes his head. But I feel it. I'm onto something viable, something that I can manage with the five grand and not piss it away. He's right though. Rent will eat too much of the startup funds.

Holding up a hand, I turn on my foot and look back at him, while trailing Rupert. "Those are logistics, Quin. We've got a consumable product and it's cold outside. People are shopping like mad after today, so we should be where the people are already going."

Quin frowns. "Are you fucking serious? You want to open a kiosk at the mall?"

"Hell no. That thing would cost more than we have and no one is cold once they're inside. We need one of those portable buildings outside the mall."

Quin frowns and stops. "A roach coach? You want to sell coffee from a fucking truck? Have you lost your mind?"

Rupert grabs three bags of coffee and a few spices, grinds the beans, and puts it into a percolator. Within moments the scent hits me hard. The guy has always made superb coffee, but I never really thought about it. His coffee was one of the things I liked the most about eating at Quin's—I looked forward to it, craved it. I tell him what I'm thinking. "If I could come up with a blend even half as delicious as yours, I'll be able to fix this mess."

"There's no need to start at the beginning. Use my blends."

Shocked, I stand there and blink. "Really? No, I couldn't do that." This guy spent years perfecting his recipes. I can't use it. It'd be like stealing from him.

Rupert clasps a thick hand on my shoulder. "You will do it, because you're a good man and I want to help you. I'll write them down for you, and make some suggestions to cut costs."

Rupert hands me a cup when it's ready, as I pick his brain about beans and suppliers. Rupert pours a cup for himself last, and then leans a hip against the counter next to Quin. Rupert explains, "There's a place where you can purchase open crate items at a fraction of the price. It's the same beans. They've either spilled or were an overage that another establishment refused."

I lean against the counter, sipping the rich, hot beverage and try not to moan as the heat slides down my throat. "Can you explain to me why I would want those beans if they were refused?"

"That's like picking beans out of the trash."

Quin frowns and then follows a server with a silver tray out of the kitchen.

Rupert smiles kindly. "Quin is a smart man and typically sees opportunities to turn a profit. The price of gourmet beans for making several different blends is expensive. Using the open bags, when possible, will give you a greater profit margin. With today being a holiday, I bet you anything that the distributor has an overage right now that he'd sell off if you offered the right price."

"Thank you, Rupert. I mean that. You've been incredibly helpful. But I still need to get creamer, milk, and a machine to make this stuff. Add in the rent and the personnel, and I don't know." I shake my head without realizing it. Rent alone will devour most of my cash.

Rupert presses his lips together firmly and then says, "If I may be so bold, I would suggest creating a reason, in addition to the fine coffee, to lure people to your location. Something that will create chatter and advertise for you."

Quin struts back in, hands in his pockets, and overhears the last few words. "Oh, you know what would have everyone talking? If you made the place like Hooters, with amazing girls wearing next to nothing. I'd pay extra for that."

I laugh for a second and then think about it.

The image, the brand, is as important as the product. I could have something amazing and if people aren't talking about it, no one will come. I point at Quin and then slap my palms together. "That my friend, is an excellent idea. We need to hit the ground running, and that would do it."

I smile as all the pieces come together in my mind. I can see it, the whole thing. It's a machine of many parts and when they're all working in sync, I'll have something amazing.

10

CELYN

It's past midnight and I'm back at my place high above Manhattan. After a shower, I pull on a pair of boxers and slick back my damp hair. I've been thinking about this nonstop, but if it doesn't work on paper, I'm fucked. So, I start drawing up the business plans.

As I get it on paper, there's one variable that's still screwing me over no matter what I do—the rent. A headache looms, so I press my fingers to my temples, trying to chase it away. I have to net two thousand bucks a week in addition to expenses. At three bucks a cup, that's six hundred sixty-six cups of coffee a week. I laugh, darkly. Holy fuck, that's a lot of coffee—and a seriously bad omen. Since I don't think the devil has it out for me—well, not unless Satan has been posing as my uncle for the past few decades—I think I'm safe.

So I need to sell roughly ninety-five cups of coffee a day. That sounds possible, but again, I need to make a reason for people to come out and pay three bucks instead of staying home. Quin's idea had merit, but it's so tacky. If I don't come up with something better soon, I'm taking the idea and running with it.

The clock chimes one and the decision is made. I'm opening a fucking hottie hut and selling coffee. I still need a location with cheap rent at Christmas. It's a laughable idea. I lean back against the couch and close my eyes for a moment. Visions of the blonde from the other night are there, behind my eyes. Her soft smile and those curvy hips. I can still picture her silky skin, and the way she laid seductively on the bed for me.

I should have gotten her name, asked for a number—anything. Life is stressful and having a fuck buddy like that to call up would be amazing. She didn't seem like she wanted anything more. I know it'd be insane to go looking for her, I'm the one who left her. I could have stayed, lingered. I'm a fucking coward. I can't go looking for her. There's no way my suggestion will sound right. Then there's the issue that arises when she finds out who I am, that's always a problem. Having money has fucked me over before. It's difficult to know if a woman is after me or my cash. I'm partly jaded and think it doesn't matter why she's there. The other part of me is a fucking moron and wants the money to be irrelevant. But cash is always relevant, in business and in life. But this girl didn't know, she didn't catch my name either. She was there because she wanted to be.

I fall asleep thinking about her, imagining the feel of her hips under my hands while feeling her naked body pressing against mine. I shouldn't have left her. That still gnaws at me. I push the thoughts away when the strain against my jeans becomes unbearable. Thinking about her isn't doing anything to address my problems. Well, maybe not. As I picture that hot body and long blonde hair, I imagine her in a sexy winter outfit —a dirndl and a super short skirt like a slutty Swiss Miss. Her tits would be perky from working the window and her cheeks would have that freshly fucked glow from the chill in the air. She's a fucking wet dream. Guys would come just to talk to her. The thought spurs ideas. More thoughts pop up in my mind, ways to ensure that the staff stay safe and keep assholes in check. A guy would need to be there too, someone who could handle himself. I can picture a fur skin vest and tight jeans on the men to give something for the ladies to admire. Add in a fuzzy cap and it could work.

Desperation's chokehold on my neck loosens as I pad over to the empty bed. I lie back and close my eyes, and drift off to sleep.

❧ 11 ❧

CELYN

The next morning I'm standing in a tiny shed at the edge of the mall parking lot. There's a huge-ass pile of dirty snow packed behind it. I'm staring at Quin like he's insane. "This is the Italian Ice stand they use in the summer."

"Exactly," he grins, his cheeks rosy from the frosty air. "And they're not using it now."

"Because there's no heat. Or windows. Quin, they'll freeze." I stand there staring at the front of the tiny building. It's a wood paneled shack, with evergreen colored paint over wooden siding. White trim lines the roof. There are two boarded up screens at the front and a counter that extends past the window making it easier for the customers to get their goodies. The entire shack can't be more than one hundred square feet.

Quin pats the side of the building like it's a lonely beast. "But the rent is so cheap. Since this place is only open during the summer and it just sits here the rest of the year."

"Because it has no windows and no heat. It's snowing, Quin." I point to the sky as if he can't see the flakes falling.

"You don't have to deal with union shit. This is a temp job, Celyn. Stop acting like these people matter, they don't. You're using their hot bodies to attract buyers to this location. The longer they linger, the more they get to look. You can't afford to pass this up."

"She'll freeze her tits off."

Quin frowns, asking, "Who? Did you hire someone already?"

"No," I backtrack to make it sound like I wasn't thinking of anyone even though I'm still hung up on the blonde. She must hate me. I banish the thought. "But frostbite and lawsuits—"

He cuts me off, "Right, and they can bite you on the ass later, regardless. I'm well aware, but it's your only option. Let them fucking sue you. You'll have your company and your inheritance. You can take the hit. If you pass this place up, we have no options. You can't afford anything else, not even a burned out roach coach."

I don't like this. They have to be protected from the elements, at least a little. "Fine, open it up. Let's take a look."

Quin unlocks the door and we shove inside. It's narrow and long with two countertops stretching down both sides. The windows open out with no glass or screen. I bump into the counter and Quin as I try to turn around. "There's barely enough room for two people in here."

"So it lowers your overhead. It also means you're not paying for employees that you're not using." Quin lifts his brows and leans on the counter. He reaches for the latch and unlocks the board covering the window and cranks it open. The board forms an awning over the little counter. He looks out at the snowy parking lot. The mall is to the right and the highway is in front. A guy selling Christmas trees is all the way at the other end of the lot. There are a few restaurants toward the highway. It's a good spot but there's no way to make this thing hold any heat.

I tap the unopen, boarded up window. "Can we put glass in here?"

"Celyn, no. It's a hut. He needs it in hut shape

for the summer." Quin beams at me. "Forget all that and ask me how much the rent is? You're going to love it once you know how fucking cheap this place is."

"Fine, how much?"

"Only $800 for now through January 1st. No deposit. No electrical hookup fees. There's a fucking generator for power. There are no utility fees."

"What about inspections, health code, and all that shit?"

Quin raises his hand toward the window. "Seasonal establishments are exempt from a lot of shit. The shack already had its inspection for the year. If you do this, we can put a space heater in here and you can afford to rent an actual percolator instead of using a fucking Keurig. Come on, Celyn. This location works."

It does. There's a lot of foot traffic already. If I'm willing to treat people like shit, I can pull this off. Maybe a space heater wouldn't be so bad. I'm not a moron. But they could hug the heater and never get warm if there are no windows. There's just one problem—I'm not that much of an asshole.

I shake my head. "We've got to have windows so this place holds heat."

Quin sighs heavily and shakes his head. "Fine,

but it'll eat into your start up. Do you really want to spend it on something you won't get back? The shits working here will still sue you. They'll still be cold."

"But it won't be as bad and I won't be looked at as a totally heartless dick. Glass is cheap. It couldn't cost more than a couple hundred bucks, less if we do it ourselves."

Quin grins. "You can cut glass?"

I shake my head. "I've seen it done a thousand times."

Quin tries not to laugh. "Right, so the glass is a few hundred, plus install. Add in the fact that it's the holiday season and you're going to pay triple to get someone out today. Plus I have to get the shack owner to okay it."

I nod at him. "Do it. I'll get signage."

Quin scoffs, "Today? How the fuck are you going to do that?"

"I know a guy." I slip out of the shack without another word.

12
CELYN

After going through the ACME Sign Center's recycled neon signs, I find the word HUT. It's in white letters, all capitalized. There's a neon sign that's red and reads HOT. I ask them to make it say HOTTIE and agree to pick them up later that day.

My heart is pounding hard. I've never been so pumped about a project before. Maybe it's because this one can't fail. Or maybe it's because there's more of me in it than the other business ventures. This is all elbow grease and manpower. The lack of funds made it that way.

Quin is helping me out. He knows how much I want my seat on the board, but even more than that—he knows how much I wanted to earn my uncle's respect. I'm not some teenager seeking affirmation anymore. I know he'll never give it—he's not that type of man. I get it. But after years under his roof, I feel like I'm finally free, even if it's for just a moment. There're no expectations here, nothing to live up to. I can do whatever I want. Creativity is bubbling inside of me. I feel it simmering from my fingers to my toes, raring to go.

After the glass is in, we scrub the place from top to bottom. The coffee grinders, cold case, and other machines will be delivered later today. I want everything spotless by the time they arrive. I already managed to find a costume shop that was willing to work with me. They have four outfits that I can rent as uniforms. If I get sued, it's going to be over that. The dirndl is a sexy blouse for the women with billowy sleeves, a scoop neckline that is nearly immodest, and a corset back. It gets laced tightly from behind which makes the shirt expose so much cleavage that there's no way I can say that it's not sexualized. Maybe the women won't care. Maybe they like big tips. Any girl with a rack worth looking at has learned how to work it to her advantage. This is no different. I tell myself it means more tips for her, that it'll be okay even though the pit of my stomach turns rancid thinking about it. There are enough dicks out there that make women feel like a piece of meat. The only thing saving my ass is that I'm equally distributing scantily clad uniforms to both genders.

My last stop is to pick up a few nametags. I grab them and head over to the shack. Quin is there overseeing the glass installation.

Quin is in the shack, pissed. He throws down a cloth he was using to clean the counter. His green eyes narrow. "It was nearly $1200 for the fucking glass."

My jaw drops as I set the things I brought down on the floor. "That's more than double the estimate."

"Yeah, well, there were issues." Quin folds his arms over his chest. "You see the owner wanted sliding glass windows so they can open them during the summer."

I cut him off. And step forward to see that's exactly what they installed. "But we were going to take them back down when we leave. It was supposed to be a sheet of glass with a small cutout in the middle. Damn it, Quin."

"I know, that's what I told him. But the shack owner insisted on it. Long story short, he ate half of the bill and we leave it for summer. So it's a bit more than expected, even after he chips in his part."

I pinch my temple firmly, massaging away the

tension that threatens to crack my head open. I glance up and tell him. "We're still okay assuming we can get people over here."

Quin points to the parking lot. It's a sea of automobiles with no empty spots in sight. Cars are circling trying to find a place to park. "They're already here, so I don't think that will be a problem."

I hope he's right. People are reluctant to try a new place. I need to think about how to get a swarm of people to mill about over here for the first few days. That'll be tricky. People attract more people. It's like this parking lot. If a car found an empty section of the lot and parked there, by the time he comes out there will be a cluster of cars around him. Likewise, if you walk into an empty restaurant, most people turn around and walk back out. It's a bad sign. People assume the place sucks. Getting some folks to mill about the front will be important. I need to figure it out.

I pull the bags onto the counter and start to unload them. "I've got signage. It lights up too."

"Sweet. Who's doing the install?"

"We are."

Quin frowns. "Seriously?"

"Yes, seriously. They're a little heavy. You can help me get it in place and I can secure it."

"Fuck. Fine. And what are you going to do if the town wants to see a permit? This guy has a hand-painted sign he hangs out during the summer."

"We don't need a permit. Come with me. I'll show you."

Quin follows me to the back of my SUV and when I open the hatch, he laughs. "Hottie Hut? Did you swipe that sign off a Pizza Hut?"

"No. It was at a recycled signage lot. It's part of a Pizza Hut sign, and then a bit of neon for the rest. They wired the two together so all we have to do is hang it. I had them put in a plug so we don't have to wire it to the shack."

"Sweet. Then you don't need an inspection. It's a modular sign."

"There's already a socket up there for the flood lights. I'll grab a splitter and we can use that socket for the sign."

Quin is staring at me. "Since when do you know shit about real life?"

"Since when didn't I?"

Quin laughs. "You weren't all Home Depot in your younger years."

"Asswipe," I smile at him and laugh. My phone buzzes and I glance down at it. "Get the inside cleaned up as much as you can. There are a few people coming over for interviews. Are you up for some hiring?"

Quin presses a hand to his chest and beams. "You mean interview hot girls. Hells yeah!"

"You have to hire hot men too. We need both."

He frowns and his body deflates, his shoulders slumping forward. "Seriously?"

"Yes, it's mandatory. These women will be working late, in the dark, and the shack is isolated. I don't want something to happen. Pick six employees. They're working six-hour shifts max, because it's cold. We open at 6am and close at 11pm. The closing crew has to prep for the next morning, so they'll end up working a few more hours. Got it?"

"Yeah," he grunts.

"Good. I'll be back in a bit. Oh, and here are the name tags." I dump them out on the counter.

Quin lifts one and laughs. "No names?"

"No, it's safer this way. No one will know their real name, so there'll be less room for stalkers and inappropriate behavior."

"As if that will stop people. I personally like the fact that you made every employee a piece of meat. The employees are going to love it." He grins wolfishly at me. "There are six different, umm, names on the tags?"

"Yeah, so if customers like someone or are complaining about them, we know who it is." I consider what he said for a moment and then disregard it. Safety trumps everything else. It's a fucking shack. I don't want problems and this will make a mental barrier between the employees and the customers.

"Nice." Quin grins and looks down at the nametags. HOT GIRL is typed in bold white letters on a dark blue background. "I can't wait to pick the hot babe who's wearing this tag."

13

NOVA

I shouldn't have quit like that. I should have used vacation days, sick days, anything, and then quit. The way the paperwork stands, the company is Ben's. A minor trying to get a loan is a bitch, so we made him the money and I was the brains. Too bad I wasn't using them the night we broke up. But I couldn't think after Ben side-blinded me. Now, I have no unemployment check and no money. Add in the fact that it's Christmastime and there isn't going to be anything but shitty seasonal jobs. I've already spent the morning on craigslist and, unless I want to be a stripper, no one is hiring. I groan inwardly and press my palm to my face. Luck could strike and I could get a decent job. I have a call out to my friend at an employment agency. She's going to contact me if something pops up. Although she reassured me that something would, I still feel sick.

I lean back against my threadbare seat in the car and tip my head back against the headrest. The first night after the breakup, I crashed in the hotel room. Hot Guy didn't come back and I had no where to go. Tonight is another story. I'll blow through the small amount of savings I have stashed away if I try to live at a hotel, even a cheap one. I need to make do with what I have and I'm sitting in it.

I SIGH DEEPLY AND CLOSE MY EYES. BEN IS gone. I moved my stuff into my trunk early this morning when I knew he'd be at work. I left behind so much, but it would be too painful to look at.

I wish I could go back and redo the past few weeks. I wish I'd seen he was unhappy. I thought it was just me. I guess I knew, but I thought that was the daily grind. Life isn't fun. Being an adult isn't a happy occasion with ribbons and parties. It's hard work. I thought we were going to work together. I thought I'd have a ring on my finger and have to slow the wedding date to a timeline I was comfortable with. But not now. He was seeing someone else. Another woman made his life so much better that he left me behind without a backward glance. The center of my chest aches and my heart feels heavy. As much as I try to ignore the pain, it's impossible. I loved him.

Just as tears well up in my eyes, my phone rings. I pick it up and steel my voice as I answer, "Hey Judy. Did you find something?" I glance out the window of my car, hoping she doesn't hear the sea gulls screeching outside. The windows do nothing to quash the noise.

Judy is a hyperactive twenty-seven-year-old with a thyroid condition that makes her super bubbly and very skinny. She's always revved up, no matter what time it is or what's going on. Today is no different. "Nova! I found a management job for you."

I sit up quickly and feel the pang of hope flood my chest. "Really?"

"Yes, it just popped up. It's from Delex Holdings. That's a Bardenbey company, so it should be a good job." I hear keys clicking as she speaks.

"Bardenbey? Like that huge-ass company in the city?" I remember seeing a tall black glass building with their red letters on the side of the skyscraper.

"Yup, that's them. They're all over with lots of

little businesses. No one realizes how big they are. This position is being filled through the main office in the city, which should be a really good sign. The interview location is on Long Island. They must be opening a new branch out here. That would be amazing, Nova. No commuting. Can you get there by two o'clock?"

"Yeah." I feel a smile tug at my lips. Bardenbey. A real job with benefits and a 401K. I could almost cry with relief. My anemic bank account wasn't planning on getting through Christmas alone. I'm never trusting a guy ever again.

"Okay, I grabbed that timeslot for you and put in your name. The address is over by the mall." She gives me the location and I scrawl it onto a piece of paper along with the time.

"So, this is a management job for what exactly?"

A few keys click as she mutters unintelligibly, then says, "Uh-huh. Right. Okay, the position is for a coffee shop manager. Oh my God, Nova. Have you seen some of their shops? They're beautiful with marble floors and exposed beams."

"The places that look like upscale warehouses?" Not to mention overpriced and bitter coffee.

"Yeah, that place! Wow, Nova, that would be a great job. I could see you in a nice suit, all sleek, telling baristas how to use the machines and doing all the office work that other people totally hate and you love. Make sure you tell them that you're a nerd and that you'd marry math and have its integer babies if you could."

I snort a laugh, "Geeze, Judy! I'm not that much of a dork."

"Yes, you are, and that's why I love you. You're all pretty on the outside and all nerdy on the inside. Just make sure they see the nerd. In the past they got stuck on your face and ignored your skills."

"It wasn't my face he was looking at, and it's more of my age than anything else. Everyone wants to know why I'm not in college."

Judy talks quickly, keys clicking as she speaks. "Avoid that topic at all cost. Give them your work ethic speech. No one will even remember college after you say that spiel."

"Got it. I need this job so badly. Thanks so much for helping me out."

"Yeah, yeah. Thank me with celebratory drinks tonight when you get the job. And, Nova —maybe now isn't the time to say it—but you could do so much better than Ben. I never liked him anyway."

My heart thaws a little when she says that. I had no idea she didn't like him. Maybe she's just being nice. Either way, it was something that I needed to hear. "You're the best, Judy. Drinks on me if I get this."

"When you get this," she corrects.

I grin into the phone. "When I get this. You're damn right." I'm going into that office and I'm not leaving without a job.

14

NOVA

I pull out my best suit, don a pair of stockings, and twist my hair into an updo. When I look in the mirror I see a young professional and hope my appearance is exactly what they're looking for. When it comes to getting a job, if you already look the part, it's easier for them to picture you in that role. The managers in those swank coffee houses wear sleek black suits and polished pumps. I hook a pair of gold studs onto my ears and tuck a loose strand of hair behind my ear. I can do this.

Jitters mix with adrenaline as I walk to my car and start the engine. Thank God that hot guy fixed the alternator the other night. I wouldn't have been able to get to this interview if it wasn't for him. I make a mental note of it and feel some bad juju coming on. Going for it with him was a plus—it helped separate me from my ex. He fixed the car. And if I get this job, then that's three awesome things. It means something sucky will probably be quick to follow. It's a stupid observation, but luck seems to come in threes, swiftly followed by a swift kick in the ass from life, reminding me that Murphy's Law was invented for a reason.

When I get to the mall, I circle the lot looking for the number on the outside of the building. It's not there. The GPS on my phone says it's here, like in the parking lot. That makes no sense. I circle the mall twice and head to a far back row to park and check the address again. Maybe I transposed a number?

I look down at my phone, shivering in the cold car, and fail to see the building. When I glance up, the ice house shack catches my eye. There's movement, people are working over there. I watch for a moment and this tall, slim, young man comes out and hangs a sign that says, #26751-B.

That's the address. I'm ten minutes early. According to Judy, this is the first interview slot, which is usually a bad slot to be in, but the rest were full. Everyone else is compared to the first candidate, but people have no one to compare the first person to so they tend to not get hired. Screw that. I'm getting this job. I bet they're working out of that shack until they build their new building over it in the spring. Maybe management will be sent some place warm to train. I'd be all over that. I'll work Christmas without an ounce of regret. This job is mine.

15

NOVA

I nearly slip and fall on my ass as my heel loses traction on a patch of ice outside the shack. My arms flap wildly as I catch my balance. Heart pounding harder, I knock on the little door on the side of the shack. A handsome young man pushes the door open. He smiles broadly at me. He's wearing a sweater under an expensive wool coat, paired with jeans and boots.

He reaches out and holds the door open, gesturing for me to come in. "Hi! You must be Nova. Great to meet you."

I return his smile and slip past him, careful not to snag my heel in a hole in the top step. "Thank you. It's great to be here." That's when I notice I'm overdressed. Compared to him, I look like I belong in an office and not a little shed in the parking lot. My lips tug into a tight nervous smile as butterflies swirl in my stomach. This place is so small that it's hard not to bump into him or the counters.

"Please, sit down." He holds out his hand to a set of folding chairs that are crammed between the two counters.

It's not escaped my notice that I'm trapped and can't leave with him blocking the door. I don't like that, but I have pepper spray in my purse. I'll use it if I have to. I scold myself for being so paranoid. This is a Bardenbey company. They don't lure young women into trailers to do nefarious things. I force myself to breathe as I take a seat. The blonde man sits opposite me.

"I'm Quin. I'm helping the owner select his management today." Quin goes on about the company, confirms it's part of Bardenbey, and tells me all about the job. I'd need to work long hours on my feet, be willing to do inventory, spreadsheets, reports, and nightly deposits. The owner will look over purchase orders but I'm the one writing them up after he shows me how he wants it done. I'm getting the importance of doing things the boss's way. Quin is making that very clear.

He stops talking suddenly and his cheek pulls up on one side as he chews the tip of his pen and eyes me. "Normally there would be three rounds of interviews and you'd start in three weeks if you were given the job. With things the way they are, we're in a bit of a time crunch so my decision is the final decision. You'll find out today, before you leave, if you've got the job or not."

That makes my heart pound harder. I want the job. "Awesome." I clench my hands in my lap and try not to wring my sweaty palms. I try to look cool, confident. "I can start right away and work holidays. That's no problem at all. In fact, I take a lot of pride in my work. I'm neat, proficient, and know how important it is to do things the requested way. I'm a team player and I work hard. You'll be glad you hired me." There I said it. I keep the loose smile on my lips as I stare him down. I've gotten jobs I was utterly unqualified to have using this speech. It's the last part that's tricky. If my tone is off or my facial expressions are too tight, it comes across as arrogant. No one hires a bitchy chick. I need to walk the line between confident and arrogant, which lands me on the intelligent and eager tightrope. Staying there until the guy makes up his mind is tricky.

Quin has his hand on his chin. It means he's making a decision about me and I feel like there's a barrier, a concern he hasn't voiced about me. I prompt him, "It seems like you're considering something. Why don't you ask me? I don't offend easily and it seems like you have a question that needs answering. Ask me, Quin."

The man laughs and his hand drops from his face. "Okay, you caught me. I'm not sure how well you'll fit in with the personality of the shop. It's a fun, hip place. There are uniforms that are quirky. It's part of the marketing plan. You seem so neat and pulled together that I can't really imagine you in this place at all, never mind as a manager."

Shit. He's deciding against me. Why did I wear a suit? Increasing the wattage on my smile, I relax my shoulders a little more so that I'm almost slouching and brush the arrogance third rail as I reply. "That's a valid concern. Hiring the right people makes all the difference in whether a business succeeds or fails. I'll tell you why your coffee house will be better with me in charge. I'm a hard worker, I'm adaptable, and I make sure every customer feels like the only customer. Repeat business is what makes or breaks a place like this. I'll keep them coming back."

"How?" He folds his arms over his chest and leans back in the little plastic chair.

My pulse is pounding in my ears. I'm making shit up, saying anything I think sounds good to convince this guy that I'm his girl, that I can kick anyone else's ass in sales and productivity. We smile, laugh, and things take a turn when I tell him about my last job. "I don't usually dress like this. I know they say dress to impress and the other coffee shops have a very elegant air to them, hence the suit and heels."

Quin laughs lightly in agreement and nods. "Yeah, the suit threw me a little bit, but you've convinced me. If you can live up to the hype—"

I steel my voice and interrupt, "I can surpass it."

He grins. "Fuck, I can't argue with that. You're hired." His hand juts forward for mine we shake pretty firmly before he adds, "Welcome to the Hottie Hut."

16

NOVA

Still smiling, with his hand in mine, I laugh. "The what now? I thought this was for a Bardenbey coffee house manager?"

Quin shakes his head. "Nope, it's for seasonal management right here."

I blink and try to hide the apprehension on my face. "Here? In the ice stand?"

"Yes, right here. Which is why heels and a suit don't work. The uniform is included in your salary and base pay starts here with bonuses if you reach certain sales thresholds each day." He holds out a piece of paper for me.

I take it and look it over. The pay is marginal, but the bonuses are pretty good. Combined, it makes the take home check enough money, assuming I can sell as much coffee as I claimed.

Pressing my lips together I ask the question, "Are there benefits?"

He shakes his head and loops his arm over the back of the chair. "Not at the this time. If you're as good as you say you are, I'd expect Bardenbey to grab you before the end of the season. This is a place to prove yourself, show that you're a good sport and an invaluable team player. It'll end up in your permanent file and when they want to hire a manager for one of the main shops, your name will be at the top."

It sounds like bullshit, but Judy works in human resources and said that's how it works. It's rare to get into a management job at Bardenbey from the outside and I'm being given a chance. I should take it. I can do this. A shiver licks my spine and I convulse without meaning to. I'm not wearing a wool coat like Quin, because I'd assumed we'd be inside a heated building.

Quin continues telling me how much promise a job like this has, that entry points into Bardenbey are rare and this one will be snatched up if I pass it up. Then he tells me about my daily tasks, and points to the places where the machines go. Apparently, they're showing up later today along with the rest of the business supplies, including cups, lids, sugar, stirring sticks, and all that.

Then he stops, stands, and looks down at me. "So, Nova—are you on board?"

I rise and force a smile, jutting out my hand to shake on it. "I am. Thank you for the opportunity." He shakes on it and then turns to grab a piece of paper from a pile of papers on the counter. "Head over here to get fitted for your uniform and report here tomorrow afternoon. You're on the night shift. We close at eleven. They'll make sure you're fitted and ready to go for tomorrow. The only thing you need to grab is a pair of shoes. I'd suggest sneakers or something comfortable since you'll be on your feet all day. See you tomorrow."

I want to ask about training, but I swallow the questions. Now isn't the time. I thank him and walk out of the shack. When I sit down in my car, I look at the address in my hand—it's a costume shop.

17

CELYN

By the time I get everything else we need to open in the morning, Quin has completed the interviews and hired the employees. He's grinning ear to ear when I see him with a cup of Starbucks in his gloved hand later that night. The sky is the color of coal and more snow threatens to fall. If they plow the parking lot again, we'll be buried from sight. It concerns me, but like everything else in a new business, you worry about issues you can't control when it's a real problem and not a moment before.

I bring in bags from the home improvement store and place them on the counter. A shiny percolator is there along with the grinder and some other equipment. The sink is spotless and the floors have been scrubbed. Quin sips his coffee. I scold him, "If you show up with that again, I'll ban you from the property. How'd interviews go? Should I be worried?"

Quin swats a hand at me. "Fuck, no. I hired a manager and a barista and two baristos. Is that what you call the guys?"

"Are they all hot?"

He laughs. "Like you need to ask. Yes, the women are smoking. The first one—actually she's the manager—had a stellar resume but she was buttoned up. I didn't think it would work, but she begged for the job and knew how to bullshit her way into convincing me to hire her. If she could sell me on that, I think she can manage to hit your sales goals. Hell, she was talking trash so much that you should increase those goals. I got the impression that she needs that bonus money. People work harder for that kind of shit."

"The position pays horrible as it is. The bonuses are attainable for a reason."

Quin takes another chug of coffee and tosses the empty cup in the trash in the corner of the room. "That's where you're wrong. Bonuses should appear to be attainable, but when it comes down to it, they're not. She works harder, you keep the cash."

I stop what I'm doing and face him. "That's

being a dick and a really horrible boss. We're still connected with Bardenbey. I can't diminish the brand, Quin."

"You wouldn't, Celyn. I mean think about it. If you didn't have to fork over the bonus money, you'd hit the goal that much sooner. And you have to hit it. It's not optional."

"I know that." I snap at him and go back to unloading my bags.

"Then stop being such a fucking idealist. This is business. You save a penny, you earn a penny, and the way this clusterfuck is set up, you need every cent you can squeeze out." Quin stands, grabs a case of cups and starts stocking the cabinets, putting them in size order with the corresponding lid size below. "Like this," he holds up the cups. "You only bought two sizes. Why?"

"Because the lids are fucking expensive and I wanted to have the opportunity to upsell."

"Right, so you needed a minimum of two sizes, but why these sizes?" He holds up the small size and then the grande size. "The comparison is obvious. You can sell this motherfucker for twice as much money. Any idiot can see it's twice as big."

I snort and shake my head. "Yeah, but that's not what I'm doing."

Quin frowns. "What are you talking about. That's standard practice."

"I'm going the snack pricing route."

Quin's jaw drops. "You're shittin' me."

"No, I'm not. Listen, if we price the regular coffee at three fifty, we can upsell them to this size for an extra $2 if they buy a cookie."

Quin sneers. "You bought cookies?"

"I ordered cookies from a bakery that's on the way here. They'll have the lot ready at 5am. I pick them up on my way here. I grabbed a display case so they can go in the window."

"Who's going to pay two bucks for a fifty cent cookie?"

I laugh. "It's not what you think, okay? Trust me. It'll work. We'll hit our average sale price a lot easier this way. Plus the cookies are cute. Women can't pass up cute shit, and if a hot guy is telling them to buy it, they will."

"Cute cookies?"

"Yeah. And I don't have a fucking dime left. The five grand is gone so all funds for payroll have to be earned this week. Thank God there's a two week delay before payday." We'd be totally screwed without it. As it is, the noose feels incredibly tight around my neck. I never do business this way. It's incredibly risky. I arranged payment on the machines and planned on restocking weekly. It took a lot of convincing to get the monthly rates broken down like that. The prospect of working with the heir to the Bardenbey Corporation was too enticing to say no to. Actually, they said no until I mentioned my name. Then they were more eager to listen, but they didn't really understand why I was being a cheap-ass and I can't tell them it's because I'll fucking lose everything if I don't pull this off.

Quin makes a sound and his face contorts as he says it, "Celyn, listen. I didn't tell them about the delayed pay. Actually, I don't think any of them could have swung it if we didn't pay weekly. I changed it."

"What? Without telling me?" I close my eyes and feel the pressure in my chest increase. Every move cost money. Every time we take a step, it could lead to failure. Imagine losing your entire fucking fortune on one shitty shot. That's this. The odds are stacked against me. I fucking know that, and withholding a week's pay fixed cash flow issues. Quin knew that.

"Sorry, man. I thought we could take a loan to get supplies and pay it back."

"No. The terms don't allow for it. None of our personal money can mix in here and I sure as hell can't have them find fault where I lose everything. Damn it, Quin."

"It was that or we work it, which also disqualifies you. You have to manage payroll, keep your manager, and show competency. I know, and I thought about it. Sorry, man. I didn't know what other options we had."

I look at him. "That means we can't have a soft start tomorrow. We have to hit the ground running. Ideas?"

Quin grins and nods slowly. "Have the hotties stand outside the shack early in the morning and hand out coupons for a free sample cup."

"What? Another size?"

"Yeah, but hear me out. Make it small and cute. Then upsell to the regular size with your cookie bait. You'll make a three dollar sale off a free coupon. It's fucking good coffee, they'll be back if they taste it. Plus, they'll see that the shack has hot chicks in it, and be willing to drive over. We can have a few mini cups for the cheap-asses who won't upsell, but 80% should go for it."

I didn't want to run things this way. I didn't want to come across as a cheap shit and that's what this feels like. It's not a bad idea and I know he's right. I just don't like it. "Fine. Do it when there's no line."

Even with the glass installed, it's fucking cold in here. My throat tightens as I realize that I can't be the type of man I want to be—it conflicts with getting my inheritance. There's a clear division in business between what's ideal and what's possible. Nothing is ideal here. The employees are going to be freezing the entire time. We're both wearing coats to stay warm. The pane of glass helped, but it's not enough. Quin says it won't matter, that the girls and guys walking in the parking lot with their scantily clad uniforms won't matter either. In the end it means more tips for them, and more money for us.

After everything is set up, I go outside with Quin to hang the sign and plug it in to see if it works. HOTTIE HUT illuminates the dark night. I wish I didn't have to stoop so low to prove myself, but I can't see another way.

18

CELYN

The next morning I'm up at 4am and out the door. I won't see Quin until much later, which is fine since I want to strangle him. He always says that I spend too much on crap that doesn't matter. Maybe he's right. Maybe that's the point of this whole thing, to teach me to be a tightwad and treat employees like shit. It's the fastest way to succeed, at someone else's expense.

Why did I have to be a fucking idealist? I try to turn it off, but I can't. There's no fucking switch, so I put on blinders and ignore it, and I fully intend to be the hard-ass boss that people can't stand. They can hate me all they want. It's only for a few weeks and then I'll be in the boardroom, back where I belong. I park my car behind a pile of snow. I don't like that it's out of sight from the hut, but there's not much I can do about it. Besides, I have more pressing matters threatening to crush me. I need to get moving. The shoppers will come in swarms starting around 7am. It's peak shopping season and I want everything to be perfect.

I'm pulling out the cookies from the bakery and putting them on a baking sheet. There's a piece of white parchment paper on top of the pan, beneath the confections. Each cookie is about the size of my hand. I angle the tray and tilt it up a bit by sticking a brick under it so the people standing outside can see. I grab the mason jar candle I bought from the dollar store and light it. This was literally my last buck of the five grand. I light the sucker. It smells like the sugar cookies. I put it in the window. We'll never bake them here and the candle was an afterthought, but it might make a difference. At this point, anything that helps is welcome.

When I finish grinding chef Rupert's concoction of different coffee beans, I put the grounds into an airtight container and stick it on a shelf. I start on the decaf when I see a POS car roll up and park. A guy with model-like features gets out wearing the sorry excuse for a uniform I required. The fur vest hangs loosely around his toned chest and the dark leather-like pants are a bit tight. A silky blonde mop adorns his head and hangs to his clean-shaven chin. He looks like a Norwegian model.

Donning the fur cap, the guy walks over to the hut and visibly rolls his eyes as if he never thought he'd have to stoop so low. That makes two of us, pal. When the Thor-like man pulls open the door a rush of cold air hits me in the face, I turn to him and nod.

"Good morning." I stop what I'm doing for a second to shake his hand. "I'm Celyn, the owner."

"Hey. I'm Shannon." He glances around the shack, bleary-eyed. I show him how to use the machines. He watches me with complete disinterest. Finally, he mumbles, "I worked a similar set up at a shop in Manhattan."

I glance at him, wondering why he's not there anymore. I don't ask. "Great, then you don't need any hand holding today." I bend down and grab my briefcase from the floor. I wedged it between the cabinet and the wall when I came in earlier. After placing it on the counter, I pull out the coupons for a free cup of coffee. I added snowflakes and other winter shit so they look more aesthetically pleasing. I still feel like the coffee should have a cute, catchy name but it eludes me at the moment. I've been operating on too little sleep for too long.

I hand him the coupons. "Hand these out and when they're gone, come back."

The guy frowns. "You realize it's cold enough to snow, right? And that I'm not wearing a shirt?"

I stare at him. My face is stern but I feel like a shit.

Shannon rolls his eyes as he says, "Whatever," to himself, and then turns on his heel and heads back out the door. He spies a pack of women and starts beaming and I can tell that the man is a bullshitter. He can turn on the charm when he wants, and he must have been at full wattage when he interviewed yesterday. I make a mental note to consider moving him to the night crew. The man clearly isn't a morning person.

Shannon points back to the hut, and hands a woman a coupon like it's a bar of gold. She tucks her chin for a moment and shyly looks at the pavement that's covered in ice and sand. When he walks away, the group of women glance at the shack several times before disappearing inside the mall.

I check my watch, wondering where the other employees are—she'll be late if she doesn't get here soon. I finish the decaf and start the corresponding machine before I take the container, seal it, and shove it on the shelf.

My heart is in my throat. I can't believe Uncle did this to me. That bastard has been vying for this since dad died, but I didn't see it. I should have noticed. How did that many years go by without my seeing the signs? Again, idealism bites me on the ass. I made excuses for him, thought he was just a hard man who never let his guard down. Rose-colored glasses did nothing but skew what'd been in front of my face for years. Truth be told, I have no idea if I can actually do this. I hope to God that I can, but I don't know. Today will clue me in. If people come over, we'll be okay. If they don't—I'm fucked.

An old gray Honda rolls to a stop in a nearby parking space. The windows are fogged but I know the car. It belongs to that beautiful woman, the one I walked away from. The one I've been thinking about every day since. My heart leaps up my throat. How did she find me? I lean on the windowsill, planning some suave line and practicing my best smile, when she kicks her car door open.

Black boots hug the lines of those curvy legs. Just above them, her skin is covered in tights that flow up to a...I gape. Shocked. She stands and smooths the pale blue, fluffy skirt, with the white slip peeking out from the hem, making sure the frilly apron that's tied around her waist is perfectly smooth. She's missing a jacket, so she shivers, rubs her arms and sighs heavily as she smooths her palms over the tight-fitting dirndl top. It hugs her in a way that makes it impossible to not notice those full tits and the way they fill out the top. She stomps across the snow-covered lot toward the door, skirt billowing in the cold wind with her golden hair in twin braids, poking out from under a fuzzy hat. Holy fuck. The woman is a force of nature. Eyes turn to her, it's impossible to look away. The curve of her back, the way she carries herself like she doesn't take shit from anyone has me seriously worried. A girl like that shouldn't be in a place like this. Quin did not hire this woman. There's no fucking way.

As much as it pains me, I pull away from the window and riffle through my briefcase, pulling out the papers and find her application. The morning crew is Shannon, Erin, and Nova—my new manager. I glance out the window again, while scanning Erin's application. There's no picture, just a vague description from Quin's notes—five foot, blonde, previous experience. Her application looks like it was filled out by a lovesick middle school girl. The I in Erin has a little heart over it. My chest feels like there's a vice crushing me slowly. I glance up again and know that it's her. Holy fuck. It's her. The sex goddess with the Chilton's manual is here, and her name is Erin. Somehow Quin hired her. As my eyes sweep over her papers, they get ensnared on one line. The date of birth. My face falls.

I mutter to myself, "No fucking way." Sweat lines my brow even though it's cold. I can't make excuses and I sure as hell don't want her to know I'm the asshole who made her wear that outfit. I panic. That's the only reason for doing what I did next.

I've regretted it ever since.

19

NOVA

This uniform, as he called it, is horrible. It's itchy and the skirt sticks out so much that if I bend forward or reach for something on a shelf, my ass will peek out. Who the hell makes their employees wear stuff like this? The shirt is so thin that I can see my lacy bra underneath. The embroidered thick belt hugs my waist and rests just under my chest. It's thick and overlaps the top of the skirt. To make it better—as if this outfit needs to be more brazen—there's a hat. It's white fake fur with two pompoms that dangle from a string on either side of my head, popping me in the face every time I turn my head. I feel like an idiot.

Who's going to take me seriously dressed like this? I want to be a team player, but this? Grabbing my purse, I manage to get out of the car without flashing anyone. I'm thankful I decided on the white tights because, holy fuck, it's cold today. The sky has that look to it—like the thin gray clouds are ready to release a deluge of snow. The air has that sharp, crisp scent like it might snow. I love that smell. I forget everything that plagues me for a brief moment, tip my head toward the sky, and breathe in deeply. The freezing air fills my lungs and makes me smile softly. But there's something coupled with it... cookies? I glance around, not seeing where the scent could be coming from. I frown. I'm too young to have a stroke, but I swear to god that I smell vanilla and brown sugar. Great. As I get closer to the shack, I see the little sign blazing and squirm.

Wonderful. I'm an attraction. Quin failed to mention that yesterday. If I didn't need the job, I'd walk in and tell him off. But I do. Screw that, I'm going to give him a piece of my mind anyway. This isn't cool. I expected to pick up a uniform suitable for a manager, not a slutty leftover Halloween costume. I stomp up the steps and kick open the door.

"This is so not cool." I'm shouting before I look up. "I specifically asked about attire and you said a uniform. You failed to mention that I'd be playing the part of slutty barista." I stand in the doorway as I shake off the cold and when I finally lift my face, it's not Quin. It's him. The hot guy from the other night. A smile tries to form on my lips as my eyes sweep over his beautiful body. I'm rendered speechless for a moment, my wrath forgotten. I breathe, "It's you."

"Yeah." He whispers, his voice deep. He's wearing a black sweater that looks incredibly soft. The V-neck has a white shirt peeking out from underneath. It's coupled with dark jeans and he looks hotter than the last time we met. He's clean-shaven and his dark hair hangs over his brow, making those blue eyes bright as sapphires.

His gaze lingers on me, a look of remorse in his eyes. His dark lashes lower like he's uncertain. The softness that lines his features is there one moment and then vanishes. In its place is the arrogant man from the bar, the one exuding confidence with a huge-ass chip on his shoulder.

He steps toward me, and shakes his head. "What are you doing here? Did Quin hire you, too?"

Quin? I can't breathe. There's something in the air, a spark between us. It was there the first time I glanced up at him and it remains even now. I forget myself, forget this silly costume, and feel something I can't identify. It swirls inside me, warming me from within. If he hadn't walked out, I would have been happy to see him. It should be awkward, but that's not what I'm feeling. It's as if there's an invisible string tied around my waist, tugging me toward him. The string pulls tight, and then snaps.

He blurts out, voice sharp, "You're nineteen?" He folds his arms over his chest like I lied to him the other night.

My eyes cut to the side as I arch a brow at him. "Yeah, so?"

"You're a fucking teenager?" He spits the words at me, glaring.

I bristle and squeeze my fingers tightly at my sides to reign in my temper. "Wow. Nice. Very smooth." I don't offer more. I don't tell him I'll be twenty in February. I don't say anything. Instead, my chest tightens and I can't breathe. The horror on his face hurts. I'm young, but I don't feel it. There are days that I feel weary and beaten by the world. Blame it on my past, I do. There's an old woman living inside of me. She's seen too many horrible things to still have the youthful idealistic tendencies of a teen. I wish I felt that way, but I don't. And I don't like it when someone thinks less of me because of my age.

His jaw gapes and he runs his hands through

his hair, tugging it. "You should have said something. I didn't know."

I frown and toss my purse on the counter and get up in his face. "When, exactly? We went straight from the bar to the hotel. You had plenty of time to ask about me. You didn't. So don't act like I tricked you or something. Besides, age shouldn't matter."

"It does!" Okay, he's either really old or I'm missing something. He places his hands on the counter and hangs his head, before continuing. "I'm thirty-five." When I don't reply he looks over at me.

I'm still standing there in my ridiculous costume, straight-faced. "Am I supposed to say eww and gag myself? Age doesn't matter. You're the only one hung up on it, so get over yourself already. Ass."

"What did you call me?" The corner of his lips twitches as if he wants to smile. I also sense a bear in there ready to rip my head off, but I don't back down.

"Ass. Arrogant ass." I step closer to him and feel the same current sizzling pulling between us, strung taut, ready to pop. "That'd be you."

"You're a kid." The horror on his face makes me feel sick.

I haven't been a kid for a long time. Life

knocked the shit out of me pretty fast. Some people age in years, I wasn't lucky enough to be one of them, but I'm not telling him that. "You're a superficial arrogant prick if you can't see past a birthdate."

"I'm your boss." He stiffens and stares at me.

Holy shit. I stiffen and shrink back a little as the warning bells in my mind clang together and shatter. They fall with a rapid thud into the pit of my stomach. My boss? He can't be my boss. This is getting so messed up.

I start muttering. "I don't know if you think I'm repulsive, or you actually think I tricked you, but..." My jaw flaps and I have no words. It seems like some distorted sense of chivalry was violated. It makes my stomach churn and something that was magical turns to ash before my eyes. The compulsion to apologize shoots up my throat, but I can't say it. I didn't do anything wrong. I was being me, living my shitty life, and he came on to me.

"You lied." His accusatorial tone is sharp, unforgiving.

My right eye narrows and I spit back, "I don't usually get proofed before sex, but then maybe you typically ask for ID. I wouldn't know because you never came back."

We're standing so close that when I inhale, my

chest brushes against his. Every light sensation sets me on fire. The memory of him, his touch, his taste—and his kiss, burns within me. His eyes lower from mine and lock on my lips, but he doesn't move. Tension laces my muscles as I resist the urge to touch him, to rest my hands on his chest and press my lips to his.

He's staring at me with that unreadable expression, a million words trapped behind those full soft lips. He swallows hard, forcing the Adam's apple in his thick neck to bob. That's the only sign that he might be nervous. It's the only sign that he might believe me.

A shiver races up my spine and the pull toward him increases. I want to step forward and kiss him. I want to taste those lips again and shut him up. Maybe I would have if he wasn't my boss, if he didn't seem so offended by me. The rejection doesn't sit right and sure as hell doesn't match the look in his eyes.

The tension breaks as his phone rings. When he turns away, I can breathe again. He pulls it from his pocket, answers, and then shoves past me into the parking lot. I watch him out the window, pacing.

An older man walks up to the window, and I notice the orange streaks across the early morning sky. The color accents his old wool coat.

He's round with fuzzy white eyebrows, a brown old dude cap on his head, and a smile on his face.

I slide open the window and return the grin. "Hello, sir. How are you this morning?"

He looks at the sign on the hut, and then back at me. "What are you selling? There's no menu in the window. I thought I'd come over and ask."

"Coffee and cookies." I glance at the counter and have no idea what anything is or how much it cost. Quin isn't here and hot guy is pacing in the parking lot, tensely talking on his phone. Talk about being thrown off balance. If I were him, I'd be more upset that I was in my thirties and working at a place like this.

"I don't know if I should have something so sweet for breakfast, but I'll take a cup of coffee."

"Of course," I'm about to turn away and grab the coffee, but I hesitate. My mouth has been watering since I stepped out of my car. I bet he smells that candle burning too. "You know, these cookies were the first thing I've smelled in a long time that made me want to eat the entire tray. I caught the scent in the parking lot before work this morning. I haven't tried one yet and I really want to." I glance between the blustering hot guy, pacing, and the old man. I lean closer to the sill and ask, "How about I split mine with you?"

He blushes slightly and smiles harder. "That's

very sweet, but my wife is waiting in the car and I think she'd have a stroke if she saw me splitting a cookie with a beautiful woman like you. How about two coffees and two cookies?"

"You got it." I have no idea how much anything cost so I guess. After pouring the coffee into the big cups, I grab two cookies from the sheet and place them in parchment. I wrap them and seal it with a piece of tape since I can't find a baggie or box. I set the things down on the counter and tell him the made up price. "It's five bucks per cup—that's amazing coffee by the way—and three bucks for each cookie. The grand total is sixteen dollars."

The man hands me a twenty and says, "Keep it. You're a sweet kid. Put the rest in your tip jar. Merry Christmas." He takes his coffee and cookies and walks away.

Hot Guy bounds up the steps and throws open the door. "You can't sell anything yet!"

"Sorry. He walked up. You saw him." I glare at him, ready to fight and then manage to keep from rolling my eyes. I lean a hip against the counter and cock my head at him. "What was I supposed to do?"

"Wait a minute." He bites back whatever he was going to say and calmly asks, "How much did you charge."

"Oh yeah," I jab my thumb at the window. "You need a menu or something. He got two large coffees and a pair of cookies for sixteen bucks."

He blinks at me. His lips don't part and he doesn't speak for a while.

It gets uncomfortable so I start rambling as I try to not to pick at my nails and avoid his eyes. He's the one who didn't tell me anything and then wandered off. It's not my fault. "Listen, I'm sorry if it was too cheap. I didn't know and there's nothing written down. He walked over to ask what we had. They should really have a sign up in the window with whatever else we sell. I guessed. If it wasn't enough, Quin can take it out of my check. He was a nice guy."

He still doesn't speak, just nods slowly. Then repeats, "Sixteen dollars?"

"Yeah." I don't know why he's so on edge. I feel like I broke his brain or something. I lower my head and tip it to the side to catch his eye. "Hey, are you okay?"

His crystal blue eyes meet mine. "Yeah...I need to make a few calls. Keep doing whatever you just did. I need to get in touch with Novous, my new manager."

I nod and try not to smile. He's such an ass. When people see my legal name on a piece of paper, they assume I'm a dude. No one assumes it shortens to NOVA. It's happened before. I'm used to it, but this time it thrills me a little bit because he's so off kilter. It's like he had an epiphany and skittered away before he could jump in the air and shout *eureka*!

Hot Guy walks outside again, plucks his phone from his pocket, and dials. A second later my phone rings. I fish it out of my frock and answer. A lazy smile snakes across my face and I lean forward in the window and say, "Hey, this is Novous."

Hot Guy stops when he hears my voice from the window. His shoulders stiffen before he turns in slow-mo and lifts those cobalt eyes up at me.

I wave at him with the tips of my fingers and smile too sweetly. "Yeah, I'm Novous, but most people call me Nova. I'm your new manager."

20

CELYN

I stand there, stunned. This girl can't be my manager. That would be horrifying. I saw her perfect tits and walked away from that beautiful bombshell without an explanation. If she's the vindictive type, she could make my life hell—or worse. She could figure out who I am and what I'm doing here. If she learns exactly what's at stake, I'm screwed. It's possible she's not that petty, but I can't have her coming between me and my fortune. I've worked too hard for this. My future is wrapped up in this hut.

Play it cool, Celyn. Don't let her see you sweat. I wipe the shock off my face as I pocket my cell and crunch across the snow back to her. I stand below the open window on the frozen pavement, gaping up at her. "So, you're not Erin." It's a statement.

As I gaze up at her, she shakes her head with that lazy smile still in place. One corner of her mouth is tipped higher than the other. She rests her elbows on the counter and leans forward on her arms, offering a spectacular view of her cleavage. I can't tell if she knows she's doing it or not. She has to know. How could a woman like that not be aware of it?

She blinks those long lashes at me and then juts out a hand though the window. "Nova Nikolaev."

I swallow hard and reach for her palm without thinking about the touch. People shake hands all the time. It should be nothing, but it's not. When her soft skin slips against mine the pit of my stomach drops and the tension from unfinished fucking laces though my entire body. I'm stiff, everywhere, and mute. I can't do more than blink at her beautiful face. I feel like a goddamn idiot, caught in a siren's trap.

Those smooth fingers lead up to slender, soft hands. They stand in contrast to her no-nonsense grip as she nearly crushes my knuckles. The handshake does something to me. It's like her touch is going to end me. A sensation that's warm and tickling spreads from my fingers, up my wrist, and into my arm. When it passes over my shoulder and into my chest it threatens to consume me. Gasping, I pull away sharply.

I steel myself, making my walls rise up faster, making sure they're thick and impenetrable. I've worked with women before, I've seen scorned exes after the fact, and nothing like this has ever happened. I can't act on anything I feel, not with her so young. It'd be wrong. Not to mention the whole, she'll figure out who I am and the last thing I need is a complication thing, but that's what's staring me in the face—a fucking sexy complication.

I force my face into a harsh smile and ask through my teeth, "Why did you say you are a teenager if you're not Erin?"

Her lashes flutter as she tries to avoid my eyes. She's perched in the window and shrugs. "Erin? Who's that?"

"The barista Quin hired. I thought you were her."

"I'm not." She smirks at me.

"Yeah, well, we know that part now. So, tell me about yourself, Nova." A wicked smirk twists my lips as I stare at her like she's the goddamned enemy.

She cocks her head to the side and narrows her gaze, annoyed. "I'm nineteen, not nine, and I don't like it when people presume to know me based on a number. Life isn't all unicorns and ponies. I'm not that girl. You don't know me, so don't act like you do."

She visibly bristles and I get the same feeling from the other night. There's a sharp mind and a wicked sense of humor beneath the beautiful face. I'm watching her, trying to make sense out of the anomaly in front of me when she raises an eyebrow at me.

"What?" She rights herself, and I notice that my eyes weren't where they should have been—on her tits. Shit. I've been looking at her face. The tightness in my chest presses harder. I need space from this woman—this girl—but I need to stay here and go over things with her. I'm going to kill Quin when I see him.

This is business, so I need to pull my shit together and act like it. I can manage sharing the hut with her for a few hours. It's not for that long, a few hours max. That's possible. Just don't tell her where you went or what's going on. Let her keep her distance. She has no love for me, I can see that. Getting rejected like that had to suck. I am wondering where the hell Erin is and why she didn't show up, but I tuck away that thought for later.

"Listen," I offer, trying to reign her in a little

bit so she's not breathing fire at me later, "you're right. I don't know you..." I would have stopped there but this know-it-all smile rises up on her face and I keep going, "and I don't care. This isn't therapy, it's a job. Do you want it or not?"

She flinches and then her eyebrows knit together and she narrows her gaze at me. "Yes."

"Then we need to go over a few things."

"I'm not the one who ran outside." She smirks.

Running away from this chick is becoming a problem. I make a mental note to stop doing it to her. I won't back down again. I won't give way and let her pass. If she needs space, she needs to be the one to walk away, not me. I'm at the door and back in the hut. We get down to work.

❧

I GO OVER EVERYTHING WITH HER, ONE STEP AT a time, expecting her to ask me to slow down so she can take notes with a pink sparkle gel pen, but she doesn't. Actually, she doesn't write anything down. She trails me as close as a shadow, looming without touching, watching me as I show her what I'm wanting—what we need to accomplish. My manager has to be on the same page as me for this to succeed. As it is, I don't know who else will be on this panel that determines my fate, but I know if I do the entire thing solo, I won't get jackshit. They want to see I can run a business and part of that skill set is handling other people. The manager is the linchpin between the staff and the owner. They need some insight into how I want things done so she can convey it to the rest of my new hires.

I was on the fence about telling the manager that we have to meet goals before, but this settles it. I'm not telling her the real reason. I'll have to skirt the truth. This one will sense a lie before it comes out of my mouth. There's just something about her in that regard. I wonder if I'm right. My guess is she doesn't take crap from anyone and that she isn't here on purpose, after getting stood up. By me. Fuck. What if she tracked me down and showed up here to sabotage me? I mentally scold myself. She's a chick with a Chilton's manual, not the devil. Cut it out. And trust your gut. Stop thinking like a dick.

Based on her disposition and that POS car out there, she's broke. That's why she's here. "At the end of the season, if you hit ninety-nine percent of your daily goals there's a bonus."

She stares blankly at me like she doesn't care.

I laugh and shake my head. "What, then? Money doesn't matter to you?"

"Come on, Kelley." She's been calling me that even though I told her my name five times already.

I act like it doesn't bother me. "It's Celyn. KEHL-ahN." I spit out each phonetic sound of my name.

"Right." She smiles sweetly and blinks those big eyes at me. "The thing is, bonuses are usually unattainable. One bad shift will make it impossible to meet these goals, so unless you have a real offer, just skip over the whole bonus part. I work hard without an incentive. I don't need it."

Did I offend her? She's leaning her hips against the counter, arms folded over her chest—defensive—with her face angled down to the floor. She shivers and rubs her arms.

I hate myself for the costume, but they work. We already sold more today than I'd thought possible. She could have done it without the costume, but that's part of the reason why people are looking. It's why people wander over. I know because several chatty women came by asking for Shannon, who isn't here right now. I sent him inside the mall to thaw out while I finished up with Nova. I didn't have to ask the guy twice.

I reach over to the space heater and turn it up. She doesn't say anything. I lick my lips before pressing them together and then tell her the truth

—well, most of it. "I need to incentivize the staff. You might work just as hard with or without a reason, but the rest of your crew won't. That's just the way it is. Case in point, Shannon. He's been gone for over an hour and I told him to come back in twenty minutes."

She snorts and nods. "I noticed that. Don't worry about him. I can ride his ass."

A visual pops into my head of her doing unspeakable things with Shannon. He's closer to her age, and it's a completely acceptable match, but it pisses me off. She deserves something better, not that slacker.

"What?" she asks, tipping her head to the side to catch my eyes. "Don't believe me?"

"No, that's not it." I watch her, my eyes resting on hers. There's a fierceness there, a tiger ready to spring, at me—at anyone—who hurts her. It's not until that moment that I realize she held back when she first saw me. She could have ripped me apart, but she didn't. Why? Unease swirls in my stomach as I consider her motivation for being here and putting up with the costume. Is she that strapped? Or am I just that unlucky? Sandy would have something to say about that, poor dog. Maybe this chick can sense the sizzle of my former four-legged best friend.

Silence stretches out so far that it snaps. Nova

sighs, "Then just say it. You don't think I can...fill in the blank, Kelvin."

I want to hear my name on her lips, but she won't say it. I growl, "Celyn."

"That's what I said." She smiles saccharine-sweet, which irritates the hell out of me.

I blurt out what I'm thinking without filtering a goddamn thing. "I don't think you can rein in Shannon and make him perform at capacity and that's what I need, Nova. I need everyone working here to give it their all and act like this place belongs to them."

She doesn't hesitate. "Then make it belong to them."

"What?"

She pushes off the counter and takes a step toward me. I can almost see the rapid thoughts bouncing through her mind. "Give your staff a share of the profits. If you do well, we do well. Bigger companies have stock, but this is a hut and I'm guessing that's not an option. Besides, stock and that sort of thing is very abstract. Offer the baristas something they need, and let's face it—we all need money or we wouldn't be here."

"That's insane. There's too much overhead." Not to mention it's a crazy-ass suggestion and hasn't been built into the business plan. Although she just tripled the price of everything and people are willing to pay it. The thought tugs at me. I need to run the numbers to see if it's possible. As soon as I think it, I hear my uncle's voice ringing in my ears, scolding me for being a bleeding heart. Sympathy is the fastest way to tank your business and I can't chance it this time. I shake my head. "Can't do it."

She shrugs and glances out the window. "You asked."

My face crumples. "No, I didn't."

She snaps back toward me. "Well, you should have. I'm not new, you know. I was running a big company before I came here. I started it from the ground up, and—"

I glance at her, and cut her off, "Then why are you here? Come on, Nova. You should have done a little more believable embellishments on your application." It's meant laughingly. Everyone beefs up their resume, adding things that they didn't really do. I call her on it. "You expect me to believe that you were a nineteen-year-old running a company?"

Her face goes slack as her jaw drops. "You think I'm lying?" I hear the bristling in her voice before it fills the shack. She steps toward me, her beautiful face full of anger. "Say it. Call me a liar if that's what you think of me."

"Nova—" I try to back away, but there's

nowhere to go. My back hits the counter and crazy Swiss Miss is toe to toe, hissing at me.

A moment later, she rounds and starts stuffing things into her huge-ass bag. "You can look down at me for being nineteen. You can look down at me because I'm a woman. I'm used to that. I can handle that, but I won't tolerate being called a liar." Her eyes bore into mine, sharp as razors. It's a look that says 'kiss my ass' and has the finality that implies I'll never see her again.

I step in front of the door, blocking her way out. She nearly steps on me, stumbles a pace, and then rights herself. She growls, "Move."

"No." What the hell am I doing? She was caught in a bullshit lie and I called her on it. She can't throw a fit and get out of it. At the same time, who would quit over it? It doesn't make sense.

She moves closer to me, and even though the top of her head is below my chin, I think she could get past me if she wanted. She sucks in a jagged breath and glares at me. "I won't ask again."

"Neither will I." She softens for a half a beat, swallows hard, and looks up at me. "Please stay." I can't believe I'm doing this. If she were anyone else, I would have let them walk, but the way she handles the customers and the brains in that head of hers make her irreplaceable. That much, I know. If I'm going to make this happen, I need her. She's a non-expendable part of the equation. I can see that already. With the few hours I've spent with her, that much is clear. If she takes ownership of this place, and I think she will, it'll flourish as if the shack was hers. I have no idea where she came from, but apparently her past experience was real. I've seen techies with mad skills before twenty, but it's rare for a person to have a mind for business at that age. I sure as hell didn't.

She swallows hard and steps back, her gaze dropping to the floor. The way she holds her shoulders stiffly and with the air filling her chest, I can tell she's pissed. Nova drops her purse on the counter and says, so softly that I can barely hear her, "Some people get upset about other things and act like lying isn't a big deal. Well, it is to me. I can't respect anyone who intentionally lies, manipulates, or omits the truth, so tell me or don't tell me—but don't lie to me. I won't lie to you."

Her fierce brown eyes meet mine. There's a story there, something painful. Deceit cost her something, and this version of Nova lays in its wake. This is the aftermath of a storm that ripped her apart. I find myself nodding, not wishing to tear her down further.

After that, she's tense, but as more customers come and go, she's back to being that swaggering woman from the bar.

21
CELYN

I admit that I'm enjoying myself, talking to her and watching her interact with the customers when I glance at my watch. It's coming up on eleven. It's been the two of us in here since early this morning. My other employee appears to have wandered off. It's possible he's still handing out fliers painfully slow, strolling from one end of the lot to the other, but I doubt it.

I ask her, "Can you see Shannon out there?"

She looks over the heads of the people waiting in line and those emerald eyes scan the icy pavement. "Nope." She glances at the people in front of her. "Anyone see a sexy guy wandering around. Furry vest and poufy hat? Looks like a hot, lost Viking?"

The lady standing directly in front of her glances at Nova with a wicked grin. "No, but I wish I had. He sounds delightful." The women waiting in line all start talking to one another. For a moment, there are hushed whispers and giggles as they peer around the lot, looking for the lost hot man.

I catch a breath and run my hand through my hair so I don't sour their pleasant moods. "Well then, I'm heading out. Can you manage alone for a bit?"

She answers without looking my way, her attention focused on the carafe in front of her as she carefully fills a white cup with rich, dark liquid. "I bet I can get him to come back without you stepping foot outside."

I arch a brow at her. "Really? How?"

Nova grins at the line of women and then turns back to me. "We can have a Where's Waldo contest, hot Viking edition. Whoever brings him back first gets a cookie."

I nearly choke, but before I can reply there's a clamoring from the crowd outside. I glance out the window. The women are eagerly waiting to see if the game is on. One of them is poised to run.

The woman closest to the window says plainly, "I want my coffee first and then I'll find him."

Her hot pink lips twist into a smile that makes my balls crawl up into my body.

I smile awkwardly and direct my thoughts at Nova. "And that's not worse than the uniform?"

She gives me a look, pinches her blouse for a second, and then drops it. "Nothing is worse than this." She hands the woman waiting at the window her drink.

The woman at the window calls up, "Thanks, uh...hon." She holds up a wad of cash as she scans my chest, then adds, "Uniforms typically have nametags."

"They do. We didn't get to it yet. The line grew too quickly." Pink lips walks away at the same time I stride over to the cabinet drawer and pull out the little baggie with the plastic badges and dump them out on the counter. As I turn them all over, face-up, so Nova can pick one, she takes the next order.

When she turns around to make the coffee, she glances down at the pins. Her jaw flaps open and she honks a laugh as she lifts one of the name tags. "Are you kidding me?"

"It's not a total dick-move." That was supposed to sound matter-of-fact, but it came out so defensive that I doubt I can recover. This chick is making me nuts. I sigh loudly as I finish lining up the tags.

She glances over at me with one eyebrow so high it disappears under her cap. "Really, tell me how this is a good thing, aka not a dick-move."

"You'll be out here every day for weeks and looking—I" I lift a hand toward her, "well, like that. You're bound to have some admirers. This makes sure they never find out your real name unless you give it to them."

She grabs a coffee cup and positions it in front of the percolator before pulling the handle. Rich brown liquid pours out in a steaming wave. "Uh huh. So, why not call us all Betty or Paige?" Her voice is light, teasing almost.

"Well, this is more—"

"I know." She swats a hand at me. "I'm just screwing with you. If I couldn't tell this job had interesting parameters by now, then I'm a moron."

I don't realize it until I'm slow with my answer, but my gaze is resting on the side of her face, on her smile. I forget myself, don't realize I'm staring at a nineteen-year-old like she's a peer, or more than that.

Nova hands the order to the older lady waiting at the window and stuffs the cash in the drawer before taking the next order. She turns and glances at me, waving me off. "Well, go on and find him. I'm fine here. Go."

I tuck my chin and nod once. I know she's got this down. Hell, she could run the hut alone from the way she's figured things out this morning. She relocated some of the supplies during a lull so that it takes her less time to fulfill each order. She mixed up a solution of bleach and water, and put it in a container so she can quickly wipe down the counter at any time. She smiles at the customers as I back away from her and head to the door.

"Put a nametag on while I'm gone."

She laughs once, and tosses her hair out of the way so she can see me over her shoulder. "Sure, whatever you want boss." That grin promises a lot of laughter. Keeping away from her is going to be difficult, at least I thought it would be, but as the minutes slipped into hours the merciless pull between us simmered down. We worked, talked, and it felt normal.

It's not until I slip out of the hut and cross the parking lot that I notice the sore muscles of my face. I've been smiling all morning. Nonstop. Somehow, being around that woman made me forget everything else. Nova's light laughter catches my ear. And I can't help it, I look back at her in that tiny window with that silly hat, and smile.

22

NOVA

After I hand an older man with the biggest jowls I've ever seen a steaming cup of decaf, I turn to the counter and look down at the name badges. Who do I want to be?

I scan the tags and my gaze falls on HOT GIRL. Sure, why not? I lift it and pin the tag on my blouse. I was afraid it'd be too heavy and make my shirtfront gape, but it doesn't. It's light. I take the other tags and palm them, ready to put them back in the drawer when an idea comes to me. I separate out the men's nametags and put them away, then stick on the rest of the women's tags.

The next customer who walks up sees me doing it and I hear her giggle. "Wow."

The familiarity in the voice makes me turn

and look out the window. I'm slightly horrified to see my sister. I flinch and stumble back, hitting my hip into the counter. "Tinselly. What are you doing here?"

She holds up a piece of paper—the coupons Shannon has been handing out. "I met an interesting man who said I needed to try your coffee." Tinselly gets up on her tippy toes and leans in, trying to see the inside of the hut. "It's freezing in there. Are you all right?"

When the shock wears off, I plaster up my emotional walls so she doesn't know. I'm not all right. I have no idea what to do next and this job is beyond embarrassing. The only thing worse than seeing Tinselly, would be seeing Gran out here. I put on my best smiley-smileypants grin and bat my lashes at her. "I'm fine. I got a new job. See? It comes with amazing perks."

"Like all those name tags?" Tinselly is grinning, her eyes flicking from one tag to the next, reading all the names.

I snort and jab a finger at one of the buttons. "Hell yeah! You'd think it'd be demeaning, but check it out. I can be HOT GIRL, BABE, and BEAUTIFUL CHICK all at once. It does amazing things for my ego. Mom should have made us these when we were girls. Our confidence would have been through the roof."

Tinselly snorts. "As if you needed more confidence."

It was all an act, but she doesn't know that. Tinselly has no idea and I plan to keep it that way. If she finds out, she'll blame herself for everything that happened that night. It was a cascading clusterfuck that still haunts me, even now. I bat a hand at her and coo, "You're just jealous because you wish you had a hat like this." I put one palm under each puff adorning the sides of my head and push up slightly, in a gesture that's typically used to fluff hair.

Tinselly bleats a long set of giggles before glancing at the menu. "So, HOT BABE CHICK. What's good here?"

"The coffee, Nova-tmas style. And you need a cookie. Okay, you need two cookies because I really want one, too. I go on break in a little bit. Hang around and I'll walk into the mall with you."

"You got it, little sis." As I prep her order, a long line forms. I upgrade her coffee, adding a little bit of chocolate and cinnamon. I hand Tinselly her items after she gives me cash and impale her ticket on the silver receipt holder by the window. I stuff the money into the drawer and watch Tinselly linger to the side of the line, waiting for me to go on break.

When I see a dark wool coat billowing across the pale gray dinge of the icy parking lot, I can't help it. I look up and watch him move. Celyn is a beautiful man. He's different than I thought he'd be. He's not one of those alpha assholes that won't talk. He seems real, like this place matters to him more than anything in the world. It makes me think he stuck his life savings into the HOTTIE HUT. That part is also alluring. A man that takes chances, someone not averse to risk. He's looking at the screen of his phone, texting someone—or catching Pokémon—when he lifts his chin. Sapphire eyes lock with mine and my stomach twists as all the air is pulled from my lungs.

I wish he came back that night.

"Miss Babe?" An elderly woman calls up to me from below the window. My chest shakes as I swallow a laugh. "I ordered one of those cookies too." She points to the sheet of confections in the window.

I smile quickly and grab one. "I'm so sorry. I'm not sure what I was thinking." I wrap it in wax paper for her.

"It's all right. You're a doll. Don't let that boss of yours work you too hard."

I'd love to let that boss of mine work me real hard. My face flames red when I think it and the old woman glances at Celyn as he stomps up the steps, kicking the snow and slush off his boots before pulling the door open.

"Ah, I see what you mean." She teeters away, sipping her coffee without giving me a chance to deny it.

Celyn hangs his coat on a peg by the door and shivers. "Shannon is MIA, so I'll take over for a while. Go on and take your break, grab lunch, and be back in an hour." Celyn grabs an apron and ties it over his sweater and jeans.

I nod, wanting to put as much distance between us as possible when he glances up at me. "Oh, and..." his voices dies before he finishes the sentence. Then he laughs when his eyes bounce between my nametags. "I'm glad you think so highly of yourself, but you can only wear one."

I frown at him and take a step closer, even though I shouldn't. The attraction tickles my skin as I grin up at him. "Really? Are we going to criticize what I'm wearing? You're not in uniform, young man."

His lips curl up at the corners into an amazing smile that reveals a hidden dimple on his right cheek. "Me? You're telling your boss to wear a uniform?"

"If you're taking Shannon's spot, then I'm your boss. And yeah, it's only fair. Unless you don't think you can pull off the Viking overlord look you picked out. Pleather pants aren't very forgiving." I lower my gaze to his thighs and an amazingly toned body. I forget that he's that easy on the eyes until I'm looking at him. I linger a bit too long, and when I meet his gaze again, I shrug.

"Seriously?"

"What?" I grin at him. "It was worth a try. I can't be the only one in here looking like this." I lift my braids by the tips and bat my eyes at him.

His eyes linger on mine too long. It feels like he wants to say something, but he doesn't get the chance. A line has formed again. Celyn tips his head toward the door. "Lunch. Go." He doesn't bark the words at me. It's more like I shocked him and he doesn't know how to respond. I love it when that happens.

"Yes, boss." I step toward the counter to grab my purse. Celyn turns suddenly, like I spooked him. But the rapid movement made it so there's no space between us. His hard chest brushes mine and when he tries to back away, he steps on my foot, and his hands fly up in the air like he's not trying to touch me. It's an awkward dance of stumbling over feet and words—anything to put space between us.

"I'm so sorry. It won't happen again." His face

is strained, each little line by his eyes etched with worry.

"It's fine. It's small in here." My voice doesn't come out. It catches in the back of my throat making it sound like I've been strangled. My heart is still racing from his touch. Even though it was only a second, it was more than that. The memories of the other night rush back as if they just happened. I swear I can still feel the pressure of his lips against mine. As it is, I've been breathing in his cologne all morning. It's something manly and light. If it were the same scent he was wearing the night we met, well, I don't even want to think about that.

I cough lightly and act like I wasn't thinking about him. I ask as I pull the door open, "Can I bring you some lunch?"

He doesn't look over at me. Instead, he hurries to take orders. "No, thanks. See you in a bit." His head is bowed as he scribbles the order on a pad, dark shiny hair covering those crystal eyes. After this morning, I thought he liked talking to me, but now it seems like he can't wait for me to leave. So I step out of the hut without another word.

23

CELYN

I prowl the interior of the mall, lapping it twice before checking the exterior lots. Shannon isn't anywhere to be found. What a dick. I wonder if he ran off with the costume or got the shit beat out of him for walking around wearing that getup.

I run my hand across my temple and push my hair back, sighing. Today isn't going as planned. Some parts have been unexpectedly good, but other parts—I can't believe Quin hired Nova.

Right before I shove through the doors into the parking lot, my phone buzzes. A text message lights up the screen.

Quin: GOT HELD UP
ME: NO SHIT

Quin: NO, LITERALLY—I GOT HELD UP. CAN'T GET TO YOU TIL 2NITE. SORRY.
ME: U OK?

Holy shit. I have a million questions, but I'm guessing he's fine if he's texting me. He's probably stuck at the police station, filing a report.

Quin: YEAH. ASSWIPES TOOK THE HUMMER.
ME: NEED ME TO PICK U UP?
Quin: NAH. TAKE CARE OF THE HOTTIES AT THE HUT FOR ME.

I smirk as I let out a rush of air through my nose. I nearly step in a puddle, but manage to avoid the icy water. I debate telling him about Nova. He'd commiserate about working with someone I nearly nailed. Walking out on her and not saying anything was a prickish thing to do, but I didn't have time to tell her anything. Hell, I just met her. She's nineteen. That number strangles me. If she were twenty it wouldn't fuck with my head so much. A lot of shit happens between eighteen and twenty-one that sets the mold for adulthood. She's still a kid, the plaster hasn't even poured yet. It's not hardening. She's still got two years before she knows her ass from her elbow. At least, she should, but it doesn't seem that way. If I didn't know better, I would have thought Nova was easily in her early twenties. The way she carries herself, doesn't take shit from anyone, and acts on her ideals—no, it's that last bit. The idealist within her is still alive. That's what makes her a kid, she still dreams that things will be better.

Swallowing hard, I think about that part of her dying the way it did with me, with Quin. Being an adult means accepting things the way they are and making the best of it. For a second, I think I'm a fucking hypocrite because I don't accept my life, my lot, or my uncle's claim on Dad's company. I'm fighting him on it. What the fuck am I going to do if this goes to shit? I glance up at the hut when I'm a few feet away.

The girl in the window is the link to my salvation. I feel the premonition roaring through my veins every time I look at her. I might be able to pull this off and it'll be because of her. It sure as shit won't have anything to do with Shannon.

Nova is speaking kindly to a customer, her face lit up. She must feel my eyes on her because she glances up and when she does I forget to breathe. Those green orbs are brilliant and filled with light that was sucked out of my soul a long time ago. For a moment, I forget she's a kid, and just look at the woman in the window. A rush of emotion washes through me, tangled thoughts, and dead dreams. It's as if they scatter into the far reaches of my mind and something in my chest feels warm and certain. If my crotch reacted, I could handle it. If lust raced through my veins and I wanted to pound her and make her scream my name, and beg me for release, I could fathom it—but this? What the fuck is wrong with me? I just met her. I can't fall for her. It's too soon, and I'm not that guy. I've been in love once and let's just say it was a learning experience. I learned that I never want to go through the aftermath again. When something so good becomes something so bad, well, it's unbearable. Maybe I'm a chicken-shit for not putting myself out there again, or maybe I fucking grew up and realized that's just the way the world works.

I step in a puddle of icy slush and feel it seep into my boot. Damn. I repress the growl clawing its way up my throat and stomp on the steps going into the shack, trying to get the caked-on snow off my boots.

When I shove through the door, I shuck my coat, put it on the peg on the wall and tell Nova that it's just us. She says a few things and I'm fine until she walks up behind me. I feel her there, and I don't know what I'm thinking she'll do, but I whirl on her.

Then I'm too close to her with my hands frozen, hanging in the air like a fucked up grizzly bear as I try not to touch her. It doesn't matter though, because the moment her body brushes against mine I remember. I see her bare skin behind my eyes and feel the memory of her mouth on mine, pressing hard and kissing deep. It flashes like an old movie, sputtering for life. I crush the thoughts and plaster a fake smile on my face while I chant in my head 'go away, go away, go away.'

Her face is close enough to kiss. She laughs awkwardly and backs off. I smirk and then turn around to face the window. I start taking orders and ignore her. I have to or I'll do something incredibly stupid.

She's watching me. I can feel her gaze on the side of my face. "Can I bring you back some lunch?"

"Nah. I'm fine. Go on." My voice is clipped even though I didn't mean for it to sound that way. Fuck. I don't turn back to look at her. Instead, I scribble the next order and decide not to turn around. I don't see her again until she's walking across the parking lot, shoulder to shoulder with another woman with cookies in hand. They seem close and I wonder who she is, but then cram the thought out of my mind. It doesn't matter.

Focus. I could kill Shannon for walking off. I have no idea where the asswipe went. The line is about half women and I'm not sure if it'll work, but I grab my phone and pull up the picture I took of him this morning. I need his ass back here. Now.

I have no idea if this will work or if I'll get slapped with a lawsuit, but there was a reason Quin hired Shannon. So I take Nova' advice and address the crowd through the window of the hut. Leaning on the sill with both hands, I call out, "We're having a contest at the Hottie Hut today. If you find this man and bring him back to the Hut, you get a free cookie." I hold up my phone so the first few customers can see.

A woman not much older than me, standing further down the line, and cranes her neck. "Can I see?"

The phone is passed around and people start smiling and joking. Laughter bubbles up from the back of the line, which is now eight people deep. My phone makes its way back to me and I pocket it.

A woman at the back of the line calls out,

"And if we find him, will you take our picture? I want him on my Facebook wall." A few others giggle with agreement.

"Sure. Bring back the hot Viking and I'll take the picture myself." I flash my best grin her way.

"Can you be on the other side?" The woman winks at me. The ladies in line around her smile and watch us.

The brunette is someone I should be attracted to. She's about my age with a killer body and the confident ease of womanhood. She's comfortable in her own skin. There's a poised smile on her lips and a set of round breasts under a fitted leather coat that hugs her body to her hips. She's polished and sophisticated. She's my type, from head to toe, but in that moment I feel nothing.

I play along, not wanting to hurt her feelings. "Anything for you, Miss."

The next hour passes and it goes from insanely busy to crickets. When there's a lull, I notice the cinnamon and chocolate on the counter. I stuff them back into the cabinet. Nova must have pulled it out. For a horrified moment, I worry that she added it to the mix. I pull down the container and sniff. It seems the same. I need to make more anyway.

I have several machines running at once, along

with a few extras available so there's always hot joe. After I start one, and it's ready, the carafe from earlier gets pulled, cleaned, and is ready to start another batch. It's great because there's no waiting as long as there's always a second batch brought in before the first is gone. When we get pounded though, it's a little more difficult. One person can't keep everything in rotation. The cookies are running low too. There's only a couple of trays remaining. I can't run out and grab more until Nova is back. If Shannon doesn't show up, I'm stuck here until 7:00pm.

With Nova.

I'm lost in thought when a female voice rings out behind me. "I found him. It's picture time."

I spin around and see the brunette in the leather coat with a triumphant smile on her face. I glance out and see Shannon skulking toward us, trailing behind her. "So you did."

"Well, come on outside. I want my picture." Her voice is smooth, confident.

A few customers wander toward the hut. "Let me take care of them first and—"

The pair of women get closer and one says, "It's okay. Take the picture. I want one too."

Her friend perks up. "Can I get one too?"

I expect the woman who found Shannon to balk, but she doesn't. Instead she holds out a hand. "That's a great idea. Why don't you ladies go first?"

There's some chatter and when Shannon finally gets to the hut, he's in full actor mode—being smooth and oozing sex appeal. After removing his fuzzy cap, he runs his fingers through his silky hair, letting it fall freely to his shoulders before donning the cap again. From the way he moves in languid suggestive poses, to his molten plastic smiles—it's clear to me that it's all fake. Sincerity eludes him. Shannon shoots me a look, making it rather clear that he thinks this job is a joke. All the same, he continues with his act and poses for pictures with them, knowing damn well that they'll post those snapshots to their profiles before walking away, which leaves me with the brunette and Shannon.

Shannon holds out an arm for her. "Come on over baby, I don't bite."

She grins at him. "That's too bad." Then she steps in front of me. "Do you bite?"

The corners of my mouth twitch. "When the moment's right."

Shannon rolls his eyes and stomps up the steps into the hut.

I glance at the woman. "Hold on, I'll get him for your picture. The guy doesn't remember his name at times." She places her slender hand on my arm, stopping me.

She tips her head to the side and whispers, "It's all right. Let's just call it an IOU. It gives me a reason to come back." She flicks her dark brows and winks at me before leaning in and whispering in my ear, "You were the only reason I bothered to find him. Maybe I could trade that cookie for a cup of coffee?" She leans back, and adds, "With you?"

I can't help it. I smile at her. "If that's what you want."

"Oh, I think I do," she purrs. "I'm Yvonne."

Nova materializes, glancing at us, before heading toward the hut. I feel like I've been caught, but I didn't do anything wrong. It pisses me off. I curb my temper, and return my attention to the woman in front of me. The woman who knows her mind and isn't fresh out of high school. The beautiful creature who isn't off limits.

"Celyn."

Her voice is deep, suggestively wrapping around my name. "Good to know you, Celyn."

Nova says nothing and passes us, heading inside. I hear the hut door close and know she's in there with Shannon.

I nod at Yvonne. "Come back toward the end of the week," I offer in a voice deeper than the one I've been speaking with all day. I flash her a smile. "And we'll do it."

She gently touches my chest, splaying a single hand just above my heart. Then she leans in and says in a bedroom voice, "Sounds amazing. See you then." She trails her nails over my sweater as she walks away. It makes my skin prickle and heart race. The weird part is that it also makes me feel guilty as hell.

I shove the thought away. While I know I have to focus on the hut, if I go three months without a fuck, I'll go nuts. I'm not celibate. And I shouldn't have to explain myself to the brunette.

A voice in the back of my mind whispers, *She isn't the problem.*

Nova didn't look twice at us and that's what bothers me.

24
NOVA

Tinselly laces her arm though mine as we wander the mall. Cookies long gone, we window shop and talk. She finally asks, "So, what happened?" She's holding a scarf in her hands, admiring the purple pattern.

I don't want to tell her. It's difficult to admit to something so stupid. "I did something stupid. Ben and I took on a bank loan a while back. The company was supposed to use the extra cash to grow."

"I saw your spring patterns. They're brilliant." She's talking about the leggings. That's all we sell, leggings with amazing patterns that are fun to wear. The overhead is limited, they're nonperishable, and the market hole demanded something other than solid black. Our expansion was going to triple the size of the company. We were going to include yoga pants in the spring line. It was perfect, until I got blindsided.

"Thanks, Tinselly." I don't really want to talk about it, but I fill her in anyway. "That decision changed things a bit. I couldn't sign, even though I have good credit. No one wants to give a nineteen year old that much money. So Ben signed for it, which required shifting the business around so he was the priTinselly officer. It had to look like he had control, and since I trusted him..." I inhale deeply and close my eyes.

Tinselly grimaces. "You signed over your half of the company for appearances. And when you quit?"

I shake my head and pick up a purse, and look at the stitching. "I was expendable and the company wasn't mine on paper."

Tinselly flinches and lifts another scarf. "Nova, oh my God. But what about all your income, savings?"

I shake my head. "I don't have any. I took what I needed to live on and no more. I reinvested the rest back into the business. I did that for three years. It's why we grew so fast. I took chances and they panned out." I stare at nothing and feel the sting of betrayal and loss. It fills my mouth with acid and regret.

Tinselly asks carefully, "And the rest?" It's as if she knows that wasn't the worst of it.

TINSELLY TURNS TO ME, FURY ON HER FACE. "Can't you do anything about it? How'd you get nothing?"

"It's my fault. I didn't draw a salary and I didn't save. Everything I had went back into the company. I'm the dumbass who signed away my half to get the loan."

TINSELLY STOPS FUSSING WITH THE SCARVES AND looks at me. Pity flashes in her eyes and I can't stand it.

A catcall rings out behind me. A group of teenage guys are leering at me. I smile at the guy who called me and give him the finger, before answering Tinselly. His friends all laugh at him and then they're gone.

"SO YOU HAVE NOTHING?"

I lift my phone out of my pocket. "I have my iPhone 7."

"Oh God, Nova. What are you going to do?" Tinselly slips her hand over my shoulders and gives me a bear hug before I can throw her off. Truth be told, I needed the hug. When she backs away, I square my shoulders.

"Well, I'm not telling Mom or Gran. Please keep them away from the hut."

Tinselly snorts and we start walking again. "I can't control Gran."

"True, but make sure they don't know where I work. I can't take their I-told-you-so attitudes right now. It's mostly coming from Mom, but Gran has it too. They think I can do better. They always think that and seeing me reduced to this, well—"

Tinselly touches my arm and we stop. She looks at me. "My lips are sealed. I won't say a thing. So, is this a permanent thing?"

"No," I mope. "It's more like an I-don't-want-to-skulk-home-and-live-with-Mom thing."

Tinselly cringes, a shiver touching her spine at the same time I feel it prickle down mine. "You could always move in with us." She beams at me.

"Thanks, but I'm okay. I'll work through this and learn from my mistakes." My chin is tipped up and she reads my thoughts perfectly.

"The lesson there wasn't about trusting people, Nova. It was about partnerships and businesses."

"Right, and tossed in the mix, is liars go to

hell and I'm never talking to anyone ever again who can't tell me the truth." I look at my sister and see the remorse in her eyes, at the way her little sister is becoming jaded and hardening. "It's that or crawl under a rock and die. Tinselly, my backbone is weak right now. A pebble could crush me."

Tinselly shakes her head and holds onto my shoulders. "Absolutely not. We're stronger than that, you and me. No man will break us." She's talking about him. That's what we'd said so long ago, over and over—but she's missing a key fact. I managed to hide it from her all this time and I'm not about to spill it now.

My trust issues don't originate with Ben. They started years earlier, before I turned thirteen. My heart starts racing as the shadow of a memory creeps into my mind. The terror courses through my veins as if he were here, now. Tinselly notices and squeezes me hard. "Nothing will ever break us, Nova. We've got stubborn in our bones, and block head in our blood."

I snort a laugh, remembering what we'd said so long ago after that night—after the red flashing lights faded and everything went back to normal. The only consolation is that the common threat is now gone, but he left a lasting mark.

I add, "All it takes is a second of bravery and a

dash of awesomeness. You've become all those things, Tinselly. What if I don't get there? What if I'm like Mom and I just keep picking the wrong guy?" My worst fear is becoming my mother and repeating her life. It felt vapid and hollow when I lived it as her daughter. It must have been a million times worse for Mom. "I thought Ben was a good man."

"He fooled all of us, not just you. Nova, listen to me. You're not Mom. You're you. You're going to make mistakes and that's okay. Don't bleed out on the sidewalk waiting to start over, okay? I know you. You've probably been castrating men from here to Staten Island." She offers a knowing smile, and I smile sheepishly. "Be you. Don't let Ben rob the world of Nova Nikolaev."

Tinselly has an uncanny way of saying what I need to hear most, exactly when I need to hear it. After a moment, she adds, "And don't make the next guy pay for Ben's mistakes."

I scoff at her. "There is no next guy." Even as I say it, my mind goes to his face—to Celyn. I hear his voice in my head. There's a hole in my chest and it's consuming me. I wonder if his arms around my shoulders would ease the pain or make it worse. I don't know, but I'm left wondering what kind of man Celyn is, if he's showing his true colors or not.

25

NOVA

Gah. When I get back to the hut, Celyn is flirting, full wattage with some woman. I don't care. Correction, I shouldn't care. He's not mine. We're not together. It shouldn't spark an ember of anger inside of me that's swiftly turning into an inferno. The only way I know to hide it is to go on autopilot, so that's what I do. I move knowing the people are there, I don't ignore them, but I don't engage either. My walls rise up, blocking out any emotional distress within me. I listen to their conversation, irritated that he'd pick her. He doesn't have to date me, hell he doesn't have to sleep with me, but her? Really? She's a mean girl on crack. Her vibes were all quick tendrils and spider quick reflexes. The woman is poison. Don't ask me how I know. I just do, after living with *him*, I know too much about people like that.

Memories boil below the surface and I'm thrown back seven years. The past threatens to consume me as the echoes of the voice pulse through my memory. I shove them into the furthest recess of my mind and hold them there. I'll never see that man's face, never feel the sting of the back of his hand, again. To this day, Tinselly thinks that was the worst of it, but there was more. Things she doesn't know. But I can recognize his evil kindred soul when I see it—when I see her. The brunette wants more than a tryst with Celyn.

I say nothing and move about the tiny kitchen, brushing into Celyn and Shannon as I wipe off the counter and then kneel down to pull out my bag from where it's wedged under the counter, held in place by Celyn's briefcase.

When I wrench it free, I stand and say, "My shift is over. I'm heading out."

Shannon snorts and continues to do nothing by the counter. Great hire. He's the poster boy employee. He glances at his watch, and wipes cookie crumbs from his mouth. When did he eat a cookie? "Hey, I can clock out too, right?"

My hands find my hips. My purse was around my wrist and slams into my ankle when I give him the 'are you kidding me?' pose. "You're shift is over when the boss says you can go, and since I clocked out, ask Celyn. See you tomorrow." I turn to the door and exit. My steps are light as I bounce down the icy steps and across the parking lot to my car but my heart feels like a stone in my chest.

When I get inside the old beast, I tip my head back and close my eyes. It's only a few weeks. I can put up with this guy for a few weeks.

I straighten, grab my keys from my trough of a purse, and slip them into the ignition. The car sputters to life, obviously detesting the cold. I can practically hear the engine promise to curse me from its cold metal bones.

No wonder Celyn thought I was lying about my experience. It's odd, I know. I graduated high school at fifteen and got the hell away from my family—and him. My childhood was erased by a prick that swore to any deity he could name, that he loved my mother with all his heart. I can still hear his voice in the back of my mind. It makes the hairs on the back of my neck rise and my stomach twist with anxiety.

I need comfort food. Badly. I know I'm broke, but I pull my emergency gas cash from the special spot in the glovebox and throw the car into gear. McDonald's, here I come.

After I get my fries and cheeseburger and tiny diet Coke, I pull into a slot at the back of the parking lot and put my windows down. The cold air rolls into the car. I inhale deeply and unwrap the burger. I pinch off a bite and pop it into my mouth, then another. I stare blankly out the window, watching silver sea gulls swoop and peck crumbs from the frozen cement. Their shrill cries fill my ears as I pop another bite into my mouth.

I'm lost in the past, caught between a happy memory and a horrific one. We were young, barely teens. Tinselly and me would walk to McDonald's which was a little far from the house for two kids to travel by foot. Mom was at work and he was at home. Tinselly took me out before something could happen. Again. She sensed the powder keg long before I realized what was happening. She made our meal last longer by making it a game to see who could take the most bites. Instead of chomping the food, she ripped off a tiny piece and popped it in her mouth. Tinselly's voice was kind and she tried so hard to make me laugh and keep me safe.

I blink and come back to the present. I'm resting my arm, hand holding the burger, on the door by the open window. I rock the sandwich between my forefinger and thumb. I was watching the meat wiggle back and forth, staring at the quivering bun, ready for the rest of the memory to slam into me. But that's not what happens. Before I'm completely lucid, there's a shrill caw and a gray wingspan bitchslaps the side of my face with a feathery wing. It lunges for my meal, and misses, careening off the side of the car and righting itself in the air. My heart slams into my ribs as all the air gets sucked from my lungs in a wild scream.

I stupidly think it's over and don't look the other way until it's too late. Another gull speeds toward me, ducks through the passenger window and lunges for the fry in my other hand. I scream as it's maw snaps at my fingers and the food goes flying. Apparently that was a stupid thing to do because then every other seagull in the area swarms my car. Since I have a bird on my lap and I haven't stopped screeching, and I'm still being beaten by its massive wings, I shove open the car door and fall outside.

There are always three. Where's the third one? Bad things happen in threes. It's just the way it is. A third bird is waiting somewhere nearby, plotting.

I stagger through the swarm of feathers and away from my dinner. I put some distance between me and the feeding frenzy so that I'm no longer being smacked by random bird limbs and stagger to a stop. I bend forward, hands wrapped around my middle, and try not to cry as my comfort food is devoured by flying rats.

I wipe a tear that's about to fall from my eye with the back of my hand. When I glance up, there's a nice car stopped across from me. I frown at it. Is that a McLaren? There's a glare on the windshield so I can't see the driver until he steps out of the car. Celyn.

He's trying not to laugh and represses a smile with such difficulty that his face is strung tight. "Are you all right?"

I feel my bottom lip still sticking out as tears threaten to fall. I won't cry in front of him. I don't care if he saw me ravaged by birds. Laugh it off, Nova. Act like it doesn't matter. Everything's a fucking act from birth through the grave. I laugh, meaning for it to sound light, but it's coated in darkness. I step on one foot, putting all my weight on it, and then the other. The dark laughter continues as I pace toward him. I don't stop until I'm close enough to shove my finger into his chest. I part my lips to say something, but he lifts a hand and plucks something from my hair. He raises an eyebrow and then shows it to me. A feather.

I can't help it. I smile. Then he smiles. I start

laughing, and then finally manage, "That had to look insanely funny."

He's still trying to hold in his chortle. "It did. Are you all right?"

"Yes, the birds are the least of my problems." I laugh again and feel the lightness restore within me. That hollowed out dark spot fills with giggles. I keep my eyes away from his, my gaze toward the ground. "That kind of thing happens to me all the time."

"There's no way." He sounds shocked. He glances at the swarm of birds like they might devour my rusty Honda too. "I've never seen that happen to anyone. Ever."

"It's because you hadn't met me yet. Animals love me, but the feeling isn't exactly reciprocal. Actually, birds freak me out a bit." I glance at the car and shiver.

Celyn folds his arms across his chest, and nods slowly. "I can see why. Let me buy you another hamburger. You look like you need it." He lets me save face, doesn't mention the sheen in my eyes.

I consider it for a second, but then wonder what he's doing here, how he found me. "So, are you stalking me? I swear, Celyn. One day and I already need to see about a restraining order. What's that all about?" I wipe at my eye, removing an unshed tear.

He grins and holds up my phone. "This is yours. I'm hoping you have mine."

I frown and glance back at my car. "I'm sorry. How the hell did that happen?" I walk over to the heap of metal and lean in after the last of the birds cleared out. I forgot the short skirt and promptly crouch so I don't flash anyone. Celyn was too close to see, at least I think he is —I feel heat radiating off of him as if he's a foot behind me, and then over my head. I pull an iPhone from my bag and flip it over. It's not mine. There's no huge gouge in the corner where I dropped mine on asphalt. That phone is the only remnant that I was once successful and I lost it.

I didn't get the shiny new car or the company. Ben took those things. I got out maneuvered and never saw it coming. I walked away from a three-year relationship with a bucket of bolts that barely runs and a gouged iPhone.

I hold up his phone. "Yup, this looks like yours."

"These all look alike." Celyn shrugs. "I'm just glad you have it."

I rise and hand it to him. We swap phones. Wearily, I glance at the sky as it transitions from blue and fills with streaks of orange and pink.

Celyn repeats his offer, "Come on. Let me buy

you another burger. That kind of bad bird luck needs to be rewarded."

I smirk and finally agree. Ten minutes later, we're back outside. I have a new tiny bag with one burger inside. I wouldn't let him buy me more than that. I unwrap my new, steaming dinner, and sit on the hood of my car intending to take a bite when I shriek and bounce off the hood. It's so cold that it stung. I hop around for a second, trying to walk off the frigid cold that bit my backside.

Celyn chuckles. "Is the hood still hot?"

"Nope." I shake my head and grit my teeth. "It's nearly frozen."

He places his hand on the hood and flinches. "Maybe I should add something to the bottom of that uniform?" He's serious and glances at me.

I shake my head. "If you require long underwear beneath this atrocity, I'll quit. I can't handle more than this. No one can." I'm half kidding, half serious. I point to my chest with my burger and lift it to my mouth to take a bite.

That's when bird number three makes his appearance. He dive-bombs me, claws outstretched for my dinner, and one taloned foot goes right into my mouth. I'm mid-bite when I realize what's happened. I chomp down on its bony leg and the acidic taste of bird foot mingles with the burger. It happens in a fraction of a second. His wings beat either side of my face before I have a chance to scream. My mouth flies open in a horrified screech. As he pulls his foot out of my mouth, his talon scrapes my bottom lip. A coppery taste coats my tongue. Mortified, I frantically look around for the rest of my coke and use at as mouthwash, spitting it onto the ground. But it's not enough. It'll never be enough.

Wide-eyed I glance over at Celyn. His face is blank but his eyebrows are rising under the sweep of hair across his forehead.

I raise my hand and hold up three fingers. "I told you. Three's my lucky number." A smile cracks my petrified face and I start laughing. It's not until that moment, that I see a small crowd standing behind Celyn. The chuckles finally roll through them too, and when they see the shows over, they start toward their cars, much more cautious of the food in their arms.

Celyn's dimple shows when he smiles this time. He tucks his chin and rests his hands on my shoulders. "I have never seen anything like that in my entire life—well, expect for a second ago. Birds really, really don't like you." The way he says it, so straight-faced, and deadpan makes me laugh so hard that I can barely stand upright.

After a moment of uncontrolled laughter from

both of us, I look up at him, gazing at that beautiful face and he stills. His eyes lock onto my mouth. He takes a step closer, his gaze not straying from my lips. There's a tightening sensation in my chest that sends a flutter through me. It ripples under my skin, starting in my heart and pulsing into my fingertips. That pull is there again, urging me to step closer, to close the distance between us. I watch his hooded eyes, the way those dark lashes linger on my lips. Longing for something more, something I can't quite put my finger on. With Celyn, I wanted a fling but if time has shown me anything it's that a night with this man isn't something I'd get over quickly—or ever. As it is, the memory of his kiss still lingers like a dream cut short.

An ocean of silence spans between us. When those blue eyes meet mine, he tips his head toward his car. "I have a first aid kit. You should probably put something on that cut."

Right. The copper tang. I'm bleeding. I press a finger to my lip and wince. It's a bit swollen and slick with fresh blood. The cut isn't too deep. I look at my fingers and see the shiny red pads. "Good plan. No amount of coke can get the taste of that bird's foot out of my mouth. I'm going to get some weird form of bird rabies."

Celyn chortles as I follow him to his car. He

pops the trunk and pulls out the little first aid kit. He hands me some antiseptic and a bit of gauze. I use his side mirror to apply it and dab at it with the piece of mesh fabric. The cut is better than I thought. Most of the damage is on the inside of the lip. As I dab, I joke, "Well at least I wasn't marred for life."

"Assuming the bird cooties don't come later." He's standing behind me, arms folded over his sweatered chest. The deadpan tone of his voice sounds completely serious. "You never know with birds."

In a mocking tone, I answer, "Har, har. But seriously, if I grow a monkey tail and fly off to be with some witch, please shoot me. I can't trade in one costume for another. The tiny hat and the vest would be so much worse than this." I jab my thumb at the dirndl top I'm wearing.

Celyn snorts and I catch a glimpse of his crooked grin in my mirror. After a moment, I think I've got ointment on the entire wound. I'm not sure if putting it on the inside of my lip was necessary, but I did learn that there are things that taste worse than chewed aspirin.

When I turn to thank him, it looks like he wants to say something.

When he doesn't, I cut my eyes to the side and offer, "Well, this has been something."

"Yes, it has." He runs his hand over the top of his head and down his neck, holding it there for a moment. "Are you all right? I need to get back to the hut. I left Shannon there alone."

I make a face, surprised he'd leave the guy there. "By all means, go. He probably wandered off already."

Celyn laughs softly. "Probably. I'll see you tomorrow." The way he says it sounds like a question.

So I nod and answer, "Yup and every day after that." Our eyes meet and there's a softness in his eyes, something that wasn't there most of today. I can't recognize the emotion, but it makes me squirm.

Celyn runs his hand through his hair, his mouth opens, and he starts, "Right, about that—"

I don't know what he's going to say but the tension between us is growing and something tells me to cut him off. A premonition tells me it's bad news and I can't let him finish what he's trying to say. "See you tomorrow, Andy."

Celyn's shoulders tighten and he corrects, "Celyn. It's Celyn."

26

CELYN

I used the find my iPhone feature and tracked Nova to McDonald's only to see her barraged by birds. If I hadn't seen it with my own eyes, I wouldn't have believed her when she told me. If she told me. Nova has some secrets. She has to. No one that age walks like that, like the world has beat them down. Like she knows about pain and suffering. Like she knows all too well how shitty life can be. Most teenagers think they're invincible. Death isn't part of their life. That wasn't the case with me. It started with losing my dog and then my dad. It sobers up that teenage defiance and dulls down the need to go it alone against the world. With the luck Nova has, I'll have to make sure she's not standing next to me during a lightning storm. I snort, thinking I'm an idiot, but the thought still makes my heart race. A fierce desire to protect her floods through my veins.

I slam my hand on the steering wheel of the car and scold myself. She's a kid. We have nothing in common. Even if she had a hard life, so did you. There's no way she's right for you. Stop thinking with your dick.

I should have told her. I should have said something. She thinks this is a permanent gig. It's not. She has a seasonal job with a shitty boss and a coworker that has some serious PMS. If Shannon isn't there when I get back, I'll fucking freak.

When I pull into the mall parking lot, I can see a swarm of people by the hut. As I get closer, it's easy to see that all these people—women mostly—have their necks craned, trying to see something at the end of the hut. The crowd is about five rows deep and pressing in toward that one point. I pull into a parking spot and cut the engine.

I slip out of the car quietly, and make my way to the back of the crowd. That's when I hear Shannon, his voice nearly an octave deeper, telling a story. At first, I think he's retelling the night before Christmas, but when I hear what he's saying, I nearly stroke out.

The woman in front of me says over her shoulder, as if she knows me. "I'd like to have that dick before Christmas." When I don't laugh, she turns toward me and flinches. A rosy flame lights up her face as she smiles sheepishly. "I'm so sorry. I thought you were someone else."

"Mmm, I gathered that. How long has he been doing this?"

She shrugs, "I got here about half an hour ago and he was already up there, sitting on the hood of that car, and reciting. He's done a few different stories, but the crowd likes this the best." She beams at me. "Isn't he talented?"

"Yeah, he's amazing." I push through the crowd toward Shannon just as the crowd begs him to tell it again.

Shannon holds up his hands and bobs his head, letting his hair fall freely around his face. "If you insist." He clears his throat and begins, "It was the dick before Christmas and all through the —" Shannon's eyes flick through the crowd and land on me. "Awh, shit."

I'm glaring at him. My arms are folded over my chest to keep from strangling him. The guy attracted a ton of people, but there's not one cup of coffee in sight. He didn't sell a thing. "Story hour is over. Get back to work."

"Lame." Shannon frowns and the women

begin to complain and look at me like I'm Satan. The guy slides off the hood of a car and smiles at the young blonde standing closest to him. "It's okay, my little admirers. I'll be back tomorrow."

The crowd mills about even after Shannon goes inside the hut, but no one buys anything. They linger by the window, talking. I've about had it. I want to fire the guy so badly, but my evening employee hasn't shown up yet. I'm going to be stuck here all night.

The mob of estrogen surrounds the hut like they're planning a siege and Shannon is the prize. They whisper as the sun dips below the horizon. Shannon uses my last drop of patience when he asks, "Are you going to get more of those cookies? I'm starving."

I blink at him. "Not until tomorrow."

"Too bad, because they were fucking awesome. I could eat another tray for dinner."

I can't help it. Something inside of me snaps. "When did you eat a cookie?"

"I ate an entire tray, man. While you were gone." He laughs at me and points to his head. "You need to put your listening ears on, dude. It was all good."

Tension lines my jaw and I swallow hard to keep my temper even. "Your shift is over. If you take coffee or food, hell if you take anything from this place ever again, don't come back. It's stealing. You can't eat the inventory."

Shannon holds up his hands, palms toward me, and behaves like I'm overreacting. "Slow down there, I'm no panhandler. I don't need your cookies, okay. I only took them because that girl took one."

I narrow my gaze at him. "Nova took a cookie?"

"Yeah, I saw her eating it inside the mall. It was one of yours from the hut."

She didn't pay for it? That would be odd, but I did see her with a cookie now that I think about it.

When I don't say anything, Shannon adds, "Check the receipts around three o'clock. There's no order for a solo cookie or that coffee she sold her girlfriend. I'm pretty sure Hot Girl is gay, because a piece of ass that fine overlooking this Adonis body—well, 'nuff said. Am I right?"

I want to punch him in the face. I could ball up my hand into a fist and just crush his arrogant face. The satisfaction of ruining that perfect nose would be worth it. Focus. You can't beat the shit out of the staff. I'm pinching the bridge of my nose and shaking my head. My finger points toward the door. "Get out. Your shift is over and you're so close to getting your ass fired. Do me a favor and leave before I tell you to not come back."

Shannon flinches. "Damn man. Take some Midol or something. I'll go, just thought you should know. I wouldn't have taken shit if that girl didn't do it first. I was following her lead."

"I heard you. Go."

Shannon is down the steps without another word. He pulls off his vest as he walks into a small group of women that lingered behind, waiting for him. He puts an arm around the shoulders of one woman and then hooks another. He glances back at me. "Get laid, man. Take some of the tension off." He smirks and the women giggle.

I turn toward the receipts and don't pull them apart until Shannon is out of sight. There's no way Nova stole anything. That's not her type. But as I dig through the paper slips, I find the orders from that timeframe and there's no single cookie on any of the orders. Shit.

27

CELYN

Night falls and Quin finally shows up. He looks a little roughed up. There's an angry red scratch on his cheek and his normally pristine clothing is rumpled. He strides over to the hut, stomps up the steps, and slips inside. "Hey, Celyn. Sorry I couldn't be here earlier. How'd you do?"

There's no line at the moment, so I walk over and look him over. "You all right? What the hell happened?"

He shrugs. "Bad timing. I was coasting through C.I. and stopped at CVS to grab a bottle of aspirin. I should have stayed in the fucking car." C.I. is short for Central Islip. It has rough patches, well, fine—the whole thing is a rough patch. Quin must have been in the wrong place at the wrong time. From the look on his face he doesn't want to talk about it. Quin pinches his temple and glances at the machines, and then the stack of receipts by the window. "Looks like you did well today."

"Yeah, better than expected. The manager you hired—"

He lights up and cuts me off. "That chick is amazing. I pelted her with a ton of situations during her interview and then told her to sell me something. She didn't waiver once. It's like her mind thrives on chaos or something. She's kind of young, but her experience and application over-rode the concern."

I narrow my eyes at him. "You hired a teenager as a manager."

He pulls a slim watch from his pocket. "She sold me this broken watch off her wrist." He holds it out to me. I reach for it and he lays it in my palm.

It's a shitty piece of crap, worse than the insult watch Uncle gave me. "How much did you pay for it?"

He grins. "Five."

I shrug and offer it back to him. "Big deal, she sold you used crap for five bucks."

He doesn't take it back. "No man, she sold me on a collectable timepiece for five hundred bucks.

Look at it. It's one of the first, early edition, 1980s Swatches. The face is cracked, but it's an authentic part. The band is original. It just needs a new battery." Quin continues to tell me about the watch and I notice my opinion of the piece of trash shifting to something of value. I'm turning it over and examining the casing as if it were worthy of inspection. Quin starts laughing. "I shit you not, by the time she was done talking about that, I wanted it. I figured a girl who can sell like that needs to be on our team. Plus, she's hot, but that was an afterthought. Her mind is a steel trap. I feel sorry for the sucker who steps in it."

Yeah, I'm getting that feeling about her. There's a soft side hidden under a ton of defenses. It's like she's battened down the hatches and launched everything she had a long time ago and now she's living in the rubble.

I say plainly, still looking at the timepiece, "I can see that about her. She's the reason why we netted our goal today. She tripled the price of everything."

Quin's eyes widen. "No shit?"

"Yeah. It was an accident. She sold something before I had signage up or went over anything with her. People have happily paid it all day."

"Except now." Quin jerks his chin toward the window. "I would have thought night time would be booming. The mall is packed." He paces toward the window and looks out across the parking lot. "We need to lure people over here."

"They wander over during the day."

Quin glances from one end of the lot to the other, and then turns toward me. "Is it mostly women?"

"Yeah, but that's because that guy Shannon doesn't stay in the hut. He wanders."

Quin laughs. "What the hell? What do you mean, he wanders?"

"The guy needs a nanny. He forgets what he's doing and wandered the mall for most of his shift."

"Did he sell anything?"

"The guy can draw in a crowd, but his sales skills suck. The people he attracted lingered and waited for him. They didn't buy anything."

Quin nods and leans his hips back against the counter. "Make the rules clear—no socializing on the job." I tell him about the dick before Christmas and Quin nearly chokes up a lung. "You're shitting me? There's no fucking way!" The grin on his face is huge, as if he wished he thought of it.

"I wish I was. What the hell do I do with him?"

Quin laughs. "Use whatever skills he's good at."

"Quin, he's not good at anything."

"We hired him because he can be a smooth talker if he tries. You gotta get him to try."

"Easier said than done."

"Yeah," Quin replies thoughtfully, still looking across the lot. "There should be more people here. You said you already met today's goal?"

"By the skin of our teeth." There are about two hours left before closing. It's been slow since five o'clock.

Quin nods thoughtfully. "We need something to attract people at nighttime. Carolers?"

"Maybe." He's right, and I'm not sure if people aren't coming over because the lot between us and the mall is covered in thick shadows or if it's something else. "Let me think about it."

Quin sighs deeply, "Well, I can stay until close. Just tell me where you need me." He reaches up to adjust one of the tins of coffee and winces. His hand flies to his side and he swears.

I step toward him. "What aren't you telling me?"

Quin smirks and laughs it off. "Nothing. I just—"

I've known Quin since we were kids and I

know when he's lying. I grab the hem of his wrinkled shirt and tug it up before he can stop me. His ribs are bandaged. "Shit, Quin." I glance up at him. "You were in the ER all day, weren't you?"

Quin pales and backs away, swatting at the hand holding his shirt. I drop it and let him save face. "Yeah, I was."

"What happened?" I ask again.

Quin shakes his head. "Nothing to say. It's behind me. I'm moving forward."

I nod in agreement. There's nothing I can say when he's like this. Whatever happened rattled the hell out of him. I know he needs to work to keep his mind from replaying whatever he's trying to avoid talking about. I make a decision right then to grab a pair of folding stools. I can shove them in the crevice between the counter and the wall if needed, but Quin isn't going to be able to stay on his feet for hours on end. He shouldn't even be here.

"I'm going to take a break, grab some dinner. You want anything?" I use the break as a pretense for grabbing time to run in and get the stools. It'll come out of today's earnings which will shove us under goal unless we sell another dozen customers before close, which looks unlikely. It's an acceptable loss.

"Nah, I'm fine. Take your time. I got this." I

show him where the pad is to take orders and point out a few things before heading into the parking lot. The icy wind nips at me as I cross to the other side and when I get to the curb, I turn back and look at the hut. There's a sea of darkness between the sidewalk and the Hottie Hut. We need more light or no one will come after sunset. I wonder if there's such a thing as used Christmas lights. If so, I need to find some.

28

NOVA

My life falls into a pattern. Sleep paws at me every night and I'm dead to the world until four in the morning, when I pull on my tacky costume and head to work. I'm on my feet all day and bone weary by the time I get off. Quitting time has gotten later and later because the second shift never appeared. Celyn has been working both shifts, along with Quin who helps him out. Shannon is useless, aside from his ability to attract swarms of women. After he does that, he seems to be at a loss and has no idea how to get them to buy anything. One day I told him, "Just tell them you can only talk if they're buying something. It's true, and they all want to talk to you."

That created some purchases, but the line

moved too slow. Shannon moves at snail speed when he's flirting, which is all the time. He has that obnoxious guy vibe. It flows off of him with such force that it's like being blasted with a high-wattage flirting fan. Personally, it's not my thing, but there are many women who like it. They linger and wait for him. No doubt, Shannon is loving the attention. I didn't get to hear the legendary story of the *Dick before Christmas,* since Celyn forbid him from reciting poetry, but periodically a blushing face will ask about Shannon and every time, she says she was in that crowd, mesmerized by him.

And things with Celyn, well, they turned cold. It's really weird because that day at McDonald's he was kind, and warm. Now he's curt and distant. He doesn't talk to me. There's no casual conversations about anything besides the weather, inventory, and work. It's as if he decided that he doesn't like me. When work is long, tense, and tedious it stretches out forever. Shannon is an obnoxious brat and Celyn, well, it's been like working with a robot. He helps, and we have a good pace. The flow of our work isn't clumsy anymore. We don't bump into each other the way we used to, but I miss his smile.

Celyn grabs his briefcase and a folder of papers. He scribbles on an order form and hands it to me with a wad of cash. "Please add that to the pile and put the money in the drawer. I'm grabbing a coffee and heading inside to finish this up before the night rush begins. Thanks."

"Sure." Pleasant. He's always pleasant and says please and thank you. But it lacks warmth. When he reaches for a cup with his other arm already holding his case and papers, I cut him off. "I'll get it."

"I can do it," he retorts flatly.

"I know you can." I stop and look into his face. He avoids my eyes. "Your arms are full and you seem like you're in a hurry. I'll grab it and you can go."

He stiffens and spits out, "You don't know what I like in my coffee."

I can feel my eyes fight to remain in place and not roll in my head. He's being such a standoffish jerk. "How about I make my special Christmas coffee for you? Something to lighten your mood?"

He doesn't say no, so I grab a few canisters after pouring the hot liquid into his cup. As I mix the drink, he watches me, his face pinched tight. "What is that?"

"Nova's famous Christmas Crack Coffee. It's really good, you'll like it." As I top it off with whip cream, Celyn makes a face. "What? Don't tell me you don't do sugar."

"No, it's just that container of whip cream is yours."

"So?"

"So, it's not mine." His tone is flatter than an anorexic pancake. There's an edge to the way he says it, so much so, that I stop and look over my shoulder at him.

"Right, it's mine and I'm happily sharing it with you." His eyes are boring into mine, searching for something that he can't find. His jaw tightens and I can tell he's debating saying something. I fold my arms over my chest and cock my head to the side. "Spit it out, Kelton." I probably shouldn't taut him, but it's too late. I already said the wrong name.

Celyn's nostrils flare as he steps closer to me. He's in my space, something that he hasn't done for over a week. "KEHL-ahN." Each sylobol is sharp. Jaw grinding, he repeats, "My name is Celyn. I don't call you *Hot Girl*, I call you by your name, Nova, and I'd appreciate if you took me seriously enough to call me by mine." There's hurt lingering there, laced with something else that I can't identify.

The smart-ass smile falls off my face and dies on the floor. My heart thumps awkwardly as I face him, a breath away. I soften and seriously ask him, "Celyn, what's bothering you?"

When he hears me say his name, something that was bound tight uncurls within him. It dulls his sharp edges and softens his tone. I expect him to tell me something real, to actually say it, but instead he straightens his spine and turns on his heel, heading toward the door. "I'll be back later."

He's down the steps and I'm torn between going after him and letting him sulk. I didn't do anything. I know I didn't. Sharing my whip cream made him super pissy and I have no idea why. I can't leave the hut abandoned, which means I either chase him now or wait for Shannon to show up—which is not a good plan.

I grab his coffee, and I'm through the door and bounding down the steps. "Hey, you forgot your drink."

Celyn stops and turns slowly. He glances at the cup, and then back up at me. "I don't want it." He turns his back on me and strides for the doors to the mall.

I stand there feeling completely stupid and make a choice. It could cost me my job, but I'm done taking blows for something I didn't do. I slam the cup of coffee down on the pavement, rush up behind him, grab the crook of his arm, and swing him around. I'm in his face scolding him, "Don't you dare treat me like that! I'm not some stupid slut, you know. I have a brain, and any ass can see you're pissed at me and won't tell me why. I've had it. Tell me! I need to know so I can tell you that you're an arrogant asshole with a whip cream aversion."

Voice sharp, he steps toward me, his face within an inch of mine. "You don't know me, princess. You don't know a goddamn thing about me. I like cream in my coffee, I enjoy a hot sweet thing from time to time," his eyes lower to my chest before flicking back to my face. The blatant innuendo isn't like him. "And after that whole speech about not lying, I didn't expect you to be a thief, but hey—I guessed wrong."

He starts to turn again, but I don't let him. "Hey!" I jerk his arm so he turns back toward me. "What the hell are you talking about? You think I stole from the drawer? Are you insane or just incapable of making a spreadsheet and checking the facts?"

Celyn growls, "I don't know how you do it, but Shannon saw you."

"Saw me do what?" I'm livid now. My fingers are balling into fists at my sides and it's everything I can do to not growl.

Celyn's quiet for a moment. He watches me, anticipating that I'll squirm, but I don't. "Shannon saw you...I saw you." His words die and silence fills the air as if he realized something. His expression softens. "You didn't steal anything, did you?"

I close my eyes for a moment and try not to overreact. It takes every ounce of strength I have to not slam my palms into his chest and scream in his face. I smile sweetly at him, "No, and that's because I don't steal things. I'm not a thief. Why the hell would you listen to Shannon?"

Celyn's eyes cut to the side like he's remembering something. "He took a tray of cookies on the first day. He said he followed your lead."

I balk, "I didn't steal a tray of cookies."

"He said you ate one on your break. I saw you."

"Yeah, and I bought it. I can eat what I buy." I'm glaring up at him, way past annoyed. "This is why you haven't been talking to me?"

"I've been talking to you."

"You have not. You've been acting like I'm a disappointment, you ass! That's confirmation bias. You thought I was a thief and you've been watching me to prove you were right all along, and you used Shannon as the voice of reason this whole time. How screwed up is that?" I throw up my hands, livid, and step back toward the Hottie Hut.

Celyn grabs my arm this time and whirls me around. He stares at me, his lips parted, as if there are words waiting to fall off his tongue, but he's mute.

I raise my eyebrows at him and try really hard not to say something stupid. "Listen, I don't know you. I never said I did. I said," inclining my head toward that cup, "that my Christmas Crack was good. I know nothing about you. And you know nothing about me. Let's keep it that way, okay?"

I sound reasonable, level-headed and... disappointed. When I walk back to the shack, I feel his eyes on me, but I don't turn back. I sold my sister an extra cookie on the day in question. There was no paper trail for a single snack because that's not what happened. All this time he thought I was a goddamn thief. My stomach sours and I don't think I can look at him when he comes back later.

❧

SHANNON SHOWS UP ABOUT AN HOUR LATER.

I'm cleaning out one of the carafes when he bumps me. "Sorry, Hot Girl. I didn't mean to touch your amazing ass with my Greek god beef cakes." He slaps his tush and grins at me. "Not that you didn't like it. I hear all the girls do."

There's a warning silence brewing around me

that Shannon doesn't read very well. I figured that out a while ago, so I make sure I say something, otherwise he'll keep doing it. "I'll sue your ass for sexual harassment if you touch me again. Keep your butt to yourself."

He acts hurt and presses his fingers to the bare skin under his vest. "Me? Harassing you? Please, if anything it's the other way around. I'm just the poor, uneducated eye candy that you two nerds hired to make the ladies come all over the pavement."

I'm staring at a spot on the wall, chanting, reminding myself that I can't kill him. I say, dryly, "Right, that's us. And you'll need to clean that up when your shift is over." He should drop it now. My tone is the same way I'm gripping my pen, like I might stab him in the neck.

But he doesn't stop. "I know, right? That's some slippery shit."

That's it. I finally round on him, snapping, "Get out. Okay, just get the hell out!" My finger points toward the door and I glare at him until he moves.

Shannon sulks toward the door, and then squares his shoulders. He stops on the top step, leaves the door open, and lets all the warm air rush out. "You know what you need?" His mouth opens to say something incredibly inappropriate, but I don't give him the chance.

Offering a syrupy smile, I say, "Tell me," before batting my lashes at him, followed by a wicked frown when I slam the door in his face. "Asshole."

Shannon swears as the metal door comes close to smashing his nose. "That just proves my point, Hot Girl. You need to get some."

I walk over to the door and lock it, before going back to the carafe. I hear him change his tune when he starts talking to a woman a few yards away. His voice fades to nothing and I'm alone.

As I prep the machine for the next batch of coffee, my nerves are totally shot. Once I get the percolator up and running, I dig through the cabinet looking for spices and pull out a few jars. I start with coffee and whipped cream, stirring in chocolate, cinnamon, and then more whipped cream. I wish I had some Godiva liqueur, but drinking at work is bad plan. Maybe I should go back to the bar where I broke down the other night and beg for a job.

I write myself a receipt and stab it on the stake that holds all the sales tickets, before stuffing a few bucks in the cash drawer. I hop up on the counter and sip my drink while looking out the small window. It's freezing in here. It takes forever for that heater to warm the space and every time I open the window or the door, all the warm air gets sucked out.

I'm done. I realize it at that moment. I'm going to quit. When Celyn comes back, I'm going to tell him that I'm done. I can't work like this. It's an all-time low for me as it is. Knowing that he doesn't respect me makes it even worse. I risk falling on my face and moving in with Mom, which isn't something I want to do. Still, I'm worth more than this. I can do more than he's letting me.

I graduated high school when I was fifteen. I got my associate's while I was sixteen. That's when I met Ben and we opened our business. In eighteen months that little company was making six figures and I have nothing to show for it. All that blood, sweat, and tears—lost.

The more I think about it, the more agitated I get. I made that company what it is. Everything from the initial idea, to outsourcing shipping, to building our first website. It was me. I coded it. I did it. Ben provided seed money and took the ball and ran with it. Now he's sitting pretty and I'm sitting in a shed in the middle of the mall parking lot selling coffee. I put my cup down and bury my face in my hands.

I'm not sure how long I sit like that, but when there's a knock on the window, I flinch. Celyn is watching me through the glass. He points toward the door. I nod, knowing what he wants.

When I pull open the door, the words are there, on the tip of my tongue. *I quit. You suck. I can't work like this.* But I don't get a chance to say them.

He presses his lips together, and steps inside. Cold wafts off of him, making me shiver. Celyn pulls off his jacket and hands it to me. "Put it on. I want to talk to you, and I know you're frozen."

I shake my head. "Actually, I have something I need to tell you."

"Fine, but let me go first. I want to hear what you have to say, and I know I deserve getting chewed out a lot more than you did. The thing is, Nova—" he sighs and runs a hand through that messy dark hair, "you shock the hell out of me. In a good way. I've never met anyone like you. And that's not a line, it's true. You have insight and perceptions that most people lack, even in the business world with all their MBA's and degrees." He sighs and looks me in the eye. "I was a prick. I'm sorry."

I'm stunned. Something flutters in my stomach and I look away, cutting my eyes nervously to the side. I'm still quitting. This doesn't change anything. But I'm civil. I nod. "Apology accepted, but we still need to talk."

"We do. Please, put the coat on and warm up. I'll buy a bigger heater tomorrow. It'll help the hut hold a more consistent temperature, even with the window opening." He holds out his wool coat toward me.

I cave and take it, mainly because my teeth are close to chattering.

Celyn grabs one of the folding stools, pulls it out for me, and holds out his hand gesturing for me to take a seat. "Sit for a second. I want to tell you something."

I feel like shaking my head and saying no, but I do as he asks. When I'm settled on the seat, he says, "I've been going over the books. We're coming up on the midpoint in the holiday season and we're really close to hitting goal. There are certain times during the day that we have lulls and I have ideas about that—and I'd love to hear yours—but before we do anything about that, I wanted to make you an offer."

I narrow my eyes and try to look neutral instead of suspicious. "What do you mean?"

"I was thinking about what you said on the first day, about the people working here being able to take ownership of the place, and while I'm damn glad I didn't flat out give a percentage of the sales, I came up with a better idea."

"Yeah? What's that?" I look at my knees and pull his coat tighter around me, getting lost in the perfect scent of it. He smells like snow and pine needles, and something sexy coated in darkness.

"Profits. They're all yours. You get to allocate how they're spent and what we do with them. You can make them Christmas bonuses or anything you want. I think you'll come up with something good, well, better than me anyway."

"Really?" I can't believe he said that. Our goals haven't been insane and most days we are well into the black. On the sheets I see, anyway.

"Yes." Celyn says, softly.

I nod slowly, and stare at the floor. When I talk, I have the words right there, my resignation speech. When I'm about to open my mouth to say it, Celyn continues, "There's only one problem right now—I'm short staffed. We can afford to replace the night crew, but I don't really have time to train anyone new, so that would leave me or you working that shift. I mean, if you want it, that shift is yours. I didn't want to assume anything, Nova. Some people like having extra money around the holidays. But I know those would be horribly long days."

"You've been doing it for a few weeks now."

He nods, looks at his hands, and then back up into my face. I don't meet his gaze. "Yes, but it's not fun."

I shrug. "Work is work, fun is fun. Work isn't supposed to be fun. It's supposed to give you a paycheck and a sense of satisfaction."

He catches my eye and asks softly, "Do you have a sense of satisfaction?"

"I didn't," I confess, "But maybe I could."

"What do I need to do?" His words hang in the air and when I glance up, our gazes meet. I can see the apology in his eyes, the one that's already fallen from his lips. I have trouble letting things go sometimes. But the way he asks me, as if he really wants to know catches my full attention.

"Can I make a suggestion?"

Celyn nods quickly and takes a step back, tucking his hands into the crooks of his elbows. "Please, do." He moves nervously and pulls out a hand, tucking it under his chin.

"You could charge an extra dollar a drink if you had some syrups. If you don't want to make it complicated and want a higher mark-up, well, taste this and tell me what you think." I hand him my coffee cup. If I hadn't kissed him once, I wouldn't have done it. Since COVID, most people don't thoughtlessly drink after each other anymore.

Celyn glances at it and takes it, drinking without hesitation. He licks the cream mustache off his mouth and makes a happy sound. "My God, that's good. What is that?"

"I make it when I'm having a bad day, it's mostly chocolate and a few spices. There are a few different variations. It's nothing major. But if you give it a cute name, you could get another few bucks for it."

I expect him to say something about the drink. His voice is soft, his expression remorseful. "I want you to name it."

I smirk. "THE MOURNFUL MOOSE has a sublime ring to it, but let's face it—normal people don't know who the Romantics were, never mind what sublime means—so how about KISS MOOSE KISSES. It'll remind people of chocolate mousse, which is an accurate way to describe the flavor. Add a pun and it's cute." Celyn doesn't say anything, and I start thinking he doesn't like the idea until I look up.

My gaze snags on his and my heart shudders. The way he's looking at me makes the pit of my stomach squirm. It's as if he didn't see me until this moment. I laugh nervously, "What's that look, Keller?" I use the wrong name to throw him off, to break the look he's giving me, but it doesn't stop. It's admiration and shock, mingled with pleasant surprise.

"Nothing, it's just that you're an unusual person. You just referenced 18th century art, 20th century marketing, science, and you can cook."

I smirk. "Making good coffee is not cooking."

He mirrors my grin and leans in close, saying in a hushed whisper while looking over his shoulder like someone might hear, "I can't boil water."

I don't believe him. I feel the grin on my face broaden. "You made the coffee mix. It's good, Celyn."

"I wish to God that I could say it was my concoction, but it's not. A friend of mine is a chef and let me use his recipe." He lingers close, his dark lashes lowered as he thinks. When he lifts his gaze to meet mine, the pit of my stomach dips. "Well, what do you think, Hot Girl? Can you put up with me through a second shift, or should I find us some new hires?"

I nearly blush when he calls me HOT GIRL. I tug his jacket up around my neck and snuggle against the soft wool. I think this is cashmere. If it is, this coat is worth more than my car. Okay, bad comparison because everything is worth more than my car, but still. Something doesn't add up. The McLaren, the coat, and the hut don't fit together. For a second, I wonder if it matters. I don't want to get caught in the middle of whatever's going on with him and it's clear something lit a fire under him to make this venture hit the ground running. I love a challenge, and his offer has *Nova* written all over it.

I smile at him, but it falls swiftly. "I was going to quit. As soon as you walked through that door, I was ready to tell you that I wasn't coming back."

He's quiet for a moment and then asks, "And now?"

I repress a smile, but it breaks through. "Now you're going to have trouble getting rid of me." I move to slip off the counter and he's there, close.

His hands slip around my waist, "Let me help you down."

A sharp jagged breath fills my lungs as his hands slip around my sides, over the coat. The memory of those hands on bare skin flashes behind my eyes and I wonder if the movement makes him remember it too. If he does, Celyn doesn't let on. He lifts me gently and sets me on the floor. I stand there a beat too long, looking up at him.

Celyn's beautiful face brightens when he finally turns away. "Hey, Hot Girl. Promise me something?"

"What's that?"

"If you ever see me doing something stupid, remind me that I took advice from Shannon. That'll sober me up fast."

I snort. "Sure thing. And," I move past him without touching, but our bodies glide within inches of one another. I can feel the heat from him there, and think about pressing him forward into the counter and trailing kisses down the slick skin on his hot back. The thought jars me so badly, that I forget what I'm saying.

Celyn turns and leans back against the counter. "And?"

I completely forgot what I was going to say. It was witty and impressive. The only thing left is the image of Celyn naked, with his back toward me. My heart hammers faster, and I mutter, "Never mind."

Celyn laughs and steps toward me as I try to move toward the sink to finish washing the rest of the dishes. "You can't leave me hanging like that. Come on, I spilled my guts, tell me what you were thinking about?"

Oh shit. I don't want to lie to him, but I can't say what I was thinking. My eyes go wide and I start stuttering, "I, I, I was, uh, I was..." I can't hide the tremor in my voice. I lower my face and look at the floor in horror as I try to figure out what to say.

Celyn is there. He tucks a finger under my chin and lifts my face. When my eyes meet his, he offers, "You don't have to tell me anything you don't want to reveal. Although from how red your face is right now, I'd love to know one day."

"I'm not red!"

"You're crimson, Hot Girl. But it's all good. It's a good look for you." Celyn laughs once and turns away as I sneak a peek at my reflection in the carafe.

My face looks like a red balloon. I detest being so easily read. I might as well stamp, 'I think you're yummy,' on my forehead. I laugh it off with a swat of the hand. "I'm just warm. It's this coat." I am warm, but I doubt the coat has much to do with it. I shuck the cashmere and hand it to Celyn, who takes the long coat and hangs it on a hook.

When he's done, he turns back toward me with a wicked grin on his face.

"What?" I ask, intrigued by that playful, sexy smile.

"Nothing," he says, waving me away.

"No, tell me."

Celyn turns to me, and whispers in my ear, "I

will," I feel his grin brush my check, as he adds, "as soon as you tell me what you were thinking."

I pout and pull back. Celyn laughs and shoves me away from the dishes. "Man the window, Hot Girl."

I walk over to the window, acting like I'm offended, and I can't help it. I smile when I look out at the evening sky and its promise of snow.

29

CELYN

That girl is stuck in my head. I'm lying in bed and the memory of Nova's voice haunts me. The sound, the light tone, is like a melody that I can't forget. I hear it when she's not there, especially when it's dark and the room is quiet. There's no way to escape and I'm not sure I want to. I can see her face with the spattering of pale freckles over the bridge of her nose and the little crinkles at the corners of her eyes when she smiles. They sparkle, those eyes. It's like she actually has fairy dust molded into her hypnotic, emerald gaze.

She's nineteen. The thought shatters the illusion that I could actually be with her in any meaningful way. Add in all this shit with my uncle and if I lose this bet and fail this test, I have nothing to offer her. Who the hell would stay with a broke failure? I can't do that to her, and since it's a real possibility I keep my distance.

I sigh and roll over, face down on the mattress, and pound my pillow flat. I just lay down and I should have passed out as soon as my body hit the sheets, but I'm still smiling like an idiot. I swear to God, my face hurts and I know that it's from being around her so much. The past few days all rolled together into one long blissful blur. Her company and chatter isn't mindless. She doesn't act her age, which throws me. There's a cunning mind in there, one that I'd hire in a heartbeat and put in a position where it could actually do some good if I weren't stuck in this nightmare.

Sleep eludes me, so I get up and pad across the dark room. The wooden planked floor has a chill clinging to it tonight. I grab a robe and head down the hall, and flick on the kitchen lights. Manhattan lies below me, covered in a blanket of white. It's nearly 3:00am and the city's constant pulse has slowed to a whisper. Not turning on any lights, I grab my laptop and sit on the leather couch and pick up the remote that flicks on the long narrow fireplace in the travertine stone wall across from me. The flames dance as I open the lid to my computer and pull up my web browser. I'm not the one who hired her, it was Quin who did that, so I didn't run her background check—he did—but the info wasn't put into her file. At least that's the rationale I offer myself for cyber-stalking Nova.

I Google her and find pages of information about her old company. As I scan the articles, I see her face, only a few years younger, in an article about changes in the marketplace—how the next generation will defy categorization and still exceed all expectation. Smiling, I shake my head and read the article. It's Nova to a T. She won't be shoved into a box or pigeonholed. The woman isn't a statistic and that's part of what makes her an anomaly, because it's true. She doesn't fit anywhere. The massive brain in that young body is an oddity, but she has wisdom that only comes with life. That's the part I'm curious about. I dig deeper, finding older articles from when she had her startup with some guy named Ben. I stare at the picture of them and notice the way her body is angled into his, like they were a couple. Shit. If that's true then things went to shit for her recently. She lost more than her job. This douchebag had something to do with her current leeriness and rough edges, but there's also something there that's older, wiser, and whatever it was—it came long before Ben.

I go further back and then try a different approach—personal background reports that include everything from speeding tickets to police reports. Something happened to her. I can feel it. I'm filling in her information and when I get to the bottom of the form, my finger hovers above the submit button. Am I really this guy? I want to understand why she's the way she is, but this seems invasive. I don't suspect she did anything wrong, but I'm guessing someone did something to her. Why else would a fifteen-year-old move away from home? And move in with a guy? And start a business? She threw her entire existence into that company and now she has nothing. A lesser person would have crumbled, but there's something there holding her together, something that's worse than losing the shirt off her back.

I swallow hard and lift my gaze to look out at the city. I could ask her. Talk to her like a regular person. I don't have to find out this way and it's probably better if I didn't. The problem is that if we talk and I know her more, I'll like her more. I can't risk that.

I shove my finger down and press SUBMIT.

I'll find out in forty-eight hours what

happened to her, if there's something there. Maybe we can't be together, but that doesn't mean she has to take on the world alone. I can watch out for her if I know who her enemies are, at least I hope I can.

30
CELYN

The next afternoon, mid-shift, Reginald calls me. I turn away from the line and answer as Nova takes over for me. I duck out of the shack, leaving my coat behind, and crunch my way across the icy pavement to the sidewalk in front of the mall exterior.

I answer as I walk, "Hey, what can I do for you?"

"Celyn," Reginald's voice is strained, "I hope you're doing well."

My breath forms a puff of white air as I exhale and run a hand through my hair. "Better than expected, actually. I think I have a shot at this thing, Reg."

There's a bit of silence, and then Reginald clears his throat. "I'm proud of you, of your attempt at this, no matter how it turns out. I went by there yesterday. Although parts of your business are unorthodox, it's doing well. You utilized sex appeal on a product with a high markup. It's impressive, Celyn."

"I didn't realize you came by. When was that?"

"Around four o'clock. There was a woman working very hard. We had a nice chat before another co-worker relieved her. I'd hoped to speak with you then. I hate to be the bearer of bad news, but yesterday afternoon something happened. I think you need to speak with your uncle right away."

I grimace and kick a spot of icy slush on the pavement. Little balls of unmelted rock salt litter the cement. I tip one with the toe of my boot off the curb. I want to ask what's so urgent, but I doubt he can tell me even if he knows. "Can it wait until tonight?"

"It can," his voice becomes deeper, more urgent, "but I'd get here as soon as possible."

Screw it. I ask him pointblank, "Why, what's going on? Is it Dad's company? Is something wrong at Bardenbey?" I glance back at the Hut and see Nova in the window, her blonde braids poking out from under her fuzzy hat as she laughs at something the man standing below the window said to her. The sound carries across the parking lot and it's hard to focus on anything else. That is, until Reginald actually tells me something.

"It's not Bardenbey. I'm not entirely sure. In years past, this month has always had your uncle on edge. His daily demeanor ranged from demon to dementor," I smile at the Harry Potter reference and nearly say something about it, but he plows on, "But your uncle is exceedingly happy, which is so peculiar at this time of year. I can't remember a final quarter where he's had a smile on his face for more than a second, and this one has lasted all day. In conclusion, I surmise that he—"

I cut him off, my mood darkening. "Yeah, got it. He's figured something out, a way to block me. Shit. Do you know what it is?" Lead fills my chest and the light hope that filled me up before is crushed flat. I've been watching my numbers all day, every day. Even with everything that's happened, I still have a decent chance of coming out ahead. But if Uncle is grinning and singing Christmas ditties, I'm fucked.

"I'm afraid not. I'll keep an eye out, but Celyn, this is a bad sign."

"Reg, I'm so damn close to pulling this off." I glance at the Hottie Hut, at the long line of people who will walk away if I take too long. "If I leave right now it could make the difference between winning the bet and losing."

Reginald scoffs, "Don't call it a bet, Celyn. That's so tasteless."

"That's what it is, Reg. I bet my entire fortune on this. I won't pretend that the board—whoever they are—will be impartial. At a minimum, it's you, Uncle, and an unknown. You're the only one I can count on to be fair. Uncle will use that third seat against me."

I hear Reginald smack his lips. "Business has very little to do with fairness, I'm afraid."

"Right, and if I don't meet goal for today, I don't have a chance in hell at winning this thing. I'll be in later tonight. Let Uncle gloat. Maybe he'll let something slip." I run a hand through my hair, wondering what else could possibly have Uncle that cheerful. The man kills bliss for sport. Being happy isn't part of his outlook on life. Success is the only thing that matters and it has a heavy price.

I glance up at the Hottie Hut. That mantra was drilled into me and I'm using it here. I'll forfeit any chance at a friendship with her when she finds out about this. There's no way she'll ever talk to me again, and if I lose—I couldn't bear to face her. The price of success is loneliness. I saw it with my father and again with my uncle. It's a sacrifice I'm willing to make to continue my family's legacy, to make a mark on this world, and make it better than it had been. I was chasing a pipe dream with the pharmaceutical division. We were so close to finding a cure for cancer. So close. That was the catalyst that caused my monstrous failure all those years ago. Idealism. Hope. I was a fool. I won't make the same mistakes twice.

After we disconnect, I head back toward the hut and help handle the line that's formed. People mill about with nowhere to go. I glance at the Christmas tree guy across the lot. He has picnic tables there and even in the cold weather, people use them. I don't have enough cash to afford seating or I'd have gotten it. People who mill about are more likely to buy a second cup or another cookie. Sometimes I wonder if that's going to be what breaks us—no seating.

When I'm back in the hut, I squeeze past Nova, my hips narrowly avoiding hers. Her scent catches me as I pass the back of her bare neck. It's vanilla and sugar. I inhale again and smirk. "Are you wearing cookie perfume?"

She laughs and swings a golden braid over her shoulder. "Do you sniff all of your employees?"

"Only the ones who smell good." I smirk at

her and the woman in the window smiles hard, watching us like we're flirting.

Nova hands her the order and thanks her before greeting the next customer. "I take it that you haven't taken the liberty of sneaking a sniff of Shannon, then?"

I laugh once, hard. "That man smells like dirt and yak."

She nearly chokes on her chortle. Nova glances sidelong at me as I hand her the next order. "Okay, you do smell all your employees then."

"You caught me." I hold up my hands, and then reach for the cups to ready the next order. Adding, "And that's why he's not in here."

She turns and looks at me over her shoulder after handing me the next order slip. "Really? I thought he was taking a two hour break after handing out fliers again."

"Leave it alone, Nova." My tone is light and she's already told me several times that Shannon is dead weight, but I'm not sure he is. I have a model working right now that's incredibly close to succeeding. My future will be secure. I'll have my seat at the table, and my life can go on as normal.

Nova holds up her hands, palms facing me. "It's not my call."

I cut off the conversation, "I'll take over in the window. You're freezing. Go buy a pair of gloves or something."

"Psh," she says, bumping her hip against mine as she passes. "I'll fill coffee cups and you work the window. I bet we can serve that last person in seven minutes or less."

The corners of my mouth tip up into a lazy smile even though worry is pawing at my mind like a determined cat. I glance at the line. "Well, let's go, Hot Girl. If you lose, you buy me a cookie."

Her head sways on her neck as she barks a laugh. Pointing at me, she counters, "And if I'm right, you owe me two cookies."

"Hungry?" I smirk at her.

"No, my sister is coming. I'm planning ahead." Her face lights up as she lifts a brow. "Well, do we have a deal or not?"

"Start the timer."

31

NOVA

Celyn I work well together. The line is gone in less than five minutes and I managed to upsell the last three people into getting my sweet KISS MOOSE KISSES drink. Most people are calling it a KISS MOOSE. They don't realize it's a pun until they say it out loud and then laugh.

Celyn had a spring in his step all day that seemed to get sucked out after that phone call. His voice sounds similar, but the sweep of his shoulders and the way his face pinches when he thinks I'm not looking makes me wonder what's wrong. But I don't ask. I decided that it was best to act like that first night never happened. Since then, Celyn has been sweet and thoughtful. He works hard every day. He's the first to arrive and the last to leave. He must be exhausted, but he doesn't complain. There's a burn on his left hand from an accident with a carafe two nights ago, but he doesn't act like it hurts either—even though the skin is still angry and raw. He barely slowed down enough to put on the burn cream.

We've made goal nearly every day, which has him excited. I'm still waiting for the other shoe to drop and find out why a guy driving a McLaren is so invested in making a coffee shack work. He's not said anything and I've not asked. We found a good pace and fell into stride. I buried myself in work and I'm not feeling the shards of my shattered heart piercing my chest at every moment of the day anymore. And I know why—it's Celyn. He makes me forget the pain, sorrow, and loss. My anger fades around him and it doesn't seem like revenge is worth my time. I've not told anyone but Tinselly what actually happened with Ben. I can't bear to face them, Mom especially. They'll think I was naïve, a fool to let it happen. It's hard to see something like that coming. It was supposed to be me and Ben against the world. But it didn't work out that way.

Tinselly's face pops up in the window. She must have snuck over, because I didn't see her. I was lost in thought, wiping the counter, when she springs up like a jack-in-the-box and yelps, "BOO!"

I startle, scream, and whip my wet cloth at her face before I realize it's my sister. Her dark head of hair sways as she stills and that huge smile on her face turns into an OH SHIT expression as she's met with a dirty wet rag. It makes a slapping sound on contact, landing diagonally across her face.

"Tinselly! Oh my God!" I lean out the window to try and grab the rag and almost fall. I yelp when I slip, but Celyn grabs onto my waist and puts my feet back on the floor.

He tries not to smile as Tinselly peels the cold cloth off her face, revealing smeared make-up and the most disgusted expression I've ever seen. She holds the cloth up at me pinched between her thumb and forefinger, then says dryly, "Yeah, you're buying today."

"You scared me! Are you okay?" I try to repress a smile and totally fail.

Tinselly's hair is stuck to her eyeball, which looks like it's bleeding black blood down her cheek. She sneers as she touches the damp hair and pushes it out of her eye. "I'm fine."

I chance a glance at Celyn who looks away fast. He reaches over and grabs a roll of paper towels from the cabinet and hands them to me before I see a wicked twitch at the corners of his mouth. He busies himself at the carafe, and avoids looking at me or Tinselly, but I can see his full grin in the silver reflection.

I shove him with my shoulder as I pass by. "It's not funny," I say softly.

"Exactly." He answers straight-faced as I head to the door.

I feel the huge grin burning through my forced frown. Screw it. I beam full wattage at him and slap my knee, laughing silently. Celyn returns the smile until Tinselly says from the window. "I can see you, Nova. And you—guy."

My laughter turns audible at that point. "Guy? That's the best you can do?" I lean against the wall and press a hand to my stomach, belly laughing so hard that I can barely stand.

Tinselly is frowning in the window, her sopping hair dripping into her eyes. "Nova..."

I say in broken laughter, "The dishrag hitting her face and the chunk of wet hair." I point toward my eye and nearly fall on the floor.

Celyn is no better, but he isn't on the floor. A second later, Tinselly wrenches the door open, and looks down at me, hands on her hips with a wicked gleam in her eye. Uh oh. I know that look. I still and wait for it. She says pleasantly, "Should I tell him what you really call him?"

"It's break time! See you later, Celyn." I'm about to fly out the door when Celyn shoves cookies in my hands.

He grins at Tinselly, "So, what does she call me?"

Tinselly opens her mouth but I talk over her and lead my sister by the hand into the parking lot. I call over my shoulder, "Bye, Celyn! Love you!" I kiss my palm and throw it back at him. I'm being a goofball, but the way he looks at me when I say it makes my chest hurt. His eyes are so melancholy that it sobers me.

"Later, Hot Girl."

While the laughter has drained from my body, my smile is still in place. "Want dinner?" Before he can say no, I tell him, "Too bad, because I'm bringing it!" I grab Tinselly's arm and lean into her.

"Where's your jacket, you lunatic?" Tinselly puts her arm around me as we make a beeline for the doors into the mall.

"In my car." I confess without much thought.

"Shouldn't it be in the Hottie Hut?"

I frown at her and tug her arm. She stumbles a little and shoves me back, giggling. "Tinselly, you're such a buzz kill. Yes, it should, but it's small in there and if I go home with my coat smelling like cookies one more time, I'll eat it."

That's what I say while I chant in my head, *don't tell Tinselly. Don't tell Tinselly. Don't even look at the car. She doesn't suspect. Just keep walking.*

Tinselly chortles. "Well, we couldn't have that."

"Nope." We shove in through the glass doors and head toward the food court, munching on cookies as we go.

"So," Tinselly throws out there and waits for me to say something.

We stop in front of the menus and I glance over at her. "So what?"

"So, Celyn. How is he?" Tinselly's heard me talk about him. I was careful though. I didn't say too much. At least I didn't think I did. She was totally bluffing before, back in the hut. I don't call Celyn anything, but I know he's going to think I do now. He probably thinks I curse him every night and complain about my bad boss.

"He's fine. He burned his hand the other night. Other than that, good." I feel her eyes on the side of my face, and I can see out of my peripheral that her grin is growing. It's big enough to eat her face. I round on her. "What?"

A huge grin eats her face and she lifts a finger toward me. "Nova has a boyfriend." She chants the words like a second grader.

"It's not like that." I'm smiling though, which

completely contradicts what I just said. "He's just, nice."

"Uh oh. Nice? Nice is the friend zone." Tinselly's gaze narrows as I study the menu too closely. She knows. I don't know how she figured it out, but she put it together. Celyn. One night guy. And me.

Her face fills with delighted shock as her mouth turns into a big O. She sucks in enough air to form a black hole when I plaster my hands over her mouth. I hiss at her, "Say it and die."

Tinselly swats my fingers away and points at me. "It was him. The guy from Thanksgiving! Oh my God!" She does a little jumpy dance, way too excited, and then tugs me to a table. "Start at the beginning. Tell me everything." She's so happy for me that I don't want to do it, but I won't lie to her.

I glance at her hands and her manicured nails. "It's not like that. He's not interested in me. Well, he was that night—for about ten minutes—then he walked out and didn't come back."

Her jaw drops and anger flashes in her eyes. "He did what now?"

"He thought I was older. I thought he was younger." I don't explain the rest of that night. I don't tell her his kisses made me forget Ben and eased the betrayal. I don't admit that his voice fills my mind, even when he's not there. I can't say that his laughter makes me feel whole and those arms—that touch—makes everything that's wrong with the world fade away.

Tinselly watches me for a moment. She lets out a slow breath and takes one of my hands and squeezes it so hard it hurts. I yank it away. "Tinselly!"

"Oh, I'm sorry, did you feel that?" She lifts a hand and smacks me gently in the side of the head, knocking my fluffy hat off. "A blind person could see you two are into each other. Why are you ignoring how you feel?"

I pull my hat on my head and frown at her. "I'm not." She lifts a dark brow at me. It's the same look Mom gave us when we were kids and we weren't telling the truth. "I'm not lying. I told you, I won't do that to you."

Tinselly nods a few times and leans back in her seat. She ticks off on her fingers, "So, you nearly went to bed with this guy, he becomes your boss, and now it's like you two are BFFs."

I shrug and can't really wipe the sadness off my face. "Yeah." I don't look at her. "Listen, Tinselly. I can't. It's easier to not admit I feel anything about him. I mean, I shouldn't feel anything. I was in love with Ben. Everything was about Ben for the longest time. What does it say about me that I can feel something so fast for someone else?"

Tinselly sighs and pinches the bridge of her nose like she has a headache. When she drops her hands she looks me in the eye. "It says you have huge balls. It says you're a survivor and you're not willing to give up. Come on, Nova. You can't beat yourself up over Ben. That was over a long time ago, wasn't it?"

My face flicks up and my eyes meet hers. "What are you talking about?"

"Maybe I'm wrong, but it seemed like things weren't good."

"They were okay," I hedge.

"Were you happy?" She asks like she really wants to know, so I think about it.

"At times, yes."

"What about work? And bed? And everything? As a whole, you seemed like you were working all the time. Toward the end, you barely smiled. When Ben touched you, you shook him off."

"I did not."

"You did. Nova, it's not a criticism. I'm just saying that maybe things falling apart with Ben wasn't a bad thing. He wasn't your guy. You need someone who can dream as big as you can, someone who will challenge you to do better, to be more. And I admit that I hoped it was Ben because he anchored your impulsiveness, but it's that impulse that made you successful. It seemed more like he caged you than anything else. Not on purpose and not in a malicious way. It's just what happens when you take a guy like him and pair him with a girl like you." Tinselly lets out a rush of air. "Celyn thinks like you, I hear it when you talk about him. So who put up the friend wall, you or him?"

"Him." I glance away, unable to look at her. I might squirm out of my seat to avoid this conversation.

"Are you sure it wasn't you?" Tinselly catches my gaze and smiles kindly at me. "Rejection sucks, Nova. But I'm not going to coddle you. Sometimes things change and if he doesn't know how you feel, nothing will happen. He'll keep everything platonic. If that's not what you want, you should let him know."

I'm shaking my head before the words have formed completely in my mind. "No," I look her square in the face. "The first day with him after that night was awkward as hell. I was angry and nearly lost any chance I had at knowing him." That's when I realize what I've been unwilling to admit—I want to know him. I want to be around him and I'll take whatever form of relationship he offers, because something is better than nothing. I can be his friend. He needs a friend and so do I.

"So you'd rather have him as a friend than nothing at all?"

I nod with absolute certainty. "Yes."

"So," she cocks her head to the side and laces her fingers together, before tucking them under her chin, "you wouldn't care if that slutty brunette was hanging all over him?"

I straighten in my chair and lean forward. In a clipped tone, I ask, "How do you know about her?"

"I've seen her talking to him, Nova. She hangs around trying to get him to ask her out."

I look at the floor. "She's his age."

Tinselly kicks me under the table. "You're his type."

"Oww, Tinselly. Quit it." I rub my shin.

"No, I won't. Listen to me, Nova." She reaches out and grabs hold of my wrist. "You only have a limited number of chances, Nova. Don't let your shot at happiness pass you by because he's not exactly the same age as you."

I glare at her. "He's older than you."

"It doesn't matter."

I counter, "He's thirty-five."

Her head jerks back. "Really?"

"Tinselly, see?" I sigh and pull out of her grip. "It wouldn't work."

Tinselly bobs her head side to side as she waves a finger at me. "Uh, you're the one that says age is just a number created by corporations to classify people like livestock."

I snort. "I said that when I was fourteen."

Tinselly touches my shoulder gently. "Yeah, but you still believe it. If he's the guy, who cares how old he is." She sees the worry on my face. There's so much she doesn't know.

"I'll think about it."

She drops her hand and gives me a look. "Fourteen-year-old Nova didn't think about things."

Her words pick an old wound open. She doesn't have any idea she did it, but I can't rein it in. Whatever broken pieces remain inside of me spark to life and rear up. I slam my hands on the table and stand abruptly. "Fourteen-year-old Nova is gone. This is what's left, Tinselly. This is what I am now. Take it or leave it, but don't become nostalgic about a past that didn't exist. I need to grab my dinner and head back to the Hut."

Tinselly watches me from the little table as I get in line at Nathan's. She's rooted everything out, except the one thing I thought she'd notice first. My car. My coat is in there, so is my blanket, and my sheets, and all of my clothes. I've had them neatly packed in the trunk for over a week now. There are a few frightful hours at night that I close my eyes and hope a deranged hobo doesn't light my car on fire, or worse. When I walked away from Ben, I lost everything. It's been hard, but I'd rather get hypothermia than go home to Mom. I can't step inside that house again. I won't do it.

32

CELYN

It's well past nightfall by the time I make it to Bardenbey. The halls are empty for the most part since workers left for the day by seven o'clock. There are a few stragglers here and there, the guys in legal who never sleep, and Uncle who is as energetic as if he just sprung out of bed.

I approach his secretary, who recognizes me. "Good evening. I hope you're well tonight." My hair is a mess and I smell like coffee and spilled milk. When I was loading the fridge, I dropped the carton and half of it splashed onto my sweater which soaked it up with sponge-like zeal. The rest spilled on the floor. When I fumbled the milk carton in front of the open fridge my quick hands acted more like hockey sticks and I literally threw dairy products everywhere. By accident. It was very manly. Thank God, Nova wasn't there.

Perky, I mean Patty, looks up at me from under a veil of inky hair. "I'm doing very well, thank you, Mr. Ryan. I'll let Mr, Ryan know you're here." She presses a button on her intercom and announces me.

Footfalls catch my ear before I can reply and the office doors sweep open. "Celyn, my boy. Come in." His high spirits are running unchecked. He reaches out, gesturing for me to pass through. Half of me wonders if there's a firing squad inside, but I venture in anyway. I need to find out what this is all about it.

Reginald was right. Everything from the spring in his step to the way he's smiling has the hairs on the back of my neck standing on end. I follow Uncle into the vast room and hear the doors quietly hiss shut behind us. "How's it going out on the Island, Celyn? Reginald told me he was rather impressed." He's smiling so hard I can see father in his face, the crinkles around the eyes and the way his lips curve at the corners of his mouth.

I'm incredibly leery, but I hide it from him. I repay his smile in kind and sit down in a leather club chair, placing an ankle on my knee while Uncle heads to the bar and lifts a crystal decanter filled with amber liquid. "It couldn't be better. I'm going to surpass that goal with flying colors, Uncle. Dad would be proud."

The last part is mostly bluster, but throwing dad onto the end of it unexpectedly makes my throat catch. He would have been proud. Truthfully, I've never worked so hard and been so exhausted for so little money in my entire life. It's taught me lessons I couldn't have learned otherwise, and I'm grateful for it, despite the circumstances that led to this point.

"He would be very proud. You were the apple of your father's eye. If he could see you now, eh? Up to your elbows in curdled milk and coffee grinds, putting your nose to the grindstone with your fellow man. He always thought a business built on the backs of its people would ultimately fail, and look at you, following in his footprint to the letter." Uncle pours two tumblers of whiskey and hands me one as he passes by. I take it, half worried it's poisoned, but that's not like him. The man would rather see me suffer and humiliated than dead.

I take a sip and place it on the small table next to my chair. I watch Uncle, expecting him to sit behind his desk, in the taller chair, and tower over me, looking down at me as we speak. The person seated in the tallest chair is perceived as most powerful. He never sits at the same level as everyone else. Even if his chair looks the same, it's always an inch or more taller and narrower, which makes him look larger than life. So when he sits in the club chair next to me, I nearly choke.

"Celyn, you fought well. I want to commend you." There's a finality to his tone that sends ice through my veins.

A trace of a smile lines my lips. "The fight isn't over yet. Congratulate me when I've won."

Uncle's cheeks bunch up on one side. "I'm afraid our little sparring match is at an end, Celyn." He lifts his phone and hands it to me, open to the weather app. There's a massive cell moving toward New York. "A nor'easter is headed this way. I was alerted first thing this morning as it could potentially affect several of our shipments. Then I thought of you in that tiny shack and three feet of snow and suggested Reginald tell you to come in. Celyn, your aspirations are noble, but it's over. You can't do anything buried under three feet of snow."

I'm shell-shocked. I stare at his phone but can't think. It's one of those rare storms that moves up and plants itself over the city. The Island usually gets more snow than the city which means three feet is the minimum. Streets will close and people will stay inside where it's safe. The few brave enough to venture out won't be headed to the mall for a cup of coffee. Shit. I could take a hit and still have a shot after one shitty day, but this—I can't recover from this. When people see a storm coming it completely changes their day to day activities. Instead they run to the supermarket and stockpile food and water. The foot traffic we rely on will die by morning. This isn't the equivalent of having a bad day, it's the decimation of having a net loss for a week. When the hut only had a few weeks to start with, it's a death sentence.

It's over.

I lost.

I lost everything.

33

NOVA

Bleary eyed and half frozen, I roll over and pray to God that it's nearly sunrise. I've managed to shower once or twice a week by sneaking into the showers at the state park. The only downside is the water is icy and the gas it takes to get there. Dodging the park rangers is getting difficult. No one is camping right now and my crappy old car is easy to spot. I can shower at Tinselly's once or twice a month and she won't know something's wrong, but I didn't want to chance it. The more I'm around her, the more I want to fall into her arms, crying. My strength is all I have left and if I can't take care of myself, what good am I?

I'm curled in a ball in the backseat, shivering. My face is frozen. Sleeping under blankets and most of my clothing isn't enough to keep me warm anymore. The temperature dropped last night and hasn't come back up. If I turn the car on, so I have heat, I'll have no gas. If it snows for long, I'm screwed. I sit up and rub my hands over my arms and crawl into the front seat. It's a little early, but I don't care. It's too cold.

I turn the engine and start the car, letting it warm the space while I tame my hair into twin braids and thank God for the stupid uniform and hat. It hides rumpled hair and clothes. The thing is polyester and incapable of holding a wrinkle. To cover the fact that I've not washed it in a couple of days, I sprayed the crap out of it with body mist. That's what Celyn smelled the other day. I keep waiting for him to figure it out. I'll die of shame when he does. Same thing with Tinselly. It's only a matter of time with the two of them.

After I'm all set, I pull out of the little cul-de-sac and crawl along on the icy roads until I make it to the hut. Shivering, I rush across the parking lot and pull on the door. It's locked. That's weird. Celyn is usually here before me. I race back over to my car and debate turning it on again. It's so cold, but I don't want to waste gas. I've been trying to save my money for the deposit on an apartment. I can't afford it, so I sit there, shivering. I glance at the mall in front of me. Sears is open for early Christmas shoppers. There's a display in the window that's calling to me.

I don't like going inside in my Swiss Miss costume, but I've gotten used to it by now. Most of the mall employees know us now. Shannon saw to that. The guy knows everyone because he stops and talks to every person with a face. Literally. He stops and chats them up, then goes to the next person. It's why a twenty-minute break turns into two hours. Celyn doesn't say much about it because he thinks it's helping us meet goal, but I'm not sure if it has anything to do with Shannon. It's all Celyn.

I haven't Googled Celyn. I don't want to. The guy is nearly twice my age and whatever I find will taint how I see him. Maybe I'm naïve, but it's not like we're dating—or sleeping together—so I'll leave good enough alone. I pull into a parking spot close to the door and sigh happily that it's getting close enough to Christmas that corporate decided to open this location at 6:00am. They're insane. No one is here, except me. I'm not complaining though. I see exactly what I want and it's a price that won't break me. Actually, it could save me some cash if I don't have to go to a motel when it gets colder at night. I rush inside, make my purchases, and when I duck back into my car, I can see the McLaren by the Hottie Hut.

I grab my bag of loot and head to the hut. When I yank the door open, Celyn is sitting there, on one of those stools with his head in his hands, eyes downcast, his fingers pulling his hair. "What's wrong?" I shouldn't ask, because he's my boss. Because it's none of my business. Because I'm falling for him and if I know, I'll want to know more—I'll want to fix it.

Celyn looks over at me as if he hasn't slept. "Nothing." He stands, puts the stool away, and starts to pull out the coffee grinder.

I don't know how to play this ¬push him or leave it alone. I shoot for the middle. "If I can help with anything, you know I will. Christmas shopping for your dog, spreadsheets for the Hut, you name it—I've got mad skills." He doesn't smile or look over at me. He seems weary, burdened. "I went into Sears a second ago and bought a new heater for my car. Wanna see?"

Celyn turns, his long lashes lowered, and when he lifts his gaze to my big bag I pull out a fuzzy white blanket. "Tah dah!"

He smiles and a small laugh escapes his lips. He touches the fabric, smoothing his hand over the blanket. "That's soft. How many Muppets did Sears have to kill to make it? You know I'm adverse to marionette cruelty."

"Oh, I know, which is why this is real fake fur.

No animals, fake or real, were harmed in the making of this super fuzzy blanket. And look," I reach into the bag and pull out the next item, "Matching socks!"

Celyn laughs and takes the socks from me. When his eyes meet mine, I smile softly at him. "I could get you a pair. They're bitchin'."

"Bitchin'?"

"Yeah, well, as far as socks go." He's still not acting like himself. "Celyn, what's wrong? It looks like your best friend just died. Quin's okay, right?" Quin's been acting damn weird lately, skittish almost.

He looks past me, outside at the parking lot. "We're going to miss goal. I was up doing the projections last night. I didn't sleep." He releases a long, slow breath through his nose.

"Like completely miss it? Or scrape it?" I ask carefully.

He glances up at me. "It was going to be close, but with the weather they're predicting—there's no way." He watches me, those blue eyes drinking me in like he might never see me again. The hairs on my arms rise slightly.

I put a hand on his shoulder because I think he needs a hug, but that would be totally inappropriate. He and I have been stuck in this spot of easy friendship, exes, and when you add in work

—it's just a clusterfuck. I don't know what we are and I don't really care if I can't label it. I still want to make him feel better, so I push, "Talk to me. How much are we going to miss by? What are the repercussions?"

He pulls away from me and says nothing. I glance around and notice that there aren't any carafes brewing. The scent of coffee doesn't fill the shack.

"Celyn, what are you doing?" I see it now. He wasn't here to open this morning, he's closing the Hut. There are no freshly ground beans, the empty syrup bottles weren't replaced. I pull open the little fridge and there's no milk or cream. "Celyn." I say his name once, my eyes wide, when I turn back to him. "You're quitting?" Something inside me curdles and I can't hide my disappointment.

"It's not quitting." He stares blankly and runs both hands over the top of his head. "I know when I've lost, Nova."

"Lost what?" He won't look at me. "Celyn, tell me what's going on." I grab his arm and pull him so he turns to face me. My voice is soft, careful. "I can help you."

His crystal eyes are framed by dark hair that's fallen forward. "It's more complicated than you realize."

I gesture toward the parking lot, "I suspected that this," I gesture to the shack with a swirl of my finger, "was an odd situation when I saw your car. It's worth more than the hut and everything in it. By a lot."

Celyn nods. "Right, it is." He leans on the windowsill and then his eyes cut back toward me. "I made a bet and I lost. This shack was part of the bet."

I don't know what's happening. The words blindside me so badly that my lips quiver. I'm going to lose my job. If he closes this shack, I'll have no income at all. Living in my car won't be an option. I'll have to sell it, along with my phone, and everything I have to try and feed myself. My gut twists as a wave of nausea hits me hard. This place separates me from destruction and to him...it was a bet.

After the anger simmers down a bit, I finally manage, "Explain."

He remains on the stool, his gaze locked on the floor. He pushes his hair back and runs his hand down his neck, explaining, "This entire setup was a joke, Nova. It shouldn't have made it this far."

"But it did."

"Right, because of Shannon and you."

"No," I tip my head sideways and get in his

face, partly because I'm pissed and I can't stand hearing him crushed. If this place was a stupid bet, why does he look so devastated? It doesn't add up. His sapphire eyes meet mine. "Talk to me, Celyn."

"There's nothing to say, Nova. It's over. I failed. What do you want me to tell you?"

"You didn't fail. This place did well because of you. It was you. It was never Shannon. You cultivated the relationships with the people. You were the one here at all hours of the day and night. It was you, Celyn. So tell me why you're suddenly taking down your shingle because of something the weatherman said? Since when are they right?"

"The shortfall is too big. There's no point, Nova." He leans his narrow hips against the counter and then reaches into his briefcase and pulls out a folder. He hands it to me.

I flick it open and paw through reports, profit and loss statements, and see one glaring money pit that he hasn't addressed. I glance up at him. "What were the terms of the bet?"

The corners of his mouth twitch. He didn't expect me to say that. From the look on his face, he expects me to beat him with the folder, but I don't.

"I made your job a joke. I'm an asshole. How

could you possibly want to help me?" Those cobalt eyes blink at me, shocked.

I gesture toward my costume. "I knew this job was a joke from day one, Celyn. I'm not that obtuse. Come on, what were the terms? What's the goal?" I thumb through a few more pages.

Celyn lifts himself onto the counter and tells me the numbers and finishes by saying, "I'm going to be nearly two grand short if it snows the way they're predicting."

"And if it misses us?"

"I'm still short and if people freak out the way they always do before a storm, foot traffic will be minimal for a few days."

"But it's possible to make it up, right? You could still hit goal in the week after Christmas."

"It's possible, but not probable. You're more likely to see baby Jesus riding Rudolph on Christmas Eve, Nova."

I snort and don't dignify that with an answer. I pull out a few purchase orders and then payroll. There's a spot to cut spending and that's one way to push up profits. Since Celyn's bet is all about profit margins, then this could work. I put the papers on the counter next to him. "What if we cut the decaf?"

He flinches and lifts a brow at me. "We'd lose over a quarter of our income."

"Right, but add in the additional carafe and beans, and the math is too tight. It's nearly a wash on decaf. Cut it. Return the carafe and get that money back." The frozen wheels in my mind are just warming up. I can see this working, buying us time. Keeping me from hobodom. I still want to know what he loses if the hut doesn't meet goal. I realize he's not said it yet. Maybe his car? It has to be something worth a great deal to him.

Celyn retorts, "I can't. We're in a contract for three machines."

"Let me try to get us out of it." I lift my eyes and meet his gaze. "If I can get them to take the third machine back and we cut decaf, then you have to do one thing and you'll have a shot again —snow or not."

Celyn folds his arms over his chest, his eyes locked on mine. "What's that?"

"Fire Shannon. He doesn't pull his weight and his paycheck will give you enough wiggle room to actually have a shot at this." I push the papers back toward him. "Numbers don't lie, Celyn. It gives you enough of a buffer that you don't have to give up, unless you've just had it and want to quit." The last few words leave a sour taste in my mouth. Celyn's not the kind of guy who works this kind of job. He's the kind of guy who drives a pricy car and wears designer jeans. When he first started at the hut, his hands were smooth. No scars or calluses. No evidence of this type of work. Now he's marred and his hands are dried and cracking.

Celyn's dark brows crinkle together as he runs his forefinger and thumb down the side of his face, asking, "You want a coffee shop to not sell coffee and to fire the only male barista right before Christmas?"

He's stuck. I can hear it in his voice. He thinks he's already failed and he won't hear it unless I beat him over the head with numbers, with facts. I don't know if I do it for me, or him. I should be pissed at him, but I'm not. Maybe it's because he's showing me the ledgers or maybe it's because he actually values my opinion, I don't know. But I come at him with cold facts that are going to feel like a brick to the head.

I snap, "It's a start-up, Celyn. Adjustments are made with the most frequency during the early months. It's a necessity. It's adapt or die. You know this. You also know that profit increases when overhead is cut. So let's hack away anything we can. You don't have to walk away. There's still a fighting chance here, Celyn. More so than when you walked in on day one. People know you now, and they'll be looking for you after the snowstorms pass. You don't need employees right now.

You have one and a friend helping you. Were there terms that said you had to hire an entire staff?"

"No, I had to have management, staff was assumed but not stated."

I raise a brow at him. "Well, you have me. Cut the chaff, Celyn. Sometimes you have to do it to get ahead. If Shannon doesn't see it coming, he's an idiot. He spends more time in the mall than in the hut."

"It's not about Shannon, although I don't like letting someone go right before Christmas." He's been scanning the sheets. "And a coffee shop with no decaf is weird."

"Decaf is for pussies."

Celyn chokes on a laugh and looks over the top of the papers at me. "I can't believe you just said that."

I smile up at him. "By limiting your product, you'll decrease your expenses and increase your profits. Besides, most people that want decaf will happily buy something else, the water, or a cookie, or regular coffee. It'll save you a chunk of change because you won't need that third machine."

Celyn stares at the papers for a moment and then nods. "It'd still be possible, even if we have a few slow days because of snow."

"Right, and even if it does snow with the three feet they're saying, you're still going to have a mass of people shopping on Christmas Eve, which will probably spill into early Christmas Day. There are restaurants on the other side of the parking lot. Get their customer's attention and they'll grab a cup of coffee while they wait. Come on, Celyn. Don't give up. If you're going to lose, do it with style, but don't quit."

He looks over the papers at me, his eyes searching mine. After a moment, he asks, "You don't quit, do you?"

"Hell no, and neither should you. That's the major difference between a business owner with an MBA and one with only street smarts—we don't know when to quit because we can't. There are no do-overs, no back-up coming to save us. If we don't bring home the bacon, no one else will. If you do this, it'll be by the skin of your teeth and that's a really stressful spot to be in, but it also will tell you exactly what you're made of, what you can do, and what you can't do. There will be no more wondering about what kind of man you are, you'll know. Most people don't want to live with the risk. They're so paralyzed by the fear of failing that they don't even try."

He considers me and then says, "I could pay

you for the next few weeks and you wouldn't have to work. I'm not leaving you high and dry, Nova."

My shoulders stiffen and I spit out the stupidest, idealistic crap. Shaking my head, I tell him, "I won't take it if you do that."

"Why not?"

"I didn't earn it." I watch him and wonder how I didn't see this side to him. Why is he giving up? What else is going on here? "I'll work for you, but I'm not taking a handout."

"I didn't mean it like that."

"I know, but that's what it would be. I'll work, but I'm not taking a going out of business bonus. It's not right." I'm so stupid. The girl who froze her ass off in my car last night is screaming at me inside my skull to take the money and run. I tell her my fuzzy blanket and socks are enough.

Celyn nods after a moment and then clears his throat. "Well, you better call the rental place and see what they say."

I smirk and jab my thumb at the coffee beans. "Right, you better start a batch of coffee before the morning crowd gets here."

I pull my phone out and head toward my car so I can do this in private. I cross the parking lot, letting out little puffs of white air as I slip inside. Celyn watches me as I pull the door closed and pull up the number. Here goes nothing.

34
CELYN

Nova has been in her car, talking with her hands for over twenty minutes, although it feels like hours. This phone call could mean I keep my place at Bardenbey. My fate lies in her hands. The reason I passed it off to her was simple, I'm good at sales, but not at begging. I couldn't figure another way around it, and since the owner of the rental company is a guy and Nova is a girl, well, she'll have some more moves than me. If I cried to get something, I'd be laughed at indefinitely. If she cries, well—who knows? Even with all sexist shit aside, there've been no tears, just a few sharp laughs and her hands flying as she speaks. It dawns on me that she must be on speakerphone. Maybe I shouldn't, but I can't help it. It's been too long and I'm dying to know what's going on. There's no line, probably because of the gray storm clouds that threaten to bury the Island.

I quietly walk up behind her car, intentionally walking over in her blind spot so she doesn't see me. I don't want to spook her, but I wonder if I can hear anything. As I get closer, I pick up pieces of the conversation.

Nova sounds poised and confident. You'd have no idea she was so young. It sounds like she's negotiating. She tips her head to the side and glares at the phone. "Come on, Greg, you can do better than that. It's Christmas, for Chrissakes."

"Right, it's Christmas and you're asking me to cancel a contract. I can't do it, Nova. Think about what it does to me and mine. There's a reason why we make these policies and—"

"I know exactly what you're talking about and it's the bottom line. And I'm not asking for a favor like that. I don't renege on my word, written or not."

"So, what do you want?"

"Refund the money from the third carafe and take it back, and for helping me out, we'll give you something you want."

"I want money and uncancelled contracts."

I cringe. There's no way she's going to get that tightwad to cancel the contract. She keeps steering the conversation the right way, but then Greg snaps it back to money. She's not going to change his mind.

"Cancel out this contract and write me a new one. Increase the rental period three months and throw in a cappuccino machine."

Greg chokes on laughter. "Are you insane? You're asking me to refund your current contract, which is only a few weeks so you can what, default later—and give you a cappuccino machine?"

"The thing is," she starts sweetly, "I know my boss likes you and when he expands next year, he'll want to work with people who watch his back."

"Expand? How," he laughs in his deep voice, "gonna do an add-on to your tiny metal shed?"

"You're a funny guy, but no. Here's what's going to happen." Nova spells it out and doesn't finish until she's laid it all out. Holy shit, she has balls.

I back away from her car and stop when I notice the mess in the backseat. Nova continues talking, but I'm no longer listening. At first I think it's shopping bags, but it's not. It's a lot of clothing and a hairbrush stuffed into the back-seat pocket. A towel is laid over the passenger chair, dangling down in back, matted in the middle like it's wet. Nova's car was spotless when I first met her. I stand there, wondering what I'm looking at. People don't suddenly become slobs. Why is her car filled with clothes?

I hear her squeal from inside the vehicle and stomp her feet against the floorboards before she kicks the door open and jumps out. She's grinning ear to ear. When she turns and sees me, she shrieks and yelps, before slapping her hand to her heart. "Celyn. What are you doing there?"

I step closer to her, unable to hide the horror creeping through me. Those clothes, the rumpled pile, the towel that's worn and damp. That shouldn't be there. None of it should. I go to open my mouth but I can't say it. She'd be humiliated if it were true. My god, has she been sleeping in her car? Nova is homeless? I'm such a fucking asshole. How did I miss it?

Her voice trembles slightly. "Celyn?" Her gaze flicks to her car and back to me.

Make something up you stupid shit. I scold myself and try to think fast but it's like my mental wheels have rusted solid. "Nova," her name wraps around my lips softly and I force myself to smile at her while steeling myself so the emotions I feel aren't plastered across my face. "Sorry, I was looking at your car and..." her voice chimes inside my mind, that plea to never lie to her. I hesitate. I can't lie, but I can't tell her I know. We stare at each other in a silence that stretches on and on.

She blushes and tucks a strand of hair behind her ear, tucking it under the fuzzy hat. "So, you heard that last part? Just say it, you wanted to hear me work my magic."

Thank God, she offered a way out. I nod like an idiot. "Yeah, so what happened? I caught the end of it."

"He will have a check for you later today, and he switched you to a monthly payment plan, and issued you a line of credit which will help with cash flow in January. He said you had to renew then anyway. I guess you were going month to month." She's looking into my eyes and doesn't sense it, doesn't see it. She doesn't know the Hottie Hut will close on December 31st. She doesn't know her job will be gone. She doesn't know any of it.

Her eyes are locked on mine and a hesitant smile creeps across her face. She steps closer to me and goes up on her tippy toes and plants a kiss on my cheek. I stiffen. What the hell was that for? I look down at her, my eyes wide.

Nova resumes her regular height and shrugs. "Stop worrying, Celyn. You'll win your bet."

I stand there, mute, and horrified while I watch her walk back toward the hut. She's been sleeping outside in this freezing cold weather, alone. Every day she walks in with a smile on her face like nothing is wrong. She's telling me not to worry. Holy shit. My chest feels like it's torn open. The floodgates in my heart crack under the duress, under the absolute astonishment I feel toward her. No, it's more than that. She's stronger than anyone I've ever met, every breath is filled with passion and life, but she's not jaded. How is that possible? Why doesn't she hate me? I don't understand why she's still here, why she wants me to succeed. She could have taken the money I offered and walked. Doing this, she risks losing her last paycheck, and if she's homeless, she fucking needs it. How could she pick me over her own basic needs? Last night while I was warm in my bed, she was shivering outside. It guts me because I would have never known. Her smile is genuinely happy, and when it's blasted in my direction I can't see past it.

That blue skirt swishes at her thighs as she walks. When she stops in front of the door, she turns back and looks at me with those blonde braids framing her face. "Are you coming, Kelvin? We have work to do."

I frown instantly and get hurtled from my thoughts. "Celyn. It's Celyn."

She laughs lightly. "Right boss, come on."

35

NOVA

Celyn seems lost in thought and I can't blame him. Although he hasn't told me exactly what he loses if the Hottie Hut doesn't meet its goal, I suspect it's more than a car. Celyn isn't materialistic. The car and clothes suggest he's well off and takes pride in the things he owns, but the stakes feel higher than just material things. I don't know, I can't put my finger on it but I feel it looming, circling my head in an ominous way.

The compulsion to Google him is becoming unbearable. Maybe I'm a fool because I won't, maybe I deserve whatever's coming. It can't be worse than being reduced to nothing and living in my car. Tonight is going to suck. If I spend some of my savings, I can get a motel room for a few hours, but it'll eat up nearly half of my savings. Rooms aren't cheap, well, not cheap enough for me. If it were summer, this wouldn't be a problem. I honestly have no idea what to do. The blankets won't be enough, and if I get too cold and iced into my car—I don't even want to think about it.

A nor'easter is coming. Imagine a hurricane, but bigger. It sits and circles over a huge chunk of the map for days, dumping snow, sleet, and ice. When it clears, New York will look pristine, shrouded in a frozen silence and sparkling snow.

There was a nor'easter when Tinselly and I were young. School was cancelled and when it finally stopped snowing, we grabbed our sleds and waded through knee-deep snow to the hill by the highway. I laughed so much that day even though my cheeks were nipped by cold and I was frozen through and through by the time we headed home. I had a roof over my head during that storm and I wasn't alone. The power went out for a little bit, but we had a fireplace and Mom was happy to light it.

This time won't be like that. This time, I'll be alone. Maybe if I keep the engine running all night, I'll be okay. It's cheaper to buy a tank of gas than a motel room. It's just that leaving the car running is a dead giveaway that I'm inside. People don't look twice at an empty parked car, but one that's rumbling and spurting white smoke out the tailpipe is another story.

Silence stretches between us, each of us lost in our own thoughts. When nearly an hour has passed and we still haven't seen a soul, Celyn grabs his coat and turns toward me. "I need to head over and take care of the return and refund. I'll bring us back some breakfast." His lips part, like he's going to say more, but the words don't come. Celyn's beautiful face pinches and his gaze drops to the floor. He looks up at me from under dark lashes and forces a smile, suppressing whatever confession he was going to make. "Bacon and eggs on a roll?"

I nod. "Sounds good. Thank you."

"All right," he nods, "I'll see you in a little bit. Oh, and if Quin comes by, tell him I'll be right back."

"Quin's coming today?"

Celyn slips his jacket on one arm at a time and then fastens the buttons down the front and flips up his collar to protect his neck from the bitter wind. If the perfect man walked off the pages of GQ, Celyn would one-up him. It's something about that shade of gray and his sapphire eyes.

"Yes, he is," Celyn confesses. "I told him I had news. I thought we'd have to pack up today, but thanks to you—" he inhales deeply, looks up, and holds my gaze so softly that it's difficult to keep my distance. "Thanks to you, I don't have to just yet."

Nervous energy flitters through my stomach when our soft stares linger after the words have stopped. I don't want him to go, not yet. I feel my mouth move, freeing the words that I wasn't going to say, "Thanks to you, I don't have to..." I realize what I'm going to say and my voice drifts off. I laugh tightly and tuck a strand of loose hair under my furry hat. "Thanks to you, I'm getting breakfast."

I turn away because I want to break the sparking current pulling me toward him. It's a million times worse at unpredictable intervals, and this is one of those moments where I'll do something dumb.

I can't tell him how I feel. I shouldn't.

Celyn steps toward me so that we're inches apart. He pushes on the back of my shoulder with a finger, making me laugh. The slight pressure shoots tingles up my arm and I turn to disconnect the touch. I'm caught in the middle and I know it. When he brushes against me, I could fly—every worry within burns to ash—and I'm light. I'm free. It's strange and completely terrifying. I've never known anyone that described anything like this. Not Gran, Mom, or Tinselly. It's all-consuming and threatens to devour me, so I repress the thoughts and steel my emotions. I can't let him touch me or I'll cave. But as I chase away the scattered remnants of thought, Celyn's finger is under my chin, tipping my face up until our gazes meet. His eyes are the blue of the sea on a winter's night, deep and unending.

Dark lashes lower against his smooth skin and he hesitates for a moment. When his lips part, he says, "You can tell me anything, Nova. I won't judge you. I swear it." The way he says it, the smooth sincerity of his voice nearly undoes me. I try to step away and hit my back against the counter, but it's enough that Celyn's hand drops from my skin. The connection between us lessens but he's still so close that I can't think. I pin my arms to my sides for fear of throwing them around his neck and crying into his chest.

I nod once, softly, and find my eyes willing to look anywhere but at him. My voice is small because half of me is refusing to say it, but the words tumble out before I can stop myself. "The same goes for you, Celyn. You know that, right?"

I lift my face and our gazes lock. The pit of my stomach goes into a free-fall and for once, I'm not afraid. I let the sensation flood me. His intense cobalt stare swallows me whole. There's so much intensity buried within this man, and it makes me wonder why he hides it, what could make him retreat so fully into himself that he'd temper his passion and put forth this anemic variation of himself? But then, I know the answer. It's the same thing I do—the reason why I never let anyone get too close, the reason why I stayed with Ben too long—distance is a defense mechanism. It's a way to hide from the world and protect your heart.

Someone hurt Celyn badly. There's a gaping hole in him. I can see it because the same thing is wrong with me. I try to fill it with work, but it won't fill. It's never full. I'm never sated, never content with life. It always feels like I'm two breaths away from drowning—except when Celyn is near. I hate it and I love it. I want to be my own woman, but is it so bad if he makes me stronger? Is that wrong?

My gaze has been learning the lines of his face, slowly tracing the planes of his cheek, mapping every freckle and mark all the way down to the bow of his pink mouth. I'm focused on his lips, the fullness of them, and lost in the remembrance of a kiss that shouldn't have happened. My heart is pounding and a warm flush covers me, head to toe. When I lift my hands to place them on his chest over his coat, Celyn tenses. The spell shatters into a thousand tiny splinters. Rejection isn't something that has to be spoken.

Celyn turns abruptly and doesn't look at me. It feels like a slap. I know it wasn't, but that doesn't change the harshness of it. He's at the door with the empty carafe under his arm, reaching for the knob when he looks my way. "I know. Thanks, Nova. You're a good friend."

The door shuts as my heart slams into my boots and fractures. Friends.

He said we're friends.

Nothing more.

36
CELYN

Holy fuck. I nearly kissed her. Again. When her voice gets low like that it softens and she seems so vulnerable and small. I just want to wrap my arms around her and hold her close. I want to tell her that I'll protect her from everything, but I can't. I can't even save myself. The walls are closing in around me, and my fascination with her has surpassed all rational thought.

It's not fascination, you fool. It's—

Don't fucking say it. Don't even think it. It doesn't matter what it is, because it doesn't belong there. It's not right, for so many reasons. I have nothing to offer her. My reflection looms in the glass on the door of my car before I tug open the handle and realize that's not true. I can help her. I just need to get her to accept it. She's so proud. An idea forms in my mind as I drive out of the parking lot. The snow is falling fast and thick now. It's supposed to switch back to sleet by lunch as the outer edge of the storm passes. I should grab food, snacks, and then take care of the carafe. Maybe I can do something more. The concept solidifies and I set my mind to it.

I run the errands and get the refund check before heading to the car dealer. The lot is filled with vehicles getting a dusting of snow and the few salesmen that are around are inside where it's warm. But when they see my car, they do what every automobile enthusiast does—they're drawn toward it. They want to touch it and see what it looks like inside. They want to hear the engine purr and ask me how much I paid. It's every man's dream to own something like this, but I see a better dream and since I have no idea how this will turn out, I'm doing what I can now. For all I know, Uncle could try to seize my assets and claim they were part of Bardenbey. It's not true and wouldn't hold up in court, but it would make my life a living hell until it was cleared up. I'm not waiting to find out, and if I can slip some of the cash to Nova—that part of the plan still eludes me. One step at a time, Celyn.

A stout, round man with a red face and

matching shirt bounces down the cement stairs and into the parking lot. His girth makes his movements jerky, but the smile on his face is genuine. "Is that a McLaren?"

I return his grin. "It is."

The man juts out a beefy hand as he approaches me. "Steve Weatherby," he introduces himself.

"Celyn Ryan."

He smirks and looks at me a second time. "Ah, so you are. Good to meet you, Celyn." He glances at the car and then back at me. "So what can I do for you today? Are you looking for an additional vehicle?"

There's a line of men inside, standing close enough to the glass storefront to fog the windows as they gawk at my car with greedy eyes.

I focus on Steve. "I'm trading this one in and looking for something less flashy."

The man's smile eats his entire round head. "Really?"

"Yes, the only catch is I need a vehicle that's ready now. So, show me what you've got."

Steve walks me through the parking lot and shows me a Hyundai SUV that's loaded. He's about to take me to a second car when I tell him, "Done. I'll take it and pay sticker price, but I need trade-in value on the McLaren. Do we have a deal?"

Steve grins like I'm a dancing leprechaun tossing gold on his head. "Let me talk to the boss. I'm sure we can arrange something."

As we head inside, the owner steam-plows Steve and reaches for my hand. He's a tall guy, dark blonde hair with a decent suit. He probably played ball in college, and has an arrogant air about him that pisses me off. Steve backs away and I wonder if the man will get his commission if the owner takes over.

After introductions are made, I politely say, "Steve here has been great to me. I've already picked something out. Sticker price for trade-in value and we're done here."

The owner laughs and then gives me a look that says I'm either stupid or I don't know how to negotiate. "Celyn, are you sure you don't need something else? I have a Stingray—"

I step toward the owner, cutting him off midsentence. "I'm positive. Oh, throw in a couple of deli sandwiches, and we'll call it a day."

The owner chuckles and rubs his palms together. "I'll get the paperwork ready for you."

Steve is about the wander away. It's like this has happened to him before and I won't have it. It's two days before Christmas. The commission on this sale could mean the difference between a merry Christmas and a shitty one if the man has a family. From the ring on his finger, I suspect he does.

"Actually," I say with every ounce of Ryan arrogance I can muster, "I'm sure I'll be back to look at the Stingray with you when the weather clears. For today, I'd appreciate concluding the transaction with Steve. We understand one another. I'd still like those bacon and egg sandwiches and need someone to make sure they're perfect. Would you mind?" It was a shit move, pulling rank like that. I wouldn't have done it if I didn't get the impression that Steve would be screwed out of his sale.

The owner's smile turns synthetic, but his eyes haven't left the McLaren for more than a second. He wants that car, probably so he can drive it to Christmas parties and show it off. "Of course. I'll take care of the deli order and Steve will get you in your new Santa Fe." The tall man walks away briskly, snapping at someone to call Jerry's and place the order.

I follow Steve to his office and the man is so excited, he won't shut up. After I sign the enormous digital contract on his glass desk and put my pen down, Steve confesses, "You have no idea what this means to me. I can bring home a tree and grab presents for my girls. Before you walked onto the lot, my job was on the line. I didn't make goal this month and then this storm —" his voice cracks and there's a sheen on his eyes. "Well, I have two little girls who can believe in magic for another year. Thank you, Celyn."

"Of course," I say, as I stand and lift up my hand. Steve walks toward me, palm outstretched, but I get duped into a bear hug with a firm slap on the back. It knocks the wind out of me.

Steve is laughing when he pulls away and grabs my check from the accountant. "I've never seen a six figure check on a trade-in before." He hands it to me and then turns to get my new SUV. "Just let me prep it and you'll be ready to go."

I take the check and put it in my breast pocket inside my coat. "Thank you, but I need to go now, I'm already late. Can you put the plates on it? I can take it from there."

Steve nods violently, still beaming. "Of course. It'll only be a moment."

The owner is back, his face flushed with cold, and hands me a brown paper bag. "Mr. Ryan, here you are, sir. Is there anything else I can do for you?"

I take the bag. "Thank you, but no. Steve is putting the plates on the SUV and I'm off."

He nods and asks politely, "The McLaren keys?"

"Steve has them and already pulled the car into the bay around back."

"Very well." The man smiles tightly. "Happy holidays to you."

"Merry Christmas," I offer back as I hold up my brown bag and head toward Steve who is kneeling in the snow to put my plates on the new vehicle.

37
CELYN

When I pull up in the silver SUV, Nova watches me climb out and meets me at the door of the hut. She ducks her blonde head out the door, her hat missing, and looks at the SUV before she backs up for me to pass through. "Where's your car?"

"I got rid of it." The downgrade didn't hurt as much as I thought it would. She looks at me like I'm nuts, so I add, "It's easier to get around in a sports utility vehicle around here."

That doesn't help. Now she blinks at me like I hit my head. "You traded in your McLaren for a Hyundai?"

"Yeah, you like it?" I grin at her and place the brown paper bag on the counter and unpack our breakfast. Tendrils of steam escape from the sides of the paper. It's still really cold in here.

I feel her eyes on the side of my face. "Are you putting the money into the Hottie Hut?"

I shake my head. "I can't. The terms were specific about that."

She places a hand on the counter, and taps her fingers. "So you just decided to sell it on a whim."

I shake my head as I hand her a sandwich wrapped in white deli paper. Nova takes it and watches me as I explain. "It wasn't a whim. It was time to move on." I avoid her gaze because she'll know what I'm thinking. *That it's time to stop acting like I can't help you. I can. I will.* I glance up at her and our gazes lock. Her beautiful face is caught somewhere between shock and awe.

Emerald eyes blink at me. "I would have thought you'd get a BMW or something more luxurious." She takes her breakfast and folds back the paper before taking a bite. Then adds, "I made coffee. Want some?"

I nod as I lean back against the counter and devour my sandwich. I've been trying to think of a way to give her some money, but nothing comes to mind yet. Pride is a fickle thing. Present it correctly, and she'll take it. Say it wrong, and I'm a dick waving cash in her face. I decide to wait until I have a plan—a way to offer it so she'll accept it.

"Thank you," I offer and take the steaming cup from her. "So, I'm thinking that today is going to be slow."

She nods. "No one has come by. The Christmas tree guy is pacing a hole into the pavement across the way."

I lift a brow and look out the icy windows, knowing how he feels. "And Shannon?"

She scoffs. "Shannon won't show up in this weather. He's probably still asleep."

"Great, so I'll get to fire him on Christmas Eve."

She laughs at me. "You really think you'll see him before Christmas, that's funny. He's not showing until the day after." Her light brow lifts and disappears under the loose blonde bangs that frame her face.

"You're probably right." I sip the hot liquid and feel more awake, more alive, than I have in a long time. I'm not just going through the motions, not today. "Well, it looks like we're going to have a slow day, so I'm going to run into the mall and grab a few things to make this space more comfortable for the day."

I'm gone for about forty minutes and when I come back, I can't get the door open. I drop two bags on the ground near the Hut and manage to wrap my index finger against the door without dropping everything else. Nova opens the door and steps back so I can enter. I'm carrying five of those humongous shopper bags on my arms. They snag on the cabinets and barely fit in through the door.

Nova teases, "Did you leave anything for the other shoppers? Seriously, Celyn, where are you going to put all that?"

When she says my name, I feel something warm ignite inside of me. I love it when she says my name. The compulsion to do something to make her say it again floods me. I drop the bags on the floor and turn to her. "It's all going in here and then I'll take it home when the weather passes."

I pull out a double beanbag chair that's covered in soft suede-like material, more blankets, another space heater, a dozen fuzzy socks, a soft cashmere sweater that's bright red—I hand that to Nova. "I saw this and thought you'd like it." She takes it from me and holds it up over her uniform. "Go grab your jeans and change."

She pulls the sweater over her head and pulls off the tags, and then moves the HOT GIRL nametag to the sweater. "Yeah, I kind of got used to the costume." She shrugs with a lopsided smile that's the sexiest thing I've ever seen. I want to lean in and kiss the corners of her lips. I push the thought away, ignoring it.

"Well, the red sweater with the fluffy blue skirt and shitkickers is quite the statement." I wink at her.

She frowns. "I'm not wearing these all day if no one is here." She attacks the pile of fuzzy socks, and pulls her boots off, replacing them with three pairs of socks piled up on her feet. "Fluffy!"

After she has those on, she pads over to me and looks over my shoulder. "What else did you get?"

She's so close that I can smell her perfume. She shifts her weight, goes up on her toes, and places her hand on my shoulder. When she shifts, I feel her breast brush my back. I tense but try to act like it was nothing.

My voice sticks in my throat and comes out deeper than usual. "Chocolate." I hand her a huge box of Godiva.

She squeals and plucks it from my hand and plops down in the beanbag chair, which takes up the entire floor. It's wedged between the cabinets and big enough to lie on. She pops open the box and tosses a chocolate in her mouth, and closes her eyes, savoring the taste. When she looks up again, I pull out a few games and other snacks. I put them on the counter before falling down next to her on the beanbag chair. She laughs when the beans in the chair shift and push her a little higher than me, bouncing her slightly.

Nova hands over the box of chocolates, offering them to me. I shake my head. "No way am I going to take those away from you. This is the happiest I've seen you in weeks. Eat the whole thing."

The corners of her mouth lift and she puts the box back on her lap. Then her delicate fingers take one from the wrapper and hold it out to me. "To Celyn, the best boss ever."

I lift my hand to take it, but she frowns at me. "What?" I drop my hand, leaving the chocolate lingering in the air.

She leans closer to me and holds it out again. My smile melts as my heart trips in my chest when I realize what she wants me to do. I shake my head and start to get up, but she grabs my wrist with her free hand.

"Are you seriously afraid of Hot Girl?" Nova represses a laugh and taunts me, "Come on, Celyn, stop being so serious. It's not sex, it's a piece of chocolate."

I watch her for a moment and then turn my gaze to the piece of candy between her fingers. I lean forward and take it with my teeth, but she doesn't let go. She snorts a laugh and makes me tug it from her hand, before she presses the tip of my nose with her finger and lounges back in the chair, pulling her knees up and resting the box of chocolate there.

This woman makes my heart pound and all rational thought flies away when she's near. I want to be something to her, I want to be the one who makes her smile. I want to be the one that elicits that warm laugh, the one that's pure magic. Hearing it lifts my soul from the dark places it's been. I feel renewed around her. I lean back in the chair and stare out the window as the snow turns to sleet. Icy slush spatters against the glass, obscuring the view.

The afternoon passes quickly. We sit on the beanbag, crank up both little heaters, and eat candy and tell each other Christmas stories, recounting tales of the past. Nova has me laughing and I forget everything until nightfall. When it's time to part ways, I'm not sure what to do. If I kiss her, she'd stay—I could do it. I could seduce her and she'd be safe for the night. Bad idea. She needs someone stable, not someone like me who will probably get hit with a lawsuit and end up with nothing. Still, I don't want her sleeping in her car. Not tonight, not ever again. A kiss is all it would take. She's at ease around me. She trusts me. I don't want to break our friendship but I'll be damned if I let her freeze tonight.

Nova is tugging on her boots and I've gone silent. I pushed the beanbag chair into the window on the counter so she could gather her things. I swallow hard, thinking I need to do it if she's going to stay. When she has on her boots, she stands and I'm intentionally too close. She brushes against me, and nearly loses her balance. I reach out and slip my hands around her waist, pulling her hips to mine to keep her upright.

"Sorry about that," I say softly and keep my eyes on her lips. "Are you okay?"

She tenses in my arms, but doesn't back away. Nodding, she replies in a breathy voice, "Yeah, I'm good."

I flick my gaze to her eyes and she's doing the same thing as me, mirroring my stance, angling her head to the side, watching me through lowered lashes. My chest has that swirling feeling like I'm falling through space and every impulse I have says to hold onto her, but I don't crush her against me the way I want to. Instead, I keep the inch or so of space between our upper bodies and am careful not to move my hips no matter how much I want to press against her.

I breathe her name as I move in closer. We're

a whisper apart and the lure between us is overpowering me. I can't have her this close and not act on it. I'm still warring with myself when she leans in and sweeps her mouth against mine. The kiss is light, careful. Her lips are slightly parted as she lingers, waiting to see what I'll do. I'm frozen, unable to kiss her back, caught between desire and something else.

She whispers, "It's all right. One kiss won't change anything." When she speaks, her lips brush mine ever so lightly.

It breaks me. The restraint I had explodes and my lips find her full mouth, warm and welcoming. She opens for me and I sweep my tongue inside, tasting her, wanting her so badly that there's no way to hide it. If she didn't know before, there's no doubt now. My jeans strain as her hands slip around my waist and under the bottom of my sweater. Those delicate fingers swirl circles at the back of my jeans, just above the waistband. Her warm fingers touch the small of my back, making me press her into the cabinet in response. Wanting her closer, desperate to feel her against me, I tangle my hands in her hair as Nova moans into my mouth. She moves one hand up my back and tangles it in my hair as the kiss deepens. Her tongue sweeps against mine as my body heats under her touch.

Her scent fills my head and I can't think. She's all-consuming and I want her, I need to be with her, and she wants me. After all this time, she still wants me.

Her fingers tug my hair as her thigh grazes the outside of my leg. I grab her and smooth my palm up her thigh until I'm under the hem of her skirt, about to cup her ass. She'd stay with me. I could make sure she doesn't freeze, but this—I can't do it like this. She deserves so much better than anything I could offer. I'm so close to being destitute and I can't do it to her.

ABRUPTLY, I LET GO AND STEP AWAY, SLAMMING my back into the other counter by accident. I lower my gaze to the floor and wipe my mouth with my wrist before rubbing my hands over my face and back into my hair. I press my eyes closed and hate myself.

I feel her light touch on my arm, "Celyn?" I move suddenly, which makes her drop her hand, but she doesn't step back.

"I can't do this." I grab my coat and step toward the door. I'm a fucking coward. I'm going to run out on her. Rationalization has taken over. She could stay in the hut, she'd be warm enough. It's safer than her car. Space will make it possible to remain friends. I just need some air. I need to think. I reach for the knob on the door.

She grabs my shoulder, trying to stop me. "Celyn, talk to me. What's wrong?"

I don't answer her question. Instead, I offer, "Stay here for the night. Lock yourself inside. I'll see you at daybreak."

"Celyn." She pleads, and the sound of my name on her lips nearly stops me. She doesn't understand, but I can't make a good decision with her so close. I can't tell her what she does to me, how I feel. She won't understand when I tell her that we can't act on it. I need to leave. I need to suck in some cold air and use my goddamn brain.

In my mind, I'm already gone and there's one glaring reason why I won't stay, why I can't be with her. It trumps everything else and there's no way she'll let it go—I've been lying to her since we met. I won't be another asshole that uses her and hurts her. I grab the doorknob and twist, pushing the door, but it doesn't budge.

Nova watches me slam my shoulder into it, trying to get away from her, but when it doesn't give after three tries, I rest my forehead against the cold metal and inhale slowly through my nose.

The only explanation I can give is weak, but I say it all the same. "I don't want to hurt you, Nova."

38

NOVA

We went from an afternoon of laughter to hot kisses that made my toes curl, but Celyn freaked out. When the door didn't open, something akin to pity rushed through me. He's afraid of me, of what he feels around me. When he can't run, when there's nowhere to go but turn and face me, the attraction doesn't die. If anything it increases. He wants me so much that it scares him.

I remain where I am, about two feet away, back by the window. "Then don't hurt me, Celyn."

He remains in place with his face toward the door, head dipped, coat clutched in his hand and dragging on the floor. He doesn't look up when he replies, "This won't work out. It can't be, okay? Please believe me." There's something in his voice, the way he says it, that's haunting. He believes it to be true, he knows a reason why we won't last so he won't start anything.

I believe him. I don't know why but I can feel it coursing through the room—fear and regret so thick it's palpable. I pull the beanbag out of the window and lean over to slide the glass open. My intention had been to slip out of the window and go around to open the door for him. The knob must have iced over, but when I remove the chair it's clear that it's not just the knob that has an issue with freezing. The pane of glass is marbled with a thick sheet of ice and a thick mound of snow. I pull on the window, but it won't budge.

When I give up, I glance at Celyn and lean back against the counter, before hoisting myself up. I slide my hips over the cold surface and ask, "Why'd you kiss me, then?" I think I already know but still, I need to hear it.

Celyn lifts his head from the door, and turns toward me. "I didn't want you to freeze tonight, and I know you're attracted to me, so I thought I could keep you with me."

"You were going to keep me here?" I don't refute how I feel about him. He knew this whole time and didn't feel the same way. But the kiss just now confuses me. He wanted me. I know he did, so why pull away? He's not telling me something.

Celyn looks me in the eye. "No, I was going to take you home before the weather got too bad to drive. I thought we'd leave after the snow started." He glances at the window. "I misjudged the ice."

I concentrate on my fingers, avoiding his gaze, "And so that would have been, what? Pity sex so I wouldn't sleep in my car?"

"No," his voice comes out in a rush.

"Then what was it?" Celyn steps away from the door and drops his coat. He strides toward me and is there, next to me, within reach, but he keeps a space between us when he nears the counter. I say sharply, "Because it feels like pity."

"It's not."

I turn to look at him. "Prove it."

"How?" His softness fades and is replaced by an emotion that's so conflicted it can't be identified. "Nova, I would if I could. It's not anything like that. I don't pity you. If anything it's the opposite. I admire you." He watches me closely, but his words feel like a fist to the gut.

My eyes remain fixed on the floor. "That's flattering."

"Nova, come on, you have to see it." He tries to catch my eye but I don't look at him.

Horror is creeping up inside of me, strangling me from within. My entire face is burning. I'd go out the window if it wasn't frozen shut. Mortification slithers up my spine but I remain still despite the urge to shake it off and run.

"I don't see it," I confess bleakly. "I see that you were horrified you kissed me. I see that you wanted to put as much distance between us as possible. I see you too ashamed to meet my gaze. I see pity and nothing more."

"It's not that—it's not any of those things. I'll prove it. I can show you."

"You said yourself, you can't. You can't prove what it was and no matter what you say, there's no way I'll believe you now. Anything that comes out of our mouth will be an attempt to make me feel better. It's fine, Celyn. I get it." I'm staring at my hands with tears rolling down my cheeks.

A moment of silence passes and he asks me, "Can I prove it to you? Will you let me?"

I glance at him out of the corner of my eye, wondering what he's getting at, when his hands—warm and firm—slip across my cheeks, his thumbs wiping away my tears as his fingers cradle my neck, moving me so that I'm looking up at him. He steps in front of me, and comes closer. His sapphire eyes are lost in mine, when he repeats, "Let me show you."

I manage a small nod. Celyn's dark lashes cover his eyes as he fixates on my mouth. He inches closer, stepping into the space between my legs, pushing my knees apart as he comes closer. His hands remain on my cheeks, holding me in place as he dips his head and presses his mouth to mine. I suck in a jagged breath at the light touch, and it's everything I can do to keep my hands on the counter and not touch him. I start to think this is a pity kiss, that he can't possibly feel anything for me, but when his lips linger doubt fills my mind. His arms are laced with tension as he cradles my face in his palms and presses his lips to mine, softly, carefully—like he's worshiping me—like he expects me to turn to vapor in his hands.

Celyn's lips move to my cheek and trace a line back to my ear where he presses small hot kisses as his thumbs stroke my cheek. He trails his lips across my jaw, tracing the lines of my face with affection, and when he presses one last kiss to my other temple, he pulls back—his eyes meeting mine.

His chest swells as he confesses, "I've tried to deny it, to not let myself feel anything for you, but it's too late. I fell for you."

I look into his eyes, searching for the lie, but not finding it. There's still apprehension there, but he truly cares for me. I sit slightly above him because I'm seated on the counter. When I pull him to me, I press his cheek to my chest, holding him close to my heart and kiss the top of his head. Celyn holds me for a moment and we stay like that, neither of us talking, his head cradled against me.

When I pull away, I smile down at him. "I believe you."

He looks up at me with that beautiful face, with worry lines pinching his brow. "Nova, I need to tell you something."

I grab the sleeve of my red sweater and pull it off, tossing it onto the opposite counter. My top is basically a variation of a peasant blouse that dips low in front. It's held in place by a fat, belt-like vest of a thing, and a string holding the neckline in place. A little bow sits low on my chest. I take one of the strings and tug, loosening the fabric. It parts, revealing the curve of my breasts covered by a white satin bra.

Celyn watches intently, his eyes flicking between my chest and my face. Celyn stiffens and looks up at me. "Nova, I need to tell you..."

"It's all right." I know what he's going to say and I'm okay with it. He's too old and I'm too young. He wants permission, my permission. It's why he asked before he kissed me. I want to make him feel more at ease, and if he wants me, I want there to be no doubt about how I feel about him. I hold my arms out to him and Celyn nestles back into the spot where he was before, but now there's bare skin and slick satin.

"Nova, I need to tell you—"

"It's all right, Celyn." I feel his eyes close against my flesh like he's warring within. "There's still a lot to say, and I trust you. It'll be all right." I don't think he's going to move, but after a moment, his hands slip up from my waist and splay across my back, making me lean into him.

Celyn presses his mouth to my skin, to the spot just below my throat and leaves a kiss. His hot lips move again, trailing down toward my waist one kiss at a time until he's caressing my curves. He loosens the rest of the top and pushes it to my waist, and then unfastens my bra, removing it completely. I'm bare, with my back to the frosted glass and feel completely exposed even though no one can see inside. I want to ask him what he thinks of me, if he likes what he sees, but I don't have to speak.

"You're so beautiful, so amazingly stunning." He hesitates before touching me. My breasts ache for his hands and his mouth, and it takes so much to not lean into him, to wait for him to do what he wants.

Celyn dips his head and slowly moves his lips over the swell of my chest. My back arches into his kiss and when he flicks my sensitive skin with his tongue I gasp. My hands are in his hair, pulling him to me, wanting more. My body is humming, wanting to get lost in him, hoping he doesn't stop. His mouth moves over me in slow, deliberate strokes, sucking, tasting, and teasing until I'm gasping his name over and over again.

Between kisses, he lifts his head and confesses, "I love it when you say my name."

His mouth is on me again, moving in a seductive pattern, caressing me, teasing me. My body grows warmer as my head become lighter. Sparks shoot through me with every touch of his lips and when his fingertips move across my bare skin, desire pools within me, dark and demanding. Gasping, I wrap my legs around his hips and desperately want to ease the heated pulsing building within. His hands are on me, his lips taking me higher than I've ever been, as I claw at his sweater, wishing it weren't there.

I can't help it, I beg him, "Celyn, please. I want to be with you. Please, Celyn."

He pulls back and looks into my eyes. His hands cup my cheeks as he smiles at me, "I love it when you say my name."

I smile wickedly at him and beg, "Please, Celyn."

A bright smile fills his face and he laughs, "God, I love you, Nova."

I tense and blink, the seduction haze clearing slightly at his words. Celyn's smile falls as his eyes fill with panic. He didn't mean to say that. His gaze darts to the side, avoiding me. Holy shit. Did he really say that? Does he love me? Why didn't I notice until now? From the way he looks anywhere but at me, I know it's true. The confession slipped off his lips—he never meant to tell me that tonight.

I place a few fingers on each cheek and lift his eyes to meet mine. "It's okay."

"No, it's not." He's visibly upset. "Nova, this shouldn't be, none of it should be—" He's about to pull away again. I feel his apprehension overpowering his feelings, rising to the surface like a caged animal about to break free.

"And yet, here we are," I say, cutting him off before he can move, before his guard shoots up again and I never get back in. I smile at him, letting the words fall freely, "Celyn, you're not the only one who fell hard."

Hope dances in his eyes as he looks up at me. "What are you saying?"

"I love you, too." I sit there, feeling more

exposed than I have in a long time, when Celyn reaches for me. He wraps his arms around me and holds me tight.

He whispers up at me, "I won't let anything happen to you."

Celyn sweeps me up off the counter and lowers me to the beanbag chair. He slowly, carefully, removes every stitch of my clothing, kissing me as he does it. I look up at him, still fully clothed, still wearing that dark blue sweater that feels like it's made out of baby unicorn fur.

My voice is soft, careful. I still worry he'll say no, but I ask anyway, "Be with me?"

In response, he pulls off his clothes and grabs the blankets as he lies next to me. "Are you cold?"

I shake my head and reach for Celyn, pulling him to me. He doesn't hesitate. He returns to worshiping every inch of my body. We're tangled together, slick skin covered in sweat, losing ourselves to lust-filled love as the night gives way to morning.

39

CELYN

I wake with the scent of Nova filling my head. I smile and roll over, reaching for her before I even open my eyes. She's there, warm and perfect, nestled against me. I whisper in her ear, "Morning, lover."

She giggles. "Morning, boss."

I cringe. "Don't call me that."

"Would you rather I called you Korbin? Oh, Korbin," she moans, saying the name the way she said mine last night.

My hands move to her sides, to the spot just above her waist that tickles the most. Her laughter fills the hut as she wriggles in my arms. "Celyn. It's Celyn. Say it."

She shakes her head between fits of laughter, her face filled with mirth. "No!"

I find the spot and tickle her more this time, until she's wriggling against me, her back to my front, and then she stills. She looks over her shoulder and whispers, "Celyn."

I hold her close, pressing my mouth to hers when the sound of Quin's voice fills the air. He raps the glass, trying to scrape the ice off with a gloved hand.

"Oh shit," I jump up and toss the covers on Nova. I whisper to her, "Don't move." She ducks below the blankets and out of sight as I pull on my sweater. That's right, I'm standing there naked from the waist down, leaning against the cold counter. It enough to make me never want to buy anything from a food truck again.

Quin manages to peel off a huge chunk of ice. It's a miracle that he doesn't break the window. He's standing there in a blue parka, cheeks chapped from the wind. "Where the hell were you?" He yells through the glass that still won't budge. There must be ice in the track. "I kept calling you last night. Did you get stuck here?"

I shrug like it's not a big deal. "Yeah, I figured why not."

Quin frowns and spits out, "Because it's a fucking shack and you're you."

I glance at the spot where Nova lies covered, hoping Quin doesn't say more. I haven't had a chance to tell her yet. I tried to last night. I was going to sit here with her, trapped in awkward hell, if it didn't go well. But she melted my brain and before I knew what I was doing, I was with her, inside of her, saying I loved her. It's the kind of thing that makes me feel incredibly vulnerable in the light of day, especially with Quin standing there and my junk hanging out. If he comes through that door, I'll never hear the end of it, but that's not the worst part. It'll shame Nova and I won't let that happen. Call it chivalry, but I don't kiss and tell. This is between me and Nova and I'm going to keep it that way.

Quin glances around the parking lot, his hand to his brow to block the bright reflection of the sun bouncing off the blinding stretch of snow. "Where's your car?"

Shit. The car. He'll never leave if he thinks I sold the McLaren. With my luck, he'll break the window and climb inside the hut to shake the shit out of me. I play along, blanching and looking around. "Don't even joke, man."

Quin turns in a full circle. "It's not here, man. Holy shit. Someone stole your car! And then the plows blocked you in the hut." Quin is still freaking out, looking for the car.

I bang on the glass to get his attention. "Quin!

What are you talking about? The plows blocked the door?" I'm thinking they parked there or something until he explains.

Quin gives me a look, brows raised, and points at the door. "You got plowed."

Nova whispers from below the blankets, "That's my line."

I grin and repress a laugh. I try to steel my voice and sound pissed, but it comes out an octave too high. "What the hell are you talking about?"

Quin walks away, takes a picture with his phone, and then presses it to the window. "You're trapped."

The plow must have come by and thought the shack was empty. They covered the steps and door in five feet of snow and ice. "Holy shit."

"I know!" Quin blurts out. He's like a squirrel when things go wrong—he gets twitchy. The man isn't someone you want in charge during a crisis. "Okay, first things first, I'll call the cops about your car and—"

"No," I cut him off, "get me out of here. I'm texting you the number of a guy I know—he has a plow. Tell him Celyn said he's calling in his favor."

Quin glances at me through the pane of glass. "I can buy a shovel."

I nearly laugh. "You can't shovel shit, Quin."

Quin frowns and looks back at Sears. "Well, no, but it'd be faster than finding a guy with a plow and—"

"Man, I'm fine. I have food and coffee in here. Go find Tim and bring him back here. There's no point in freezing your ass off out there and it'll take hours to dig me out." Leave, please leave. I chant the words over and over again in my mind. He can't stay. He can't see her, or know about us. Not yet.

"You sure you're okay?"

"I'm fine. Go already."

Quin presses his face to the glass and I nearly back off the counter. Thank God I don't because he's looking down and sees the blankets on the floor. "Did you have some quality time with yourself last night, Celyn? Light some candles? Play some Sonatra?"

"Fuck off," I laugh, "and go find Timmy. Go on, girl." I mock him using Lassie quotes because I can't think of anything else. "You can do it. Timmy's in the well."

"Asshole." He backs away and looks at me again. "You scared the shit out of me, Celyn. I thought you wrapped your car around a pole or something. Answer your goddamn phone next time."

"Yes, Mom." Quin scoffs, but he finally wanders off and leaves. I'm alone with Nova once more.

She comes out from under the blankets, tossing them aside. "So, that's a nice look." She stares up at my ass, my legs parted so she can see every stitch of me below the belt. She dips her head to the side and smiles.

"I think the health department would have a stroke," I chuckle.

"Screw them. I'd have a stroke, Celyn..." she pauses and then says, "I don't know your last name."

I kneel next to her and kiss her forehead. "Ryan."

She grins. "Ryan, so you're like super Irish, right? You eat corned beef and cabbage all year? Have a stash of leprechauns in your trunk?"

"If I did, the Hyundai dealer has them now." I pull her against me, wishing for more time. She's heard my name before, but it's the kind of thing that unless you hear both names together, it doesn't register. I can tell she still doesn't realize who I am, and that's bad. I need to tell her before it looks like I was intentionally hiding it from her. I suppose I am, but it's because I want her to know me before her opinion shifts to align with the press.

She snorts a laugh and cuddles into my chest. I wish I could hold her against me all day. If we could get out of here, I could lose Quin and take her to my place. *You have to tell her first, asshat. Tell her*.

I press my lips together and jump head first. "Nova, I need to tell you something. I'm not—"

She leans in and kisses me softly, silencing my words. "Do you still love me?"

Her question is jarring and I forget what I'm saying in order to answer. "Of course."

"Then, the rest is details." She smiles softly, leaning into me.

The contentment on her face is perfect. I don't want to shatter it, but she needs to know. "Nova, I need to—"

She turns toward me and presses her body against mine and then grabs my bottom lip with hers, and nips me. "Shut up and kiss me, Ryan."

I do as she asks, muttering, "Celyn," into her mouth. I feel her smile against me and then my plan goes to hell because she wants me. Her hips rub against mine and I'm so ready for her, but Quin will be back soon. I pull away and she groans. "We can't. Not unless you want Quit and Tim to know everything."

She frowns. "Not really." She lies on her back,

her breasts beautiful swells, pale and perfect in the morning light.

"Then let's get you out of here before he comes back. Do you think your car will start?"

"It should." She stands and looks out the window.

I grab her wrist and turn her toward me. Her naked body curves into mine. "Promise me that you'll never sleep in your car again. Please." I'm looking into her eyes when I say it, when I plead.

She plays with the hair at the base of my neck, curling her fingers in it. "It's just for a little while."

"Stay with me." The words come out in a rush and I'm not sorry. Every part of me meant it.

She looks at me and considers it. "I don't know."

"Then, I'll stay with you."

She snorts. "I don't think we'll both fit." She glances at the little Honda and back at me.

"Which is why we should stay at my place tonight. We can stay at yours in the spring."

She laughs as she traces a line with the tip of her finger along my shoulder. "All right. I'll stay with you tonight. But just for the night."

I repress my smile but it doesn't matter. My entire face hurts from grinning so hard. I place the space heaters against the glass while Nova and

I dress, hoping it'll melt the remainder of the ice caught in the metal window track. After I tug on my boots, I work the glass, moving it a few inches and rocking it back and forth until it finally rolls to the side.

"You really want me to go out the window and leave you here?" She arches a delicate brow at me before tugging the furry hat onto her head.

"Yes, and I'll see you later. Go spend the day with your sister and tell her about the hot guy you nailed last night." I turn toward her.

Nova's lips pull into a bashful grin. She dips her head, looks at the floor, and then meets my gaze. She laces her arms around my neck and whispers in my ear, "And the one from the night before, and the night before that. The list goes on and on."

I'm tickling her again and as she tries to wriggle away, I press her body to the door. "You're mine."

"And you're mine. I don't share, so if the brunette shows up, tell her you're taken, Hot Guy."

I lift a brow and cock my head at her. "How'd you know about that?"

She shrugs. "I have my methods and I know you were interested, so what made you pick me?"

Her face scrunches up and I can tell she didn't want to ask, so I tell her.

"It was always you, Nova. That woman never stood a chance with you around." Her arms are around my neck and she's on her tiptoes, kissing me. Telling the truth never felt so good.

40

NOVA

Celyn suggested I spend the day with my sister, which wasn't a bad idea because when I don't show up first thing tomorrow, she's going to be pissed. It's Christmas Eve and we always spend Christmas morning together, even when Ben was around. I'd run over first thing and he'd catch up later. It's a standing tradition that I'm okay with skipping this year. The thought of waking up on Christmas morning with Celyn in my arms is too much to pass up. Heading over there today gives me a chance to tell her. Celyn wants to pick me up at her house and take me to his place tonight. Since the roads are crap, I agreed.

When I get to Tinselly's picture perfect house and approach the steamy glass door, I pull it open and am delighted to hear twin-sized chaos. "No! No! No!" They shout in unison, almost singing it with glee.

"Tinselly?" I call out to my sister and step inside the warm house. A fire is crackling in the brick fireplace. When I walk into the living room, Tinselly is standing with her hands on her hips staring down at two little boys who are buck naked and covered in red and green glitter smears.

Tinselly turns toward me in slow motion, not blinking, her face glazed over with horror. She's two ticks away from stroking out. Not only are the kids a mess but the entire room looks like a unicorn was murdered. There's glitter and glue everywhere.

I shout to her husband, "Lucas, you better get out here!"

Tinselly's left eye twitches so I go straight to the liquor cabinet after ushering her to a seat. She's speaking softly, with her palms up, explaining to the air, "They were making the place cards for tomorrow. I had the entire house clean and it seemed like a good idea." She looks up at me as I mix a strong mimosa. "It would have been cute. I put the glue and glitter out, turned around, and when I came back—"

Lucas walks into the room at that moment and flinches. "This isn't good." His eyes travel to the boys who are rolling around on the floor, smearing glue and glitter everywhere—then he glances at his wife. "Boys, what would Santa say?"

One of them, I can't tell which on account of the massive amount of glitter, says, "Santa loves glibber—mommy says."

His brother nods in unison. "Mommy says."

Tinselly mutters, "Mommy says. I says that."

I repress a smile and hurry to her with the drink. "I've got this, you get that." I point toward the boys. "I'll help with the glitter later when her eye stops twitching."

Tinselly frowns, "It is not." When she tries to stop the tick, it just gets worse. She swears and grabs the glass from me, downs the whole thing and stalks to the sunroom on the back of the house.

I get her a refill as Lucas wishes me good luck and chases his naked children, corralling them toward the tub.

I hand Tinselly a second drink. She holds it and rants, "I had everything done. All of it. The decorations, the tree, the food prep, and the last thing was the cards. I was going to sit down in front of the fire and read a book." She glances up at me, her eyes wide and weary. "Do you know how long it's been since I had time to read a book? I haven't sat down for four days."

I point to her drink. Tinselly puts it to her lips and drinks this one slower. Her eye twitch slowly fades and she looks at me, I mean really looks at me. Her dark brows furrow and then a smile forms on her face. "Nova?" She asks as if I have something to tell her.

I'm ready to burst and it all rushes out. Everything from the time I took the job until last night. I leave out the homeless part, because that'll freak Tinselly out and make her eye twitch more. When I'm done with my story, I'm smiling so hard my face hurts. "I did what you said and made sure he knew. I kind of hated you for a little bit there, because he freaked out and nearly bolted. If the door wasn't covered in ice..."

"But it was," Tinselly's features fill with happiness. She comes over and wraps her arms around me. "Will you bring him by tomorrow?"

I give her a look. "It's our third date. He's not meeting my family. He'll run the other way."

"Hey, he will not." She plops down next to me on the couch, drink in hand. "And if you guys want to come, he's welcome here. You don't have to show up until dinner, since I'm assuming you have better things to do in the morning. Like him."

I swat her with a pillow and giggle. "Thanks for understanding. And just to be clear, never say anything that raunchy again. You're Miss Prim and Proper. I'm the crass one."

Tinselly tips her head back and honks a laugh. Finger raised, pointing toward me, she agrees, "That's true. And to show you how great of a sister you truly have, I'll even buffer him from Mom and Gran if you guys come. Please, please, please." She begs, hands clasped together, as if she were praying to her mimosa.

I blanch. "Oh God, Gran. Can you imagine?"

Tinselly giggles. "She'll be asking for his sperm count before he leaves."

I grimace and then Tinselly and I start laughing again. We tell the old Christmas memories of our favorite times. I retell my favorite, "Remember when we were snooping through the presents when I was eight years old?"

Tinselly nods, a huge grin on her face. "Yeah, mom tried to hide them in the attic that year thinking you were too afraid to go up there. Then I found you with the stairs pulled down and half way up."

"Yeah, I nearly fell off the ladder when you yelled at me. I thought you were Mom."

Tinselly smirks. "You were always so afraid of getting caught. I couldn't believe you had the audacity to pull the stairs down, never mind actually go up there."

"Hey, you followed and then trapped us up there."

Tinselly snort-smiles and points her glass at me. "Only to save your ass from Mom. I heard the car door slam."

"It wasn't even mom! We spent half the day waiting in a pitch-black attic so we wouldn't get caught."

"Hey," Tinselly corrects, "we didn't get caught and you got over your fear of the dark. Add in shaking a few boxes and it was a day well spent."

The tales go on, from year to year, and then fade as my fourteenth year approaches. Tinselly and I had thirteen Christmases before him, before Frank. Before I ruined everything and ran.

Silence falls between us and after a moment Tinselly asks, "He's the one, isn't he?"

I nod slowly, and lean against her shoulder. "If there is such a thing, yes. I don't know how I know, I just do."

Tinselly smirks, "And there it is—the infallible logic that lets you know love has totally screwed up your brain." I tickle her and she tickles back. We both sigh contently before settling onto the couch again. Tinselly adds, "I'm glad for you, little sis." Then she changes the subject, "I'm headed to Mom's tonight. You should come."

I'm caught off guard. "No." I feel my throat

tighten and Tinselly doesn't push it. She thinks it's from all the fights between me and mom, but it's not. It's because of him. The memories of that house are so tainted that I can't see past the last thing that happened there. I fake a smile and offer to refill our drinks.

Tinselly holds up her glass. "I'd love that."

I'm on my feet walking toward her liquor cabinet. "And how about that book?"

Tinselly looks up at me and confesses, "I don't have one." She starts laughing. "Isn't that sad? I knew I wasn't going to get a chance to sit down today. I figured I'd go out and buy one, but the storm came in."

I glance over my shoulder at her as I mix her mimosa. "I have one that will make your toes curl."

"Where are you hording books?" she calls after me. "Is it in that massive purse you carry?"

"Nope, it's on my phone!"

41
NOVA

After giving my sister an ebook that was tawdry at best and completely, uh, naughty—her face turned fifty shades of red. She flips the pages of my phone, her eyes wide, like she's been missing out on something. She glances at me, "You've done this?"

I'm sipping my mimosa and nearly choke. I put the cup down and scold her. "No! I don't have twin sugar daddies with huge schlongs that do it every chance they get. Geeze, Tinselly—it's a story."

She blushes delicately and shrugs. "Just checking. You never know with you. It's like you have a secret life or something."

I bark a laugh, "Yeah, that's not it."

"Do you ever wish it was? I mean, if you had

someone who could make everything instantly better and all you had to do was sleep with him, would you do it?" She's not looking at me, instead she's still reading the book with her eyes getting wider as she goes.

"I think you forgot who you're talking to. I don't take handouts."

"It's not a handout. You'd have worked for it."

"Okay, in my hypothetical career as a hooker, I suppose I'd take on two men. Are you happy?" Tinselly looks up at me and my cheeks burn wildly.

"Oh my God! Did you ever do this?" She points at the screen.

The rest of the afternoon goes on like that. Somehow we start talking about lovers and positions when the doorbell rings. I hear his voice before I see his face. Celyn walks into the room with a toddler on his ankle. "Does this belong to someone?"

My nephew looks up at Celyn, grinning. Celyn continues, "I found him. He says I can keep him if I give him some *glibber*. Since I don't have any of that, you'll have to make do with this nice lady. Do you know her?" Celyn gestures toward Tinselly who he's seen several times at the hut.

The little boy giggles, "That's Mama."

"Maybe she can provide you with your highly

sought after *glibber?*" Celyn lifts the boy off his ankle and the toddler runs to Tinselly.

"Mommy says Santa loves glibber." The little boy beams at Celyn, hands behind his back, swaying at the hips. His little blonde head is still wet from his bath and he's wearing a red sweater with a Santa head plastered on the front. Black corduroys and shoes finish off the look. He's ready for Grandma's house tonight.

Tinselly's eye twitches slightly and I laugh. I swat her arm and get up to tell Celyn hello. I wrap my arms around him and kiss his cheek. "Glad you got out of the Hottie Hut."

Celyn waggles his eyebrows at me. "I'm glad you walked into the Hottie Hut."

Tinselly holds my nephew on her hip and hands me back my phone. "Are you sure you won't come?"

I shake my head and manage to keep the smile on my face. "One family meeting per day. I've filled my quota. Celyn, this is Tinselly. Tinselly, Celyn. We're done here."

Tinselly scowls. "You'll come tomorrow night though, right?"

I wrap my arms around my sister and hug her tight. "I wouldn't miss it."

42

NOVA

As I step into Celyn's apartment, I can barely keep my hands to myself. I don't look around too much. My mind is elsewhere. Tinselly talking about that book all day made me crazy. I couldn't wait to have him alone, doing whatever I want to his beautiful body. Once we're through the door, I push him back into the wall, pinning his hips with mine. My mouth finds his and I purr, promising him more.

That's when the lights flick on. I startle and pull away from Celyn as he puts a protective arm around me and steps in front of me, shielding me from whoever is in the apartment.

There's an older man sitting in the living room with a dog at his heels. It whimpers at Celyn and then cowers behind the armchair. The seated man doesn't move. He's dressed in a fine suit, his leg crossed at the ankle. His dark hair has grayed at the temples, giving him a salt and pepper look. He reminds me of Celyn, something about his posture. For a second, I wonder if it's his father.

"Celyn, Miss Nikolaev." He taps the pads of his fingers together, leaving a yellow envelope on his lap. "I've heard we've had quite the day."

Celyn is across the room and inches from the man before I can blink. "How did you get in here?"

Familiarity jogs at something. I don't know if it's his face or his voice, but I know that man. I step into the room, but linger back. If Celyn is this upset, the intruder isn't welcome here.

The man rises, the dog at his heels. It skulks away from Celyn as he passes by, head lowered like he's afraid. The older man strides in my direction and stops in front of me. "It's the holidays, Celyn. Where are your manners. Did you not consider telling me you had a significant other—a plus one? I'm his Uncle Aldrich, dear." He reaches for my hand, but Celyn steps between us and cuts off the touch.

"You're not welcome here," Celyn growls.

"Of course. I thought maybe this year we

could let bygones be bygones, but apparently not." The old man looks at me with silver eyes, sharp and shrewd. "Does she know about your wager?"

I speak up, not liking how this is going. The hairs on my arms stood on end when he first announced himself and they still haven't relaxed. There's an icy feeling slithering over my skin, like something bad is about to happen. I look the old man in the eyes and say sternly, "I know everything."

"And you're still here, so you're either a gold digger chasing an empty vault or you're after power. Either way, it's unbecoming." His gaze rakes over me as if I were a piece of trash. "New year, same story, isn't that so, Celyn? Every Christmas, he'd bring home a bright-eyed hopeful whore that wanted nothing more than a shot at his bank account. Well, after our exchange the other day, I took things a step further."

Celyn growls again and steps forward, trying to get his uncle to move toward the door, but his uncle doesn't back down. "Get out or I'll call the cops and have you removed."

Uncle Aldrich stands stone cold. "I'm afraid not, my boy. It would seem that your mental state has been called into question. Undue duress, working long hours will do that to you, as well as choosing unbecoming bedfellows. She's a child, Celyn. Really."

The vein in Celyn's neck is throbbing like it may burst. His hands fist at his sides as he hisses, "You have no right—"

Uncle Aldrich cuts him off. "I have every right. It's the way your father left things to make sure you weren't taken advantage of or lead around by your—"

I step between them, gripped by a fierce protectiveness that I know too well. I know what type of man this is, I sensed it the moment I saw him. He's a predator poised as prey. He's the type of man who will pretend to love and protect you, but the moment your back is turned the knives come out. I know his kind.

"That's enough." The strength in my voice shocks me, but he's dredged up some old shit and I can't stand there and let someone I love go through this, not if I can help it. "You can walk yourself out right now or I can tase your ass and kick you to the curb myself." Celyn watches me, shocked as I snarl, "Leave. Now."

A smile snakes across his old lips. He claps once and then twice, loudly. "Bravo. Did you know she'd round on me like a bitch, Celyn? Is that why you had the background report run? Or is it because you thought you'd have your assets to protect?" His words blindside me and it's not until that moment that I see the envelope in his hand with the seal ripped open. He pulls out the papers thrusts them toward me. "Well, have a look. See if there's anything he missed?"

I falter as the papers are shoved into my hands. A background check. He didn't. If he did, then he knows what happened—what I did. I glance over at him, unable to hide the betrayal spilling across my face. "Is that true? This is a background check?"

Celyn is frozen, his face pale. When I look to him to deny it, he doesn't. Instead he tries to say, "Let me explain. Nova, it's not like that."

"Then what's it like?" I glance down at the crumpled papers in my hands and see my name, date of birth, and work history. At the bottom of the page is my expunged record with the details typed out in black and white. My hands tremble as my eyes fill with tears making the words blur. This part of my past that was never supposed to resurface is here in black and white, and Celyn is the one who conjured the demons. My heart turns to ice and shatters inside my chest. It's all I can do to stand and face him. The papers fall from my fingers and flutter to the floor as I turn and rush out the door. I run as fast as I can and when I'm at the curb, I race down the street and turn before the tears catch up. I walk swiftly through the icy streets, making a beeline for Penn Station. My plan is to head back home, back to Tinselly's house, grab my car and disappear.

43
CELYN

Uncle stands there smug and I know there's more. He steps in front of me, blocking my path, keeping me from immediately chasing her. "It's not always obvious, is it?"

"Get out of my way," I snarl, ready to rip his fucking throat out.

The dog whimpers and cowers as it crawls under the couch. Uncle smirks, confidently. "When a pretty face like that shows up, you'd never think she was capable of such malice, but you knew. Deep in your heart you knew something was wrong with her or you would have never ordered this report."

Every muscle in my jaw is strained, tensed,

and ready to fight. If I swing at him, he'll have me for assault. It's exactly what he wants me to do. He's baiting, hoping I'll snap and let my fists fly. No matter how much I hate him in that moment, there's no way in hell I'm giving him the satisfaction. I sidestep him without a word and rush down to the street. I call out her name, pacing the wet pavement, searching the road for her face, but she doesn't answer. She's gone. Nova is gone. My uncle ripped my heart out of my chest in one swift movement.

I didn't pull the report because I thought she did something. It was the opposite, I thought she was hiding or hurt by someone. Is it possible that I misjudged her so badly? What the hell did she do that gave her a criminal record that would make her run away like that? The look on her face was more than embarrassment, but I won't know why she ran unless I look at the report myself.

Anger floods me as I shove through the door. The man has the audacity to linger. He strokes Karma's wide head from his seat in the center of the living room. "Well, that was predictable," he says softly without looking up. "Really, Celyn. She's too young and violent."

I glance around at the papers littering the floor and pick them up. I shuffle through, reading as fast as I can. What did she do? I read quickly, seeing things I already know—her birthday, her old address, and her old business. Then I see she graduated high school at fourteen. That alone isn't odd, but it corresponds with an arrest record that fills the bottom of the page and spills onto the next sheet.

Uncle says from his seat. "She's practically a felon. Well done. They make for the best fucks, assuming you're looking for a cheap thrill."

Nova was nearly fourteen years old when it happened. I scan it quickly, my heart breaking as I read it. Her mother's boyfriend was living with them at the time and they'd since parted. There was an incident, but the details are missing. The man, Frank Cecil, broke her arm and Nova bludgeoned him with a trophy. When the police showed up, the officer tending to Nova tried to help her and she attacked the young cop with the same trophy. She wouldn't release it or say what happened. Nova said she was guilty, but the officer seemed to intervene and had the charges dropped. He's the one who arranged to have her record expunged. I turn to the third and fourth pages, looking for more of the story to explain the rest, but there is no more. Just a note that says additional details cannot be found at this time. That can't be all of it. I sift through the papers.

Uncle speaks up. "It's not there. I already read through it. Nice touch, by the way. Having her background checked that thoroughly was something I would have done. You paid for expunged records, which shows you never trusted to her start with—ordering a search that deep."

I slap the papers down on the table and growl at him. "She matters to me more than anything. If you destroyed any chance I had with her—"

He cuts off my threat from his seat. "You did that yourself when you ordered the report." Uncle stands and sighs loudly. "Celyn, you know what I want. Stop this childish claim on Bardenbey and things can go back to the way they were. I'll leave you with the apartment, the car, and still offer you the allowance. It's more than gracious. Take it. This is the last time I'll offer you such grace."

I shake my head and fold my arms over my chest so I don't murder him where he stands. "If anything, you just made me more determined to win. When I'm on the board at Bardenbey, your power won't run unchecked and I'll hold you accountable for everything you've done. Your ass will end up in a jail cell and there's nothing you can do to stop me."

I rush out of the apartment and down to my

vehicle. I pull out slowly on the slick streets. I have no idea where she's gone. I should have talked to her. I should have told her. It feels like I've been gutted alive. Then it comes to me and I know where she went—to Tinselly. She has to be headed back toward her sister's house for her car. If I can get there first, I can stop her.

44

NOVA

I lean my head on the window of the train, watching the world rush by in a blur of white. The tears finally dried up and I stare at my reflection as the world dies in my ears. I keep hearing his voice, seeing his face—the shock, the confession—he knows about Frank Cecil. Even Tinselly doesn't know all of that. Sure, she knows that I hit Frank in the head with a trophy and then did the same to the cop, but the rest—no one knew except me and Frank.

When I scanned the papers, it wasn't just line items and dates. It was written out. I saw the bottom of the first page, where it said I confessed. I didn't have to keep reading to know that all the details would be there. That record was supposed to be erased, gone. I stayed out of trouble. I did my part. I didn't assault anyone else or have problems with cops again after that night.

Truth be told, I wouldn't have touched the officer, but I was in shock. That was determined later. Something he said triggered my fight or flight response, which was still roaring in my ears. I didn't run. I stayed and fought the cop who was trying to help me. I reacted without thought. My arm swung and the trophy hit his temple hard. I can still see the crimson trail on his dark skin. Even so, he didn't yell at me. The policeman was patient and tried again to find out what happened with Frank. He wanted to know how my arm broke, but there were no words. I remember my heart racing so hard that I thought it would burst as sweat trickled down my spine. The roar in my ears was deafening. If I think about it too much now, it comes back. The past and the present collide and it's terrifying because I can't separate the memory from reality. They merge together and maul me.

Assaulting a cop is a felony. They took me to the station and processed me. I spent the night in a holding cell, alone, as they pressed me for answers that I couldn't give. They sent in a shrink, a female cop, and a CPS agent. I said what I needed to say to leave, to show them I was fine, but they all knew I wasn't. Later, they determined I was psychologically unstable when the officer approached me. Sometimes people don't realize when they can stop fighting. The shrink told me I was stuck like that. I just nodded. Mom bailed me out the next day and the charges were eventually dropped, but the arrest record was still there. No one understood what happened. Mom thought I broke my arm and then threw a fit, hitting Frank with the trophy. I didn't contest her theory, so that's what she believed. The young cop, the one I struck, took pity on me and spent his own money to have my record expunged. Nothing should have shown up on that search.

I swallow hard, knowing that there's a good chance Celyn raced to Tinselly's to cut me off. If he tells her what I did that night, I'll lose it. I protected her from that man—from Frank—for as long as I can remember. I don't want her to find out. I need to get there first.

When the train reaches my station, I jump off and race down the street as fast as I can manage without falling on my ass. I'm running for Tinselly, now. My mind is singularly focused on keeping Celyn away from her. When I get to the house, my car is parked out front and his is missing. Thank God. Traffic must be at a crawl because of the weather. It's late, but her front door is cracked, light shining onto the snow in the yard. She's home.

I rush up her shoveled steps and pull open the door. "Tinselly." I say her name in a rush and when I see her standing there in her red holiday sweater, I run to her, and throw my arms around my sister. She hugs me back and it's not until I look up that I see Celyn standing behind her, a black form in that dark cashmere coat.

I freeze in Tinselly's arms. She takes the moment to back toward the door to trap me inside. She says carefully, "Nova, it's time to stop running from this."

I glare at Celyn. "You told her?" I didn't think he would. Part of me didn't want to believe that he'd be malicious with the information, but when Celyn doesn't deny it what's left of my sanity collapses.

Tinselly watches me with worry pinching her face. "Nova, you can't keep running."

I round on Celyn. "How could you?" My eyes flash with fury as I rush him, my fists pounding into his chest. "She didn't know!"

Tinselly tries to peel me off but I push her away. "Nova, stop!"

Celyn wraps his arms around me and pins me against his chest. Tinselly steps back, but doesn't leave the room. I buck and kick against him, screaming the entire time. Tears streak my face as I thrash. "How could you do it? How could you tell her? She spent her entire life hiding from that man! I made sure he didn't touch her! I STOPPED HIM!"

I feel Tinselly's eyes on me, but it's not until Celyn releases me that I notice the quietness of her voice. "What are you talking about?"

I sniffle and look into her face, and then back at Celyn's. "About Frank, about that night at Mom's house—how he threatened to rape you. He wanted you, Tinselly. I heard him saying it and..." my voice trails off. There's no recognition in her eyes. She doesn't know what I'm talking about.

Tinselly's face crumples and her voice shakes, "Nova, oh God. I didn't know." Her hands are pressed tightly together and she holds them to her lips. "No one knew why you attacked him and you never said anything. Why didn't you tell me?"

My bottom lip quivers as I try to hold it together, but I'm failing. I almost failed her then and I failed her now because I couldn't shelter her from this knowledge. "Because he was still there and he kept looking at you like that. What was I supposed to do? I made sure you felt as safe as possible and I told him I'd do worse next time. I stayed until he left, until he broke up with Mom and walked out. I threatened him, Tinselly, and I had every intention of following through if he went near you. I couldn't let him do that to you."

Tinselly's face is streaked with tears. She stands there mute, her fingers pressed to her face.

I feel Celyn watching me. Anger mixes with pain and remorse for having the story come out like this, now. It's Christmas Eve. Tinselly should be kissing her little ones goodnight and playing Santa, not dealing with this shit. Not finding out that her little sister is completely warped, that there's a very scary person living inside of me. I didn't want her to know. I never planned to tell her.

I bite my lip and try to hold it together when I address Celyn. "I would have told you if you'd given me enough time, but you had to go behind my back."

"Nova—" He starts, raising his palms, stepping toward me.

I shake my head and step back. "But you couldn't wait. I thought you were a piece of shit when I first met you, an arrogant rich brat that thinks he can buy anything and everything. Well, fuck you, Celyn Ryan." I hear it. His name, the first and last names together places his uncle's face—that voice.

Celyn pales as he holds up his hands and steps

toward me. He tries, "Nova, please, I tried to tell you."

I smile bitterly and feel the corners of my lips quiver as they fight between a sadistic smile and horror. "Celyn Ryan. You're that spoiled brat that nearly bankrupted Bardenbey. I remember the papers that day, and how your greediness pushed out a drug that wasn't ready and it killed people." Horrible things are streaming through my mind, so close to coming out of my mouth. I temper the words, but not enough. "Your uncle saved your ass back then. Apparently he's not as forgiving now and frankly, neither am I."

Celyn backs away toward the door. Tinselly tries to stop him, "Celyn, wait."

But he doesn't stop. He says nothing countering my claims.

I narrow my eyes and it takes everything in me to remain where I am. "Let him leave. He's a coward, he always will be."

"Nova," Tinselly sounds horrified, but Celyn finally takes the cue and leaves without a word.

I sit down hard on the couch and bawl into my hands.

45

CELYN

I'm in my SUV barreling down the Long Island Expressway, headed for Manhattan. There's no way to explain—there's nothing to say. I shouldn't have pulled her report. And from the look on her face, she had no idea what was in it. She assumed the reasons were there, that I'd dug deeper than I had. Uncle baited her and she took it and ran. The look on Tinselly's face when she realized what her sister sacrificed to keep her safe, why she went nuts that night, and never went back to that house. Tinselly had no clue what kind of danger she was in at the time, or what Nova did to keep her safe. That burden shouldn't have been on a fourteen-year-old, but it was—and it shows. That's the weight on her shoulders, the thing that stole her youth and tempered her into a much older mind. While her body remained young, her soul didn't. She'd seen things a child shouldn't see, and done things that no kid should have to do and then she condemned herself for it. Whatever transpired between Nova and Frank, Nova still blames herself. She thinks she's the felon, the horrible person who had to do bad things. Holy fuck, I screwed this up and there's no way fix it. The entire situation exploded and there is nothing left of us.

The darkness that threatens to consume her is always there, but it's not pride propelling her forward. It's her sister. It's always been Tinselly. They're best friends and have been since they were girls. I don't have a brother in that sense—Quin is as close as it comes. Add in blood and the same mother, and things get a lot more complicated.

The world whizzes by in a rush of white and gray. The roads are slick and covered in slush, sand, and salt. The back of the SUV fishtails slightly when I take a ramp too fast, but I keep the vehicle under control. The night replays in my mind and sticks on what Nova said about the lethality of the drug. I can't let my Uncle do whatever he wants, when he wants. There's no way that people should have died. Every medication has its risks, but ours was better than the rest of the medicines on the market at the time, and without adverse side effects. Death sure as hell wasn't one of them. After the scandal came and went, I spent hours looking at our research and still didn't see how it happened. But the fatalities weren't isolated incidents.

I lost my future and my fortune, and tonight I lost Nova too. I can see the number on Uncle's legal pad in the back of my eyes. Rage makes the numbers burn and I have razor sharp focus at the moment, along with a lot of hatred that's unspent. Uncle is sitting in my apartment with the dog, gloating. He won. He took away everything that matters to me in one night.

As I drive, dots form in my mind, tugging me toward something, but I can't put it together. That's always been the problem, but I'm so livid that there's no way I'm leaving this alone. Not tonight. Not ever again. My uncle isn't the kind man watching out for me, he never was. Everything he did was to better himself and displace me. He wanted my father's fortune and most of it is wrapped up in Bardenbey. I suspected his intentions weren't pure a long time ago, but after tonight it wouldn't surprise me if he had something to do with my colossal failing. I've walked around with blood on my hands for years. I accepted that I was the reason those people died, that it was my foolhardiness, my stubbornness that created the mess in the first place. But what if it wasn't me at all? How dark does that side of Uncle go? I need to find out.

I pull up Quin's number and when he picks up, I blurt out, "Can you meet me at Bardenbey?"

"Merry Christmas Eve to you, too." Quin mutters and then adds, "Your uncle will be there. I thought you were avoiding him so you don't accidentally kill him for Christmas."

"He's not there tonight." My throat tightens as I grip the steering wheel harder. "He's gloating in my apartment. He was there when I brought Nova home."

Quin chokes so hard that it sounds like he swallowed a chicken leg. When he finally stops, he manages, "Shit, man. You and Nova? Really?"

I fill him in, telling him that she's the woman from the hotel room. She was the chick with the Chilton's manual. Then he hired her and things happened. When I'm done, I blurt it out, not caring what he thinks, "She's the one. I love her and I shot everything to hell. While she was telling me off she said something and I can't let it go."

Quin's stunned silence speaks volumes. I've never told him I felt that way about anyone.

When he finally talks, he asks, "And where is she now?"

"At her sister's house."

"Shit, man. This is bad. I can't believe your uncle did that to her."

"It wasn't him. I ran the report. I did this." I'm gripping the steering wheel so tightly that my fingers are going numb. I loosen my grip as I navigate the shiny dark roads.

"You'll figure out how to patch things up with Nova. I'll help you."

HOURS OF RIFLING THROUGH PAPERS HAS DONE nothing. Maybe it's not the date after all. I'm sitting on the floor of the filing room with my head tipped back against the cabinet. It's fucking late and the adrenaline that was flowing through me earlier is long gone.

Quin on the other hand is high on candy canes and peppermints when he bounces to another cabinet and rifles through the folders. After a second, he stops sucking the piece of candy and calls over to me. "Hey, there's a thumb drive in here."

"In a folder?" I rub my hands over my face and glance up at him. Quin is holding a black drive between his thumb and forefinger, lifting it up in the air.

He waggles his eyebrows. “Weird, right?”

“Yeah,” my brain wakes up a little bit and I lean forward. “Which cabinet are you in?”

Quin backs up and tips his head to the side to read the drawer label and grins. “Bardenbey Pharmaceuticals interoffice memos. That’s the biggest bunch of bullshit. There shouldn’t be a drive in here. Everything else in this drawer is paper.”

I jump up and race over to him, plucking the drive from his fingers. “Maybe they didn’t want anyone to find it.”

Quin mutters something and then heads to Perky’s computer. “Well, then let’s take a look.” Quin keys in her password.

“You know her code?” I ask, shocked since the man doesn’t know her name.

Quin shrugs. “I saw her key it in the other day. She didn’t change it from the factory settings. 1, 2, 3, 4 isn’t hard to hack.” Quin then inserts the drive.

We both watch as one folder flickers onto the screen. My stomach is swirling. I want to find something. I’ve been such a fucking moron trying to play by the rules with this man.

Quin double clicks and a file opens. He shakes

his head when he's looking at a long string of numbers and letters. "What is this?"

At first glance, I recognize it. I lean in closer to the screen to confirm it's what I think it is. "This is the formula for the cancer drug. It looks like the patent papers." I squint at the screen and frown. Something is different. I've seen this a thousand times but I can't put my finger on what changed. After scanning the screen for a moment, I spot it, the glaring difference. I press my finger to the screen. "That's not supposed to be there."

Quin is sitting next to me on Perky's desk and dips his head to look at the item on the screen. "What's europhen?"

"It's diisobutyl ortho cresol iodide, and it's an archaic antiseptic. It's a substitute for iodoform, which no one has used for much in the past seventy years, so what the hell is it doing in here?"

"Why do you know science shit?" Quin asks, while he crunches up a candy cane in his mouth.

"I worked in a lab every day for years. You learn things."

"You mean you'd learn things. Your brain is a fucking sponge. You never forget anything."

"True." And it's a good thing too. I flip through the pages with the cancer drug formula to look for CHI3, and find it. There's no way that was in the formula. I pull out my phone and

Google the drug index for 429 and swear. It takes everything I have to keep myself in check and not smash my fist through the computer. This is it. This is what Uncle Aldrich was hiding. He's the one responsible for this, for all of it.

Quin is on his feet, looking at the phone in my hand. "I don't get it? What'd he do?"

After I inhale sharply and rub my palms over my face, I look up at him. "Uncle altered the formula on the patent application. This shouldn't be there. Iodoform is lethal in large doses. It's why people got sick when they took the RequimX. It's why the drug was recalled. It's why it didn't fucking work—he changed the paperwork and no one saw it."

"How is that possible?" Quin is there, staring at the patent papers and then he takes my phone. "Shit, this stuff killed people. Are you saying he knew? That it was done on purpose?"

I nod, still staring at the screen. "That's why I was ushered out of the pharmaceutical division so quickly, he was covering his tracks."

"Why?" Quin is shaking his head. I feel his gaze on the side of my face. "Why the fuck lose close to a billion bucks and nearly bankrupt the company?"

"He wanted it for himself and this was the best way to push me out. It made me look incompetent and when it came time to take my place at the company, he had an ironclad reason to deny me. He made sure that I made a mistake that I couldn't recover from, not just by losing money, but by showing the public and the board that I couldn't be trusted." It's exactly what Nova said to me before she threw me out. The public's perception of me tainted by something that I didn't do.

"Shit, man. That's twisted." When I don't respond, Quin asks, "Why keep this around at all?" He points at the thumb drive.

"Because it's the patent and it's a tax write-off. That's why he was talking to the accountant and flipping out. The thumb drive went missing. It was misfiled."

Quin smiles slowly. "And we found it, so now what?"

I close the window, shut off the computer, and pocket the drive. "I need to talk to the lead chemist, Dr. Snow and confirm my thoughts. Then we expose him."

"Celyn, if you do that, you'll destroy Bardenbey." Quin pauses, candy cane midway to his mouth. "You won't have any company to take over by the time the suits and papers are through with you."

"I don't care. This was wrong and he did it."

I'm out of my chair and walking down the hallway to the elevator bank when Quin stops me. I have Snow's number on my phone.

"I know, but think it through. Celyn, you'll lose everything. This could backfire and your uncle could blame you, say you did it."

I shake my head. "The last person to touch the patent papers and send the final formula to manufacturing was Uncle. That's why no one saw it. Snow was ruined because of that incident and so was I. Snow has a right to know it wasn't his fault."

"And if you destroy yourself in the process?"

"Then so be it."

THE NEXT MORNING, DR. SNOW CONFIRMS MY thoughts and echoes my outrage. This wasn't carelessness, it was sabotage. Uncle bypassed the safety checks in place and oversaw the initial distribution of the drug himself. He's to blame for it, for all of it. By the time I'm done exposing him, there'll be nothing left of the legacy my father created. That's the only thing that makes me hesitate, but if I don't act now and strike when he least expects it—I'll lose my shot.

My mind keeps drifting back to Nova. I've

tried to call her, but she won't answer. I want to apologize, but I don't deserve her forgiveness. I never deserved her in the first place, and now I've caused her pain that I can't take away. I assumed she was running from demons that were in the present. I had no idea the threat lay dormant in her past. I woke the dead and made her relive the entire thing again, bearing it to the one person she tried so hard to protect. I'm a shit. She should do more than spit on me if she ever sees me again.

I'm dressing quickly and ready to fix this mess. It's Christmas morning and while other people are opening presents, I'm handing over my last living relative on a platter to the New York City police department. I spoke to the detective last night and we agreed to meet at Bardenbey this morning. I know damn well that Uncle will try and take me down with him, and I've accepted that fate. It's worth the risk.

When I get to Bardenbey, the halls are empty save for a few top executives hurrying to do some last second work before rushing out for the day. I meet Detective Tatch, a tall tank of a man in his late forties. "I'm sorry to call you out on Christmas."

Tatch looks over at me, the olive skin on his face slack with age. His hardened eyes reveal nothing. If he didn't speak, I'd have no idea what he was thinking. "It takes guts to do what you're about to do. Waiting will make it worse. If you're ready, let's get it over with."

I stop before Uncle's large office doors and look at the cop. "Let's go." I shove inside, and walk straight up to my uncle and drop it on him like a bomb.

46

NOVA

I'm lying on Tinselly's couch while the twins play with their new fire trucks. They roll them over my legs, pretending that I'm a road while I stare bleary-eyed at nothing. Tinselly's tried to get me to move, wash, sit up—anything, for a while now, but I can't find the strength to do it. Failure creeps through my spine and keeps me face down on the sofa.

One of the twins sits down hard on the remote and the TV turns on. I stare blankly, eyes open, but not seeing him until I hear his voice. Celyn? I look up and see the man I love wearing a polished suit, standing in front of Bardenbey. The ticker on the bottom of the screen says: Aldrich RYAN ARRESTED FOR MURDER.

I sit up suddenly and turn up the volume.

Tinselly notices and walks in behind me. She's watching as intently as I am. Celyn confesses that Bardenbey didn't do its due diligence with the formula for the cancer drug RequimX. It was tampered with by his uncle, resulting in the poisoning and deaths of so many loved ones.

His voice is somber as he stands there in front of the cameras and adds, "I'm so sorry that this happened and I'll do everything in my power to see justice served." Before he can say another word, he's ushered off stage to a waiting car.

The news reporter starts talking, saying, "It's unclear what this means for the future of Bardenbey. The findings were brought to the attention of the police late last night by Celyn Ryan." They go on to speculate that Celyn just forfeited his fortune and his family legacy. They talk about his late father briefly before switching to his uncle. My heart hurts when I look at Aldrich, when I see that horrible man.

Tinselly is standing at the back of the couch and looks down at me. "Did he know? When he was here last night, he seemed upset, but I don't think he knew about this. It must have happened after he left."

"I don't care." I'm about to flop back down on the couch and cover my head with the blanket when Tinselly yanks it away.

She snaps, "Yes, you do care. If anything, you care too much. How do you want this to end, Nova?"

I gape at her. "What do you mean?"

"With him? That's the only question that matters. How do you want this to end with Celyn? Do you want to see him on the street with someone else? Do you want the brunette to help him through whatever happens next? He decimated himself to bring his only living relative to justice. It's Christmas day and he's alone." She looks at me like I'm a heartless bitch.

"Tinselly, he betrayed me!" I'm on my feet and in her face. "I can't believe you're defending him."

"I'm not. I'm simply asking you if you'd rather live with him or without him. You have a choice here." She puts her hands on my shoulders and speaks kindly. "You're good at protecting everyone except yourself. You have a good heart that's been hurt too many times for someone so young. He made you smile again, Nova. I saw how you looked at him. If you can forgive him, with all the stuff going on today, well—it's Christmas."

My voice catches in my throat. "I don't want to lose him, but I told you and—".

"And I needed to know why my sister won't go home. I needed to know what made you act like that. Nova, you moved out and I thought I'd never see you again. I thought Mom allowed you to be emancipated to get rid of you. You two were always fighting. I didn't think you'd come back."

My face pinches as my heart buckles. "Of course you'd see me again. I'd never let anything happen to you."

Tinselly inhales deeply and nods a few times while blinking away the tears in her eyes. "I know that now, and that's why I can't let you mope on the couch all day. Nova, you saved me that night. Let me save you for once." I can't help it, the corner of my mouth rises a little. "I'm your big sister and I know better. I know that look on his face and I recognize it in you, too. You get to choose how this ends."

"Tinselly, I can't just walk back over there."

"Why not?"

I start shaking in her grasp as I try to hold back sobs. "Because, I'm not the one who blew everything up, he did that."

Tinselly's expression softens. "You were the one who didn't wait and talk to him. You were the one who tried to protect me for so long that you didn't see what it was doing to you. Nova, you're not wrong, and that's not what this is about. If you want to work things out with him, you need to go talk to him." She pulls me into a hug before shoving me down the hallway. "Go take a shower and then find him. Bring him some food. He's probably eating Taco Bell or something equally unfestive."

I snort. A holiday lacking proper food and decoration is Tinselly's worst nightmare. I grin at her, "That's what worries you the most about this? His meal?"

Her voice stops me in my tracks. "No, what worries me the most is that you found your soul mate and because of a manipulating, asshole of a relative, you're going to lose him. Your chance at love doesn't have to end like this. That's what I'm afraid of Nova, that you won't forgive yourself enough to be able to talk to him."

I push my matted, frizzy hair out of my face and stare at her. "I love him, but I have no idea how to fix this. I still hurt, Tinselly. I feel violated, almost. Why'd he have to do that?"

Tinselly smiles softly. "You're asking the wrong person, sweetheart. Get dressed and borrow my car. Go patch things up."

I pad across the room and then turn back and ask, "What if he doesn't take me back?"

"Then you'll know and knowing is better than wondering."

47

CELYN

The sun sank below the skyline of steel and glass nearly an hour ago. I still haven't eaten anything today. It doesn't feel like Christmas. There are no presents, no ribbons, no tree. My only companion is silence. After the police took my uncle into custody, I went home and sat down on the couch. It feels like I've been gutted, like my insides were scraped out. I've been decimated. Everything I cared about is gone. The man I wanted to be my protector, my kin, manipulated me for years and I would have never known—never noticed if Nova hadn't told me off last night. Something she said resonated and drove me to those filing cabinets. It was a fluke, a complete act of God, that I found that thumb drive. Bardenbey will crumble and there will be nothing left of my father's legacy. I traded that card in to make sure justice didn't pass over my uncle a second time.

Flurries flutter from the darkening sky and pass my windows. I sit there on the cold leather couch watching them fall, wondering how the hell I'm supposed to move past this because that's what's paralyzing me—I'm completely alone. No one will care if I do anything significant, there will be no one there to catch me when I screw up, and at life's greatest moments—marriage and children—my half of the church will sit empty. There won't be a single soul there. Well, that's not true. There will be one—Quin. He lingered this morning, but aside from handing me whiskey and telling me to get drunk, he can't help with this. It feels like my fucking heart is missing, despite the rhythmic beats.

I lean forward and put my elbows on my knees and run my hands through my hair and clasp them at the base of my neck. This is the shittiest Christmas I've ever had. Karma canters by and sits as far away from me as he can, but he's no longer shaking around me. I didn't have much of an option with the dog. It was adopt the nutcase of a canine or take him to the pound. I couldn't do that no matter how much he hates me. Some of Uncle's feelings for me clearly translated to the dog, but over the past few hours, Karma seems calmer. His dark coat glistens as he sits by the window, tail wagging, like he wants to run outside and eat snowflakes. The animal doesn't know what happened today, how much was lost. Lucky bastard.

My doorbell rings. Karma jumps up and slides across the floor, trying to beat me to the door. He probably wants to escape before the threat of lightning later tonight. I can't blame him. Grabbing hold of his thick green collar, I pull open the door. Karma barks and then wags his tail furiously when he's confronted with a fat Christmas tree in the foyer.

"Hello?" I try to glance around the branches, but I can't see who's holding it. Quin doesn't have enough sentiment to send me a tree or realize that I even wanted one. "I think you have the wrong address." I'm turning on my heel to go back inside when I hear her voice.

"I'm sorry, I thought Hot Guy lived here. He has this little coffee place called the Hottie Hut—you know, amazing coffee with girls dressed like a slutty Swiss miss." She peaks her blonde head around the branches and smiles carefully at me. Her lips press together making her mouth form a thin line, before she continues, "I was afraid you were having a crappy Christmas."

I'm shocked she's here, that she hauled a tree upstairs. It's taller than her. Something inside me wants to send her away and I'm about to when Karma pulls hard and I fumble his collar. He rushes at Nova and plows into her, knocking her to the floor, followed by the tree which topples sideways and lands on them both. Nova screeches and Karma howls.

"Shit! Karma, you crazy bastard. What the hell are you doing? Bad dog! Sit!" I shout out a bunch of other commands, all of which the dog ignores. I can see his tail tangled in the branches as he happily yips and tries to climb out. At least I think that's what he's doing. The animal is insane and with Nova's luck, the dog is probably chewing her face off.

Nova shrieks and then giggles. When I pull the tree upright, Karma is licking her cheek. She's smiling wide and purely happy. There's a rosy glow on those cheeks, like she's been out in the cold. My gaze sweeps to a large red box and some white bags scattered on the floor behind her. I don't understand why she's here, but I'm not stupid enough to ask. Instead, I look down at her beautiful face and hope for a miracle.

When Karma runs back into the apartment, I'm left standing over Nova, holding the tree. "I'm so sorry. He doesn't usually act like that." He usually cowers and pees on the floor. I suppose this was better.

Nova sits up, wiping the dog drool off her face. "Karma seems to think I'm magically delicious."

"Yes, he's charming." Part of me is bristling. "What is all this, Nova? You were pretty clear that things were over. If this is pity—"

"It's not pity." She's on her feet and tries to grab the tree from me, but she's too small. She yanks it hard, I pull back. Basically, we're playing tug-of-war with a large conifer in the hallway.

"Then what is it? Because you don't have to make a show for me." I yank the tree again and end up with pine needles in my mouth when she doesn't let go.

"It's not making a show." She yanks the tree hard.

I snap it back. "Then what is it?"

"I don't want things to end like this. I don't want—" She tugs the tree.

"What *do* you want, Nova?" I pull back a lot harder this time.

"I want you, you idiot." Nova stumbles forward and we fall through the door of my apartment with the tree sandwiched between us. She rolls off the tree quickly and pulls it off of me. She's on her knees, examining the spots where the branches scraped my cheek. When those emerald eyes meet mine, I don't have the balls to hope, to believe I heard her right. "What?" I blurt out, sounding annoyed and defensive.

Kneeling by my side, Nova lowers those long lashes and when her eyes meet mine, my chest aches. "I love you, Celyn. What happened before was horrible, what happened to you today was unthinkable. But..." her voice drifts off as she looks around the room.

"But what?" I ask softly, urging her on.

When she looks at me my heart pounds harder, and my throat tightens. I can't tell if she's here to decimate me further or make up. There's no way she'd forgive me after what happened. I blew a lifelong secret from the one person she loves the most. I manage to keep my mouth shut. I want to listen, I want to really hear her because it might be the last time we ever talk.

Nova inhales, filling out her red ribbed sweater. It's the same one she had on the night we met. There's a black leather jacket over her shoulders and she's wearing the fuzzy hat from the Hottie Hut. She looks like a goddess in a silly hat. Nothing diminishes her beauty. The woman could wear a lampshade as a hat and it'd be sexy, because her face, her spirit, her soul is perfect. She's beautiful inside, so she has this ethereal glow about her. It's hard to look away, and even harder to ignore.

Silence spans between us and Nova's eyes are glassy when she speaks. "I don't want things to end like this. I love you and I always will. I can't really see how to get past what happened, but I know I want to and I was hoping that maybe we could figure it out together."

I push up on my elbows as she speaks and I think my jaw has dropped. Is she forgiving me? I can't fathom it. What the hell is going on? I'm too stunned to speak. I remain mute with my lips parted and my brow knitted together.

Nova averts her gaze and nods slowly. "All right. I understand. Either way, I want you to have the tree and the gift. There's a cinderblock in one of the bags. It's for the tree. There weren't any more stands, so tree guy gave me the block." She smiles sadly at me. "Merry Christmas, Celyn." Her back is to me and she's leaving.

I'm on my feet, and all I can think is that I'm going to lose her again because I'm such a fool. What she said formed a lump in my throat and I can barely make a sound. I rush toward her, tripping over the tree in the process. My body collides with hers and I accidentally shove her into the elevator doors. Her curves press against me and my mind is screaming at me to say something, say anything!

I'm still a sputtering fool, when the elevator doors open. Nova tries to catch herself, but I'm there. We fall to the floor, me on top. Nova lets out an *oof* as her back hits the wooden floor. Speech returns to me in a rush when I think she's hurt. "Are you all right? Nova, I'm so sorry. I'm sorry—for everything. I should have never pulled that report. I could tell something was weighing on you and I convinced myself that I could help if I knew what it was. I was an idiot and it was wrong. I'm so sorry, about that and about Tinselly. God, Nova, I have no way to tell you how sorry I am...and now you're here. I love you, Nova." Tears well up in my eyes and spill down my cheeks. "I always will."

I start to roll off of her, but she grabs hold of my sweater, holding me in place. Her face crumples and she sobs, "I thought you didn't like me anymore. I thought—"

I cut her off and take her face in my hands and tell her, "I'm in love with you. I have been for a long time and nothing could ever change that. You're my heart, my home. Everything I was missing, everything I ever wanted has been staring me in the face. I love you now and I'll love you tomorrow."

Nova swallows hard and throws her arms around my neck. When she releases me, I pull back and smile down at her. "Will you help me trim my tree?"

She snorts loudly trying to conceal an out of control giggle. "Celyn," she scolds. "We need to go inside first."

My face burns as I stand up and then offer her a hand. "That's not what I meant!"

She doesn't comment on the blush rushing across my cheeks, but she smiles harder. "Can I trim your tree?" she teases, taking my palm in hers and then standing. "Really."

I point to the massive pine sprawled across the floor of my apartment. "I was serious!"

She takes my hand and walks us over the threshold. "So was I. I'll trim your tree if you ride my sleigh."

I laugh and lean in, whispering in her ear, "I'd love to ride your sleigh, and maybe even stuff something up your chimney."

She laughs and swats my chest, "Celyn!"

"That makes you blush? Really?" I'm grinning at her, leaning down, my mouth close to hers with a smile tugging at the corners of my lips. I lean in closer and drop my voice, "You are the most precious," I kiss the corner of her mouth, followed by the other, "wonderful gift I've ever gotten. Will you stay with me tonight?"

She nods sweetly, those long lashes focused on my lips. "Yes."

"Will you stay with me the night after? And the night after that?"

Her smile increases and she looks up at me. "Yes, if you want me."

"I want you every night, every day. When I thought I lost you, it was clear."

"What was?"

When she looks up at me with her green eyes, I bare my heart to her. "I want you in my life, in my bed, and I don't want you to leave. I couldn't have dreamed of a better life than one with you. What I'm saying is, will you marry me?" It's too fast, too soon. We've barely had any time, and I hate myself for being so weak, for saying it now.

But when her eyes widen and I think she's going to push me away, she blinks rapidly as if trying to keep tears from falling. "Yes."

48

EPILOGUE

- CELYN -

The wedding was three months ago. Nova and I went to town hall and eloped. Tinselly was there, and Quin. Then we spent a little money on a honeymoon and lay around on a beach for a week. I loved her in every way possible and she still wanted more, wanted me. She's insatiable and completely perfect.

When we got back to the real world it was clear that we needed to act quickly to keep my apartment. I offered to sell it, but she wouldn't let me. Nova wanted that decision to come later, not under duress. I showed her the cash from selling the McLaren and told her it was all we had until everything was sorted out with Bardenbey. It's possible that when it's over, there will be nothing left.

"You married a man with very little to his name." I felt like a shit doing that to her, but Nova just cocks her head at me.

"I was sleeping in my car. You have a lot, we just need to use it wisely and we will. We're in a nosedive right now, but we can pull out of it." Nova is the optimist, and kept her promise.

We went back to the Hottie Hut and strategized how to handle it year round. Our offer had to be big enough to make the owner want to rent it to us instead of opening the ice shack in the summer. We found agreeable terms that wouldn't cripple me and Nova—and that's where we've been working all day, every day.

Nova makes a monthly drink and puts a picture in the window. The night she visited the tree guy, she saved his ass and helped him sell trees in exchange for the one she brought me. She worked the lot that night and he sold out. As thanks, he gave us his picnic tables, which also helped tremendously. Now we have several places to sit, right outside the hut. Nova landed a few banks and brings the tellers their coffee every morning, which increased cash flow quite a bit. People are crazy when it comes to their coffee and she made it possible for a lot of people to try it easily. I would have never thought of bringing it to them.

Days are long and I've never been so tired in my life, but I've never been so happy either. Every night we drive home, and talk about the day and what we can do to make tomorrow better. By the time we walk in the door of our apartment, she's back to being Nova—my sexy goddess.

One night, Nova lies in my arms, her body slick with sweat, and she looks up at me. "I think we can do it."

"Do what?" I'm so sated that I can't do anything but sport a lazy smile.

"Expand." She rolls onto her stomach and crosses her ankles before pulling them toward her perfect naked ass. "If we opened more shacks, we could manage them, instead of working them. It'd pull in a lot more revenue and it wouldn't matter if it takes years to see what happens with Bardenbey. It gives us more options. If Bardenbey survives, then we can sell the shacks and go there. In the meantime, it would give us more stability. What do you think?"

I rub my hand over my head and tuck my wrist behind my neck, letting my eyes rove over her naked curves. "You can see it? How all the moving parts have to fit together to work, can't you?"

She nods and smiles at me before leaning over and brushing a strand of hair away from my eyes. "Yes, I can, but it'd be a risk. We can keep things the way they are and we'd be okay, Celyn. I was just thinking that having more shacks would allow more flexibility and if one hut did poorly, then another could shoulder it. It creates a buffer that we don't have right now. It's up to you."

I lean in and kiss her temple. "If you think it works, I trust you. Let's do it."

As days slip into months, Nova makes it work. I'm good working with concrete notions and numbers, but Nova can pull ideas out of the air and make them materialize. It's uncanny how long shots work for her. We open a second hut and learn from those mistakes before opening a third. By the time the holiday season rolls around, we own seven Hottie Huts scattered across Long Island. So much has changed in a year. We no longer work the machines or stay in the shack serving customers all day. Nova and I have an office in Commack and our workweeks are no longer one hundred hours long. Those days have finally passed, which means I can spend every night tangled together with my wife, enjoying her body and getting high on her happiness.

On Christmas Eve, we set out for Tinselly's house. The normal festivities were relocated now that Tinselly knows why Nova avoids her mother's home. Tinselly never told her Mom, she just said it'd be so much easier with the boys if we went to them. Mom and Gran didn't refuse.

Nova sits quietly in the passenger seat, probably worried about her family being over the top —they always are. I reach for her, take her hand. "It'll be all right. We have so much to be grateful for, stop worrying."

Nova bobs her head and squeezes my hand. "I'm not worried."

"Yes, you are. You've been quiet for days. Are you feeling better?" She was sick a few days ago, caught a stomach bug and stayed in bed most of the day.

"Yeah, I'm good." She looks over at me, smiling. "I'm looking forward to Tinselly's stuffing, and I won't even mind Gran's crazy questions."

When we're all seated at the beautifully decorated table and the usual conversation ensues, Nova doesn't balk. Instead, she keeps her head down and picks at her food like she's not hungry. I lean over and whisper, "Are you feeling okay?" Worry creases my brow as I try to catch her eye.

Gran notices and snaps the other conversations to a halt when she says, "No secrets, it's Christmas! If you knocked her up, it's time to fess up, Celyn."

I'm mid-sip on a glass of wine and choke. Tinselly mouths apologies and grabs me another napkin, but she freezes in place when I turn to Nova. Our eyes meet and the dots connect—she's been tired, sick to her stomach, and unusually quiet. I smile at her, knowingly. "Really?" She nods with a soft smile. "Are you sure?"

She beams at me brightly, trying to repress a smile and happy tears. "Yes."

I jump up so quickly that I knock over my chair. I scoop up Nova in my arms and spin her once before pressing a kiss to her lips. "Oh my God! Do you know what this means?" I laugh, and feel the happiest I've ever been in my entire fucking life. My chest is going to explode with pure joy.

The twins frown, as Gran cackles, pointing at Nova. "Ha! I knew it!"

Mom hasn't followed and is sitting next to Tinselly, who is still frozen between the table and the counter, holding an extra napkin in the air. Mom looks up at her, "I missed something. What's going on?"

Tinselly sits down hard in her seat and watches me kiss my wife. "They're going to have a baby."

The toddler twins cheer in unison. "Hooray! More friends!"

I don't want to put her down. I want to hold her like this forever, but I place her back in her chair and kiss her cheek. Then I lift a glass of wine, and everyone stills. "To the most amazing woman that I've ever met. A year ago tonight, I thought I'd lost everything. I sat alone, broken and beaten when she showed up with a Christmas tree and cinderblock and changed my life. Nova is my other half, my soul mate, the piece of me that was missing. I thought I couldn't possibly be any happier than I was on the way here, but I was wrong. To my beautiful bride and mother to be. Merry Christmas, Hot Girl."

Turn the page for more romance by H.M. Ward!

MORE HOLIDAY BOOKS BY H.M. WARD

A LITTLE CHRISTMAS ROMANCE

CHRISTMAS KISSES

And more.

To see a full book list, please visit:

http://hmward.com/books/

EXCERPT: OVER YOU

CHAPTER 1

I sprint down the hospital corridor, dodging patients, other visitors and a delivery guy with an enormous bouquet of flowers. My heart is pounding so hard I'm afraid it'll crack my ribs. There's not enough air, and the stitch in my side brings tears to my eyes, but I don't stop—I can't.

The overhead fluorescent lighting casts an eerie glow on the sterile decor, and the sound of the bulbs makes my tired eyes twitch. I focus on the sound of my footsteps, rhythmic and reliable. He'll be okay. Things won't end here today.

Seven hours ago, I was in Texas, about to eat dinner. My only worry was studying for the graduate school admissions test I planned to take next semester. But that was before my sisters called to let me know they were rushing our father to New York City's Mt. Sinai Hospital. They didn't say much, only that I needed to travel as fast as possible.

When I walked away from New York, it seemed like a good idea. I wanted my own life, my own space, and two thousand miles in the middle made it impossible for my mother to meddle. I didn't expect this. I never thought my dad could slip from this world before I returned home.

Turning the corner, I see an information desk and a friendly looking nurse. She's a little older than me—late twenties, early thirties at the latest—with bright violet eyes and a stethoscope slung casually around her neck.

"Excuse me," I pant, "can you please point me in the direction of room 651? I'm David Bennet's daughter, Beth."

She reaches up and squeezes my hand reassuringly. "It's down the hall to the left and around the corner. You're a good daughter flying up here so fast."

"Thanks," I say, grateful for her kindness. I take off down the hall at a quick clip. I increase my speed when I'm away from the nurse's station and round the corner without slowing. I see the tall man in the dark suit just seconds too late.

We collide and I bounce backward. I tilt dangerously, preparing myself for an ungraceful landing, but he reaches out for my elbow and pulls me to his chest, steadying me.

His bright blue eyes gaze down intently into mine and—just for a moment—I forget why I'm here. Those eyes hold a lifetime of pain and a wealth of secrets. For a split second, the depths of his torment are reflected in those twin blue pools, and I sense a kindred spirit in him, like he understands my fear of loss all too well.

He blinks, clears his throat, and sticks his hands abruptly in his suit pockets, letting me fall away from his chest and out of his spell. "Darcy. William Darcy."

"Beth," I say my name instinctively, as a warning bell goes off silently in my mind. "Elizabeth Bennet."

He looks around nervously as if he'd rather be anywhere else right now, but he doesn't leave. He runs his hand through his dark hair and then glances at me again.

Darcy. Why does that name sound familiar? Wait a minute!

"William Darcy of Darcy Biopharm?" I take a step forward, poking his surprisingly muscular chest right in the middle of his expensive designer tie. I'm normally not so aggressive, but this man is a shit, I know that for certain. "What are you doing here? Putting my father in the hospital wasn't enough? Did you come to pull the plug, too? Or just kick him while he's down?"

Darcy blinks and takes a step back. "I had little to do with it. Maybe you should ask your father what he's been hiding."

"Don't insinuate you know my father better than I do." I glare up into his face and narrow my gaze to thin slits. My fingers twitch at my sides, wanting to ball up into fists so I can clobber this monster.

William Darcy has a strong reputation for being a heartless dick. He destroys without remorse, completely calloused from the inside out. His calm exterior irritates me. "Miss Bennet, I suggest you—"

"What? Take advice from you? No, thank you." I push past him without giving myself a chance to feel guilty for my manners. Fuck him. I wish I could say it to his face. As I start to rush away, I round and walk backward for a moment. "And don't show your face here again. You're not welcome."

"It's a free country, Miss Bennet."

"Kiss my ass, Mr. Darcy."

CHAPTER 2

"Beth, thank God you're here," my older sister, Jane, cries as I enter the hospital room. Her blue eyes look as tired as I feel. She rushes across the room, throwing her arms around me in a hug. "The doctor is just about to tell us if Dad can go home."

"I still don't see what all the fuss is about," Dad says in a weak voice from the hospital bed.

"You passed out at your meeting with William Darcy. It's a damn good reason to fuss since he hates you and the feeling is mutual," my baby sister, Tinselly, says from her perch in the window. She looks like a raven in a tree, her dark, Goth-style clothing contrasting vividly with the stark white window facing. "I imagine he prefers people consciously listening while he talks."

“Manners, Tinselly,” Jane echoes mother, but more sweetly. Tinselly rolls her eyes.

"Technicalities," Dad says lightly. "Sit with me, Beth. I'm happy to see you, but you shouldn't have flown all the way here on my account." He shoots a sideways glance at Tinselly, who shrugs in response.

"She was long overdue for a visit. If she doesn’t fly home every six months or so, she’ll be wearing cowboy clothes and talking with a twang.

Nobody wants that, raht, Beth?" Tinselly smirks, trying not to laugh as she does her worst Texas accent impression.

No one in my family understood why I chose to go to school so far away. It was a necessary evil. I needed to figure out who I am and how I fit into this world. I couldn't do it with certain people present. Okay, not people.

My mother.

She's like gravity—you can't escape her downward pull unless you leave for outer space. Texas might as well be outer space to my family of pedigreed New Yorkers. I like it, though. People are always nice, going out of their way to help a stranger, and no one hurries anywhere for any reason. If you walk slowly on a city sidewalk in New York, you get shoved to the pavement and trampled. Nothing moves slowly here. The city is always breathing, beating, pulsing like a rave, with no end in sight. In comparison, Texas is quaint and charming, a respite from the energy of the life the rest of my family lives.

I sit down on the bed next to Dad and take his hand. It feels lighter than usual, and his skin is yellow and paper-thin. All of him is paper-thin—when did he change so much?

Dad licks his dry lips and glances at me disapprovingly. "Stop looking at me like that, Elizabeth, it's just a virus. The doctor is going to get me some elephant antibiotics, and I'll be as good as new in no time."

Before I can respond, the door opens, and my mother breezes in with a doctor in tow.

She's speaking in overdrive, running her words together. "Now, of course, he'll be going home tonight! Don't be silly, Dr. Wade, a man heals best at home in his own bed." The doctor opens his mouth to speak, but she talks over him. "Dear me, no, we won't hear any more about it. Imagine! Expecting us to sleep here? Overnight? No one could get any proper beauty sleep in a place like this—the noise, the sheets, the sick people! No, Dr. Wade, you'll write us the necessary prescriptions, and we'll be on our way." Her gaze lifts, and she notices me. "Elizabeth, how nice to see you."

Translation: How could you run out on your family!

She smiles tightly and tips her head to the side.

Translation: I'll deal with you later, and you won't like it.

I skip the pleasantries, which also irritates my mother. "Mom," I begin, "if the doctor thinks Dad should—"

"Nonsense," she interrupts in a tone that

means there will be no discussion. "David will be happier at home, won't you, dear?"

Dad nods silently from the bed, suddenly mute. I hate it when he does that! He just sits back and allows Mother to steamroll him. He openly adores Mother, but she's much less affectionate toward him. Their relationship is so one-sided. I sometimes wonder how they got married at all.

Dr. Wade finally finds a moment of silence large enough to voice his concern. “Mr. Bennet, I strongly suggest you consider staying here this evening for observation. It's only one night. I know it's not the Ritz, but I'm sure you understand.” His eyes bounce from my mother to my father, as if deciding what to do, then he begins scribbling furiously on Dad's chart.

What the hell is going on here? There's more to this story, a lot more.

"Girls, would you give us a moment, please?" Mother gestures to the hallway with one hand.

“Mom, let us stay.” I'm not ready to act like nothing is wrong. That's all we ever do—smile, nod, and talk about the weather. I'm sick of it.

Mother shoots me an icy glare. “No slang, Elizabeth. Call me Mother or nothing at all. I asked nicely, and won't repeat myself a second time." She clasps her hands tightly on the rail of Dad's bed, narrowing her gaze dangerously at me.

"Come on, Beth. Mom doesn't want us here." Tinselly takes my hand as she walks by, tugging me away from Dad.

Reluctantly, we shuffle into the corridor, the door shutting resolutely at our backs and muffling everything said behind it.

"What's going on? Why didn't you tell me Dad was sick?" My eyes flash accusingly from Tinselly to Jane.

"We didn't want to distract you from school." Jane blushes and looks at the floor before continuing. "Dad insisted nothing was wrong. He was going to work, attending meetings, and gone for most of the day. He seemed more stressed than usual, even a little run down, but we thought he just needed more sleep. He hasn't had seizures until today, and we texted you the instant he was on his way to the hospital."

"Beth," Tinselly says, her eyes staring straight into mine, "we don't know any more than you do right now. I promise. I'd tell you everything. Mother is, well, Mother." She rolls her eyes. "And you know how Daddy is. He takes pride in being able to care for us. This experience must be weird for him."

I sigh and lean back against the wall, sliding

down until I hit the floor. Tinselly and Jane join me, all of us staring blankly at the gray wall across the hallway. One minute turns to two, two minutes turn to five.

Tinselly rests her head on my shoulder. "I've missed you."

"Likewise, Little Lamb." Old nicknames stick, even after years apart.

Tinselly smiles, and I see a moment of peace on Jane's face. She may be my older sister and have her shit together in front of everyone else, but in front of me, there are no walls. She tells me everything. The truth is, Jane struggles with such a massive amount of pressure she's usually doped up on Xanax to cope with it.

She's the eldest daughter, the most talented of the three of us, and swiftly passing prime age for a first marriage. The thought makes me want to puke. Who plans a first marriage with the expectation there should be a slew of others after that?

Not me.

I want love, marriage, and forever. One man, one love, one life, and a shoe full of kids. Needless to say, the odds of my becoming a spinster increase daily. Prince Charming must be trapped in a tower, somewhere, unable to get free and waiting for rescue. Maybe a dragon ate him, and I'll never find him. I'm not even certain what I'm looking for, just that I don't want to settle for the first eligible bachelor my mother suggests.

Jane, on the other hand, is too sweet and obedient to stop Mother from meddling in her life, always ready to please anyone except herself. It makes her miserable, but she can't stop. It's who she is, and why she needs Tinselly and me. We're the defiant ones, acting as a buffer between Jane and mom.

Jane leans forward and wraps her thin arms around her ankles. I think she's lost weight. Her silky blonde hair falls forward, hiding her face. "Do you think he'll be all right? Mother wouldn't have kicked us out if he wasn't seriously sick."

"I don't know," my voice is soft, careful. "I haven't seen him look that frail, ever."

Tinselly clears her throat and kicks her feet out, so we are all staring at her shit-kicker boots. "Beth, you haven't visited for nearly a year. The change looks more sudden to you. We see him every day. I noticed him changing a little bit, but I thought he was getting older. I didn't see any more to it."

"And Mother acts like nothing is going on," Jane adds softly.

"Maybe she doesn't know?" I ask.

Tinselly snorts and looks me in the eye. "When has our mother not known everything?

No, she's fully aware of the situation and doing what she can to play defense."

"It feels more like keep away." Jane has tears in her eyes. "It's not fair. Dad is a good man—he shouldn't have to suffer like this!"

"What do you mean?" Tinselly leans forward and stares at her. "Dad's not suffering. What are you talking about?"

Jane has a natural ability to sense the emotions of another human being without trying. It's nearly impossible for her to ignore her family, and insanely difficult to hide things from her. "He is. Something's wrong, but I didn't think it was physical pain. I thought it was stress, but now I'm not certain. It's hard to tell. I'm sorry, Beth, I should have called you sooner. I thought..." She sighs, and I know what she's thinking. She doesn't trust herself anymore, not since Xanax dulled her senses. She walks around in a trance most of the time.

"Fuck it, I'm not going back to school this semester. I'm staying here. We'll figure out what's up with Dad, and, Jane, I love you, but we need to get you off the meds. They're screwing with you."

Jane ignores my last comment. She sits up and drops her knees to the floor. "You can't quit school!"

"I'm not." I shove in the two words before they freak out on me.

Tinselly blanches. "What about Mother?"

"I'll deal with her. I'm not quitting. I'm about to graduate. I can finish the few credits I need online from here and study for the grad school entrance exam. I don't have to be in Texas right now."

"I'd love for you to stay, but are you sure?" Jane looks at me with those big pale blue eyes, and I want to hug her until her head pops off.

I smile. "I've already decided. Now, all we have to do is find out what's wrong with Dad and play nice with Mother."

Tinselly snorts. "Is that all?"

We sit silently, staring at the wall again for a few minutes, none of us speaking—none of us daring to wonder out loud if Dad will still be with us in a few months.

Continue reading OVER YOU now!

COMPLETED SERIES BY H.M. WARD

ROMANCE

-SECRETS & LIES-

-STRIPPED-

-THE PROPOSITION-

-DAMAGED-

-LIFE BEFORE DAMAGED-

-SECRETS-

-SECRET LIFE OF TRYSTAN SCOTT-

-SCANDALOUS-

TEEN PARANORMAL

-DEMON KISSED-

MORE FERRO FAMILY BOOKS

Trystan Scott

-BROKEN PROMISES-

Jonathan Ferro

-STRIPPED-

Bryan Ferro

-THE PROPOSITION-

Sean Ferro

-THE ARRANGEMENT-

Peter Ferro

-DAMAGED -

Nick Ferro

-THE WEDDING CONTRACT-

Please turn the page for a suggested reading order.

SUGGESTED FERRO SERIES READING ORDER

THE ARRANGEMENT 1

THE ARRANGEMENT 2

THE ARRANGEMENT 3

THE ARRANGEMENT 4

THE ARRANGEMENT 5

THE ARRANGEMENT 6

DAMAGED 1

DAMAGED 2

SECRET LIFE OF TRYSTAN SCOTT 1

SECRET LIFE OF TRYSTAN SCOTT 2

SECRET LIFE OF TRYSTAN SCOTT 3

SECRET LIFE OF TRYSTAN SCOTT 4

SECRET LIFE OF TRYSTAN SCOTT 5

THE ARRANGEMENT 7

THE ARRANGEMENT 8

THE ARRANGEMENT 9

THE ARRANGEMENT 10

THE ARRANGEMENT 11

SCANDALOUS 1

SCANDALOUS 2

STRIPPED 1

THE PROPOSITION 1

THE PROPOSITION 2

THE PROPOSITION 3

THE PROPOSITION 4

THE ARRANGEMENT 12

THE ARRANGEMENT 13

THE ARRANGEMENT 14

THE PROPOSITION 5

THE ARRANGEMENT 15

THE ARRANGEMENT 16

THE ARRANGEMENT 17

THE ARRANGEMENT 18

THE WEDDING CONTRACT

SECRETS & LIES 1

SECRETS & LIES 2

SECOND CHANCES

LIFE BEFORE DAMAGED 1

LIFE BEFORE DAMAGED 2

LIFE BEFORE DAMAGED 3

LIFE BEFORE DAMAGED 4

LIFE BEFORE DAMAGED 5

LIFE BEFORE DAMAGED 6

LIFE BEFORE DAMAGED 7

LIFE BEFORE DAMAGED 8

LIFE BEFORE DAMAGED 9

LIFE BEFORE DAMAGED 10

THE ARRANGEMENT 19

THE ARRANGEMENT 20

MANWHORE

BROKEN PROMISES

THE ARRANGEMENT 21

STRIPPED 2

SECRETS & LIES 3

SECRETS & LIES 4

SECRETS & LIES 5

SECRETS & LIES 6

THE ARRANGEMENT 22

SECRETS & LIES 7

A DAMAGED WEDDING: DAMAGED 3

THE ARRANGEMENT 23

THE ARRANGEMENT 24

THE ARRANGEMENT 25

THE ARRANGEMENT 26

CAN'T WAIT FOR H.M. WARD'S NEXT STEAMY BOOK?

Let her know by leaving stars and telling her what you liked about this book in a review!

ABOUT THE AUTHOR

New York Times bestselling author H.M. Ward continues to reign as the queen of independent publishing. She is swiftly sold more than 23 MILLION copies of her books, placing her among the literary titans. Articles pertaining to Ward's success have appeared in *The New York Times, USA Today,* and *Forbes* to name a few. This native New Yorker resides in Texas with her family, where she enjoys working on her next book.

You can interact with this bestselling author at:
www.hmward.com

www.ingramcontent.com/pod-product-compliance
Lightning Source LLC
La Vergne TN
LVHW050919080826
845145LV00001B/135

* 9 7 8 1 6 3 0 3 5 2 4 8 6 *